TWINS OF WAR

Part I: The Vow

DANA LEVY ELGROD

Producer & International Distributor
eBookPro Publishing
www.ebook-pro.com

TWINS OF WAR

Part I: The Vow

DANA LEVY ELGROD

Copyright © 2023 Dana Levy Elgrod

All rights reserved; no parts of this book may be reproduced or transmitted in any form or by any means, electronic or mechanical, including photocopying, recording, taping, or by any information retrieval system, without the written permission of the author.

Translation: Shira Carmen Aji

Contact: dana.elgrod@gmail.com

ISBN 9789655754643

Contents

Prologue 5

Chapter 1 7

Chapter 2 22

Chapter 3 32

Chapter 4 41

Chapter 5 55

Chapter 6 68

Chapter 7 86

Chapter 8 97

Chapter 9 108

Chapter 10 115

Chapter 11 126

Chapter 12	138
Chapter 13	153
Chapter 14	163
Chapter 15	170
Chapter 16	185
Chapter 17	196
Chapter 18	204
Chapter 19	213
Chapter 20	226
Chapter 21	241
Chapter 22	250
Chapter 23	255
Chapter 24	278

PROLOGUE

Selfishness.
1939 is a great year.
Warsaw, my incredible city, bustles with life, commerce, and culture. My mother's fashionable boutique prospers, my father's position is growing stronger, and my twin sister – my other half – isn't overshadowing my radiant light.

I was born into a life of luxury. I have a wonderful family, many suitors, and financial prosperity.

I love my life, and I thank the universe for the gifts it continues to bestow upon me.

But I know no satisfaction.

I want more.

I long for more.

I hunger to be the center of attention.

I'm not afraid to hurt others to get what is mine. I don't feel bad when I take, and I don't give back.

This world was created just for me, and I'll milk it for all it's worth.

1939 was supposed to be a great year.

But a horrible secret that was hidden from me threatens to destroy the world I know and love.

This year, I was also exposed for the first time to the power of a vow.

Promise. One word that encompasses an entire world.

It could save me, but it may destroy me.

A promise demands to be kept.

CHAPTER 1

The streetlamps flash in an even rhythm as I stare at them and spread my arms to the sides with delight. The adrenaline in my body refuses to subside, and I'm sad that the evening's amusements are about to end. I slide my palms down my hips, feeling the delicate weave. The magenta gloves I'm wearing were made to measure, just like the beautiful ankle-length dress fluttering in the lovely late summer breeze. The beret, which arrived by special delivery from Paris, adorns my head like a crown, and the lustrous ringlets of my hair hang lightly over my bosom.

The sounds of jazz coming from the restaurant have stopped already, and the last reveler has come out into the street. He ambles slowly on the heavy cobblestones singing in a loud voice.

The long avenue, which was full of life just a few hours ago, is practically deserted. The dense rows of buildings have pulled the crowds of people to them, demanding their nightly rest. The horse-drawn carriages have disappeared, the rattling of automobiles has ceased, and the shop windows have gone dark.

I love the hustle and bustle of my beautiful city, but the quiet is unsettling.

"Anushka, come sit with me." My sister pats the bench.

"An-Yah," I stress the syllables of my name irritably. "Please don't call me by that childish nickname." I sneak a glimpse at Anton, who's sitting by her side on the bench. He doesn't return my look. His gaze is fixed on the man who just came out of the restaurant and is now meandering gaily down the street in front of us.

"You'll always be Anushka to me." My sister smiles at me.

I take two steps back and lean against the lamppost. I grab the material of my dress with both hands and swish it around. The rustling of layers of material brushing against each other sounds like the soft caress of the wind, and it slightly alleviates the aggravation my sister has aroused in me.

"I hate my name." I drop the cloth resentfully. "Ania... what a boring, common name. And you, who came into the world only two measly minutes after me, got such a unique name. Maybe if you hadn't been so sluggish 20 years ago, you would've pushed out first, and I would've gotten your beautiful name."

Anton's face is contorted with scorn, but he still doesn't look at me. He never looks at me.

"Michalina isn't a prettier name than Ania," declares my sister. "And you already know it's not our names that matter, but what we choose to do with them."

I roll my eyes and press my lips together, determined not to get into this dreary discussion again. This evening exceeded all of my expectations, and I won't allow anything to dim my fabulous mood. The atmosphere in the restaurant was electrifying. The band played jazz all night, and I received considerable attention from admirers, old and new. I felt like a daughter of nobility, as if the dance floor were my kingdom.

I lift my face toward the night sky, take a deep breath, and imagine I'm outside a restaurant in Paris, the fashion capital of the world. I love Warsaw, but sometimes I feel that the city is too small for me. My gaze shifts again to the buildings in front me – a long row of impressive, old residential structures standing shoulder to shoulder. There are large rectangular windows on each façade, and narrow front balconies hang off some of them. The advanced age of the buildings doesn't detract from their beauty – on the contrary, I can imagine the residents who lived in them generations ago. I can clearly picture the aristocrats wandering between the rooms after coming home from an extravagant ball. Each home retains a magical, exhilarating history. I, on the other hand, was born into a period during which my city is attempting to be modern and breaking away from its classical past.

"I should escort you home," Anton says to Michalina in a low voice, awakening me from my reverie. "I promised your father I would ensure your safe arrival."

"No!" I cry. "Come with us to Peter's café. I forbid you to announce the evening's end."

He ignores my plea and turns to face the avenue leading toward our apartment.

"Anton." Michalina slides her hand up his arm, and when he turns around to meet her gaze, a blush rises in her cheeks. At once, she lowers her hands to her knees and looks down. "I'm sure Peter's café is already closed, but I'd appreciate it if you would sit with us for a few more minutes. Ania is still dizzy from our exciting night out."

Anton nods in consent and sits down.

My eyes dart from Michalina to Anton, and instead of feeling satisfied that he gave in to her request, I feel my stomach cramp up with pangs of envy.

My eyes are locked on Michalina, my identical twin. Her hair is golden and wavy, her complexion as pale as porcelain, her bright blue eyes shaped like thin almonds. We both have the same slim figure with impressively rounded feminine curves. Until just a few years ago, no one could tell us apart. Even our closest friends had to pull back our hair to expose the skin between the cheek and the right ear, searching for the beauty mark that is Michalina's trademark. In addition to her special name, she's also been blessed with the sun's kiss, while my face remains banally smooth. Nowadays it's hard to confuse us.

My sister endeavors to obscure the gifts nature has awarded her, while I flaunt them. Michalina wears prudish clothing. Her dresses are always dark, dull shades, and even the cuts she chooses are old-fashioned and conservative. Her hair is always gathered in a tight braid that hangs down her back, and she only lets it down when we go out on the town. While I keep our mother company at her fashionable boutique, Michalina diligently studies nursing. She reads newspapers with unwavering dedication and conducts discussions in public like some intellectual gentleman. She is, without a doubt, the most boring girl I know, and it's no surprise that, unlike me, she rarely wins the attention of any captivating suitors. It transcends my ability to understand how a man like Anton is so spellbound by her. She never goes out socially without him. He's the only one who invites her to the dance floor. And he constantly walks next to her and always listens attentively to her tedious speeches.

"Thank you for watching over us, Anton," I say flirtatiously and go back to twirling my dress in the desperate hope of winning even one single glance from him.

He bows his head, but his eyes are now fixed on the street corner.

"Maybe you'll agree to tell us about a serious crime you recently prevented," I say, trying my luck once more.

"I refuse to share any information that may upset you." He leans back on the bench and rubs the back of his neck.

"But you seem so troubled." I feign a despairing tone. "I'd like to think that a senior police commander in Warsaw can keep the criminals off our streets and soothe my battered nerves. When you look uneasy, it scares me."

"Anushka," Michalina chides, "you have no idea what criminal activity Anton has had to deal with at work. The fact that he's troubled only proves that he's human and that he truly cares."

He rewards her with a quick smile, and she blushes again.

I bite my tongue to keep from retorting. Her self-righteousness always makes me look bad. She's incapable of appreciating basic female flirtation.

"Then promise that if you happen upon some shocking crime, you'll share the story with us." I won't relent.

"Anushka, Anton never makes a promise he doesn't intend to keep."

I narrow my eyes and stare daggers at her. By his side, she looks tiny. His masculinity announces itself far and wide, even as he leans back comfortably on the bench. He's wearing a black suit jacket with a white, button-down shirt underneath that emphasizes his broad shoulders and highlights his robust, sturdy torso. His hair – the color of dry earth – looks lush and soft to the touch. His jaw is chiseled, and his brown eyes gleam, veiled and mysterious behind long lashes. I suppose I have suitors as handsome as Anton, but none of them radiates with the same intensity.

I'm trying to think of what to say to gain his attention this time, but I'm distracted by the clomping of boots walking up behind me. I spin around and see two men in blue uniforms approaching us.

"The beautiful twins from the house of Orzeszkowa," Łukasz shouts, and I quickly stand up straight and shape my lips into a dazzling smile.

"This night is getting better by the minute." Stanisław smooths his uniform, and both men stop in front of me, looking at me with pleasure. When they notice Anton, their expressions turn sober.

"Commander." They face him and salute.

I bite my bottom lip sullenly. My excitement over encountering the young policemen is quickly replaced by disappointment. Both are handsome, and both chase after me determinedly. But the moment I see them standing next to Anton, they look like two children dressed up in clothes that are too big for them – as though they are playing cops and robbers.

Anton acknowledges them with a slight nod and goes back to surveying the avenue uneasily.

"Ania..." Łukasz rolls my name over his tongue, then grabs my hand and kisses it. "You... You look like a flower in a field of thorns." I giggle at his stupid compliment.

Stanisław shoves Łukasz aside and pulls my hand toward him. "Ania, you look like a rainbow peeking through the clouds of a gray and gloomy sky."

I giggle again and glance at the bench. Their compliments are precisely what I need to make Anton finally realize that his affections are directed at the wrong sister.

"My brave policemen!" I grasp the skirts of my dress and daintily sit close to Michalina on the bench. I brush imaginary dirt off the delicate fabric and grin at them. "Tell us about the vicious outlaws you fought today. Anton refuses to entertain us with heroic tales," I protest miserably.

"Ania," Michalina scolds me softly.

"What?" I play dumb. "Anton isn't on duty right now. I have no doubt that he'll allow our friends to share exhilarating accounts of their bravery with us."

Anton doesn't respond, so I seize the opportunity and wave my hand, gesturing to the policemen to start talking.

"Unfortunately, we didn't experience anything too thrilling." Łukasz grins. "Someone smashed the window of some Żyd merchant's shop in the Muranów neighborhood again."

Michalina's body tenses up. "That term is inappropriate, Łukasz."

He frowns, perplexed, and I exhale in aggravation.

"Michalina." This time I scold her. "What's wrong with that nickname? People shouldn't have to watch their tongues when they're around friends. It's like how I call Masza a stinking Christian. Because she literally smells like rotten onions."

Łukasz and Stanisław burst out laughing and bob their heads in agreement.

"This is different." Michalina sticks out her chin. "In no way do I mean to justify your decision to mention her religion while slandering her, but Żyd is a slur that denigrates all Jews, regardless of their actions."

I try to understand her argument, but to no avail.

"Don't mind her," I say as I wave my hand dismissively. "She's determined to dissuade you from amusing me with your heroic stories."

"Ania, how would you feel if they called our grandfather a Żyd?" Michalina won't let it go.

"Which grandfather?" I shudder.

"Grandpa Szymon," she whispers, and for a moment it seems as though she regrets bringing up his name. "Do you remember him? Mother's father. We met him when we were little."

"You fool! Why would they call him a Żyd?" I snicker.

Michalina stands up, and Anton rises to his feet next to her.

"Our mother's parents were Jewish," she states reproachfully. "When Mother married Father, she decided to leave the Jewish religion and not convert to any other religion. If not for that, we would be Jews, too."

I open my eyes wide, totally aghast. "Michalina! I won't tolerate such insults." I cross my arms over my chest. "To claim that we are of Jewish ancestry is malicious." I stand up and look at Łukasz and Stanisław. "Tell her to please stop upsetting me."

They both face her sharply but immediately fall silent when Anton softly clears his throat.

The realization that I will have to defend myself unaided fills me with rage. I stick out my chin and put my hands on my hips, defiantly.

"Tell me, do I look like a Żydówka to you?"

Both policemen shake their heads vigorously from side to side.

"Am I any less Polish than you?"

"No," they reply in unison.

"You're as Polish as they come," Łukasz adds, pointing at me. "You should be on our flag."

"Exactly." Stanisław smiles. "Your name should be added to the national anthem."

Their compliments help calm the fury that is rising in me, and I bat my eyelashes. "Imagine if I had to live as a Jewess in Poland." I burst out laughing. "If I had to go to their bizarre places of worship, dress like a beggar, and marry a man who grows long ringlets in front of each ear."

They both chuckle loudly, and I rebelliously ignore Michalina's muttering and walk ahead.

"I give you permission to escort me home," I announce without breaking eye contact with Michalina. Within seconds, the two policemen are striding on either side of me.

I listen to Łukasz and Stanisław with half an ear while trying to catch the conversation between Michalina and Anton that is going on behind us. Sentence fragments about religious distinctions, Nazi Germany, and even history echo toward me. Michalina is talking, and every so often Anton contributes his thoughts to the discussion. His sentences are articulated clearly and communicated with great patience.

A moan escapes my mouth involuntarily, and my companions fall silent. I quickly fake a giggle and bolt ahead.

I no longer want to eavesdrop on their conversation although I'm sure she's boring him with her self-righteous sermons. The day will come that he'll realize that he's wasting his time with her and will yearn to court me. I make the decision to relish every moment of our courtship and celebrate Michalina's downfall.

Suddenly I hear a faint cry coming from behind the gate of one of the nearby buildings. I hurry in my heels, click-clacking towards the noise, and push the gate open. A tiny, ginger-colored kitten is standing there alone, yowling; he looks like he's starving and exhausted.

I scoop him up in my arms, clean the dirt from his fine fur, and gently pet the back of his neck. I've always had a weakness for cats. Unlike loud and annoying little children, cats soothe me. They remind me of myself: proud, naughty, and spoiled.

The kitten's claws get caught in the lace of my dress's collar and scratch my skin.

"Anushka," Michalina exclaims. "Your dress! He's ruining your dress."

Her yelling awakens me from my trance, and only then do I notice the whole group crowded near the gate, watching me.

"I don't care." I shrug my shoulders, hold him close, and walk out onto the avenue. "His mother has abandoned him. He won't make it through the night if I don't take care of him."

"Mother will abandon *you* if she sees what the cat is doing to your new dress," Michalina remarks prissily.

"She won't find out." I jut my chin forward defiantly. "If you don't tell her, she won't notice."

"Of course I won't tell," says Michalina, offended. "I never tell her about your daring exploits."

"In that case, we can continue walking," I resolve.

Anton steps back. His stare is focused on the cat resting in my arms. Then he looks up at my face. A slight shiver runs down my spine at the sight of his pupils concentrating so intensely on me as I realize that this is the first time he's ever really looked at me. I look down and try to regain my composure.

Łukasz and Stanisław walk up to us and peer at the cat. Our steps echo between the quiet buildings, and I decide to take a shortcut home through the beautiful neighborhood park. The sight of the barren benches arranged among the lush trees captivates my soul.

"Tell me another story," I order them, attempting to distract myself from the look I received from the gentleman who never even glances at me.

"Around noon, two gypsies arrived at the police station," Łukasz says, snickering.

"Gypsies?" I ask, wrinkling my brow. "I don't believe I've ever seen gypsies."

"And you're better off for it." Stanisław grimaces. "They're filthy and smell terrible."

I laugh.

"They wanted to file a complaint against a Polish merchant who bought carpets from them but didn't pay," Stanisław explains.

"Those gypsies are as despicable as the Żyds."

"They also multiply like the Żyds," Łukasz snorts in irritation.

"So what did you do?" I ask, stroking the kitten's fur.

"We got rid of them, is what we did!" Łukasz says proudly. "They need to learn as soon as possible that they're not welcome in Warsaw and should roam elsewhere."

"Excellent," I conclude and peek behind me.

Michalina bites her lip, straining to hold back, and Anton stares into my eyes. His look sends chills down my whole body. I can see that he's repulsed.

I wrinkle my brow, not comprehending what I possibly said to provoke such a reaction in him.

We leave the park, go into the well-kept street and stop before the gate of the three-story building that we live in – which is without a doubt the most exquisite structure on the entire street. I keep stroking the kitten's fur, knowing full well that I won't be able to bring him into the house; instead, I pick several leaves from our garden and create a soft bed where I put him down delicately. He immediately starts yowling again.

"Don't cry, Dziecko. You're a cute little baby, and I'll bring you some milk soon." I stroke him behind the ears and stand up.

Łukasz pulls my hand to him and kisses it, and Stanisław instantly follows suit. They then turn towards Michalina and award her the same gesture.

Anton opens the front door, holds it ajar for both of us, and ascends the unlit stairs to the second floor after us. On the first floor lives a lonely old man, on the third floor an elderly couple, and in the apartment next to them, a middle-aged widow. A quarrelsome old couple used to live in the apartment next to ours. But after they died, Father bought their apartment, and now it stands empty. I suppose that whichever of us marries first will live there, and I have no doubt that I'll effortlessly beat my sister in that race.

Anton lingers as Michalina opens the door to our house. He kisses her hand. She beams shyly at him, and I extend my fingers impatiently, waiting for him to wish me farewell in the same way.

"Good night to you as well, Ania," he says curtly, then turns around and walks down the stairs.

I stifle a grumble of discontent, push Michalina out of my path, and walk into the apartment ahead of her. My heels clop loudly on the tiled floor as I cross the foyer and step into the room next to the kitchen.

"Maria." I call for the maid.

"Why are you waking her?" Michalina whispers behind me.

"Maria!" I raise my voice and knock twice on the door of her room.

Our young domestic opens the door, bleary-eyed. She looks up at me in bewilderment, her thin body shrouded in a simple robe, yet when she spots Michalina, a faint smile appears on her lips.

"I need a saucer of milk." I step back a bit and motion toward the kitchen.

"Of course, Miss Ania," she nods, and turns in the direction of the kitchen. "I'll warm up two glasses of milk for you."

"We don't need two glasses of milk," I reply impatiently. "I asked for cold milk in a saucer."

She nods again and shuffles into the kitchen.

"Anushka..." Michalina mumbles my god-awful nickname. "Why did you wake Maria for such a silly chore?"

"Mind your own business."

Sighing, Michalina heads toward the long hallway that leads to our bedrooms.

"Do you require anything else, Miss Ania?" Maria hands me the saucer of milk.

"Not at the moment," I say as I feign a smile. "But I may later on."

She bows her head and goes back to her room.

I cautiously walk downstairs to the garden, put the saucer down next to the kitten, and encourage him to taste the milk. His fuzzy face is soon painted white, and I go back inside giggling with amusement.

I hang my coat on a hook next to my parents' coats in the entrance hall and stride under the archway into the dining room. A solitary lamp floods the space with warm, comforting light. I slide my hand over the long mahogany dining table and, with my fingertips, brush the napkin arranged on the porcelain plate that Maria has already set out for breakfast. I'm still tingling with adrenaline from our night and debate whether to pester Maria again, but in the end, I reconsider. I turn on my heels down the hall, cross the drawing room, and continue to the sleeping quarters.

The door to my parents' bedroom is closed. I am mindful not to thump in my high heels and tiptoe quietly past. Michalina's door is ajar, but I don't dawdle and go into my own room.

My thoughts stray to the evening's events, and twinges of anger rise in my chest. From the very moment I became aware of my feminine charms, I have never met a man who didn't reciprocate my flirtations. I have set goals to attain the unattainable many times and have always had great success – although, in truth, it's the challenge that thrills me, and after each triumphant conquest, I lose interest. Now, for the first time, I feel the ache of defeat, and the sensation is unfamiliar and overpowering. The shocking revelation of our questionable lineage has left me uneasy, and I can't help but wonder if Michalina told me that just to ruin my good mood. Oh, how I will rejoice when she finally loses her only suitor to me!

"Anushka," Michalina softly whispers my name from the doorway of my bedroom. She's dressed in a white nightgown and has a sad look on her face.

"What do you want?" I wriggle around, straining to unhook the clasps at the back of my dress.

"I can feel your anger," she pats her gut. "I have an inkling that it's directed at me, and I don't want you to go to sleep mad at me." She comes up behind me and gently undoes the hooks.

"You should have considered that before you ruined my evening with your lies." I remove my beret and take off my dress, flinging it onto the armchair.

"I have never lied to you." She sighs and picks up the dress.

"If so, I cannot understand why you chose to begin lying tonight." I remove my chemise and tug a nightgown off a hanger in my closet. I know she's incapable of telling a lie. Back when we shared our mother's womb, I absorbed the shrewd cunning, and she the integrity and the just system of values. Whenever I beg her to lie for me, she stutters, becomes pale, and looks grief-stricken.

"Anushka, please sit on the bed and listen to me," she tells me as she shakes out my dress and hangs it in the closet.

I ignore her request and take a seat at the vanity, wrapping my hair tightly around the rollers.

"The winds of war are blowing from Germany," she says in a hushed tone and sits down in the armchair. "I need you to understand the situation so we can prepare for it together."

"I'm not interested in your ominous announcements." I raise my voice. "Haven't you gotten enough pleasure from insinuating that we're tainted with Jewish blood? Now you're trying to scare me by talking about *war*?"

"Do you know why the people around us overlook our Jewish blood?" she continues to whisper calmly.

"Because we aren't Jews," I snort with disdain.

"Because our father is Polish, the deputy manager of a bank, rich, and well-born." She stands up, and through the mirror, I can see that she is hugging her arms to her body. "We belong to a very wealthy family, and we don't lead a Jewish lifestyle."

"So, you admit it yourself." I shrug. "We are not filthy Jews, and no one can force us to be."

"Anushka," Michalina sighs and grabs my shoulders with her hands. "Father donates money to my university; he makes sure to reward the municipal officials and the police and maintains a close relationship with the city's politicians. He does all this to strengthen his position and to protect us. It's the reason I wasn't segregated along with the other Jewish students, and it's why the strict laws against the Jews don't apply to Mother and to us. If you were even slightly interested in our family history, you would already know this."

"Get out of my room." I shake her off of me and stand up. "I'll wake Mother and tell her you're frightening me with horror stories before bed."

"You need to open your eyes and accept reality." Her voice is harsh.

I refuse to let her harrowing revelations penetrate me and decide to make things difficult for her, too.

"So, you're saying that Father pays Anton to spend time with you?" I snicker.

"Of course not." She puts her hand on her heart. "Anton is a dear friend of our family's."

He may be a dear friend of hers, but he's never invested in building a friendship with me. "I don't like him, and I don't want you spending time with him." I jerk my chin.

Michalina drops her head and shakes it from side to side in desperation. "I'm trying to explain to you that we have to plan for difficult times ahead, but instead of listening, you've decided to slander Anton."

"Then go plan," I tell her as I shrug and lie down on my bed. "Maybe you should ask our dear friend to teach you to shoot his gun? Who knows? Maybe he'll even lend you his uniform!" Venom is rising fast inside me, and I embrace it. "Maybe he'll take off his uniform and kiss something besides your hand. Would you like that? Would you like his lips to kiss your...?"

"Ania!" she interrupts, almost shouting, and I look at her wine-red cheeks, amused. "Please stop embarrassing me and being mean. You're my sister, and I love you." She lowers her voice again. "You are brave and resourceful, and I have no doubt that when the time comes and things begin to change, we'll overcome everything together."

"Hmm..." I yawn and cover myself with the duvet. "Excuse me, but your boring speech has tired me out. I'm going to sleep, to dream about my many admirers. Soon I'll have to decide which of them will win my heart, a task that will certainly require bravery and resourcefulness. And just so you know," I giggle, "you can continue clinging to Anton like a leech. But Mother will never consent to him anyway. He's not at our social and economic status, and he never will be."

"I don't cling to him." The soft tremor in her voice betrays her wounded feelings. "He's just a good friend, that's all." A few seconds pass, and I hear her footsteps walking away.

My stomach cramps up the same way it does every time I hurt Michalina. It's as if we were never really separated from each other at birth. I hate feeling her pain, especially when I've caused it.

To calm down, I let my thoughts glide to the dance floor, where I spin and twirl to a perfect waltz. I raise my eyes to face my dance partner, and my bosom quivers when I meet his burning stare. His brown eyes dart to my right cheek, and he pushes my hair behind my ear. When he sees that her beauty mark isn't there, his expression goes cold in an instant, and he hastily breaks away from me.

Why has he taken over my most intimate thoughts? And why does Michalina keep terrorizing me with her horrifying scenarios? Her harsh words echo in my mind, and I roll over onto my stomach with a groan.

"Damn sister," I murmur, hugging my pillow.

CHAPTER 2

Porcelain plates with delicate floral embellishments adorn the table, and a matching teapot stands in the center. I take a freshly baked roll from the basket and delightedly inhale its magnificent aroma. The beautiful breakfast plates are loaded with delicacies, and other wonderful fragrances swirl through the dining room, awakening my senses.

Father is sitting at the head of the table in a black, three-piece suit with a blue necktie flawlessly tied in a full Windsor knot. His light hair is combed neatly to the side, and he is clean-shaven. Michalina sits, her back straight, on the side of the table nearest the window. She's wearing a drab brown dress in an old-fashioned style, and her hair is in a long braid that goes down her back. They are both thumbing through the morning newspaper with the same serious expressions on their faces.

I tie the sash of my satin robe and examine the abundance laid out on the platters with great interest. Sunday breakfast is always richer and more decadent than the rest of the week.

"Ania, quit staring at the food and sit down next to your sister," Mother scolds me and goes back to slicing the kielbasa sausage. She sits with perfect posture, modeling a dress the color of champagne, her black hair arranged stylishly. She looks like an aristocrat.

I sit next to Michalina and scowl. "Mother, why on earth are you cutting the sausage yourself? Call Maria to do it."

"Your father asked her to leave." Mother's upper lip curls in irritation.

"Forever?" I shriek. "Who'll serve us? Who'll cook for us and pour our tea?"

Father turns the page of his newspaper and looks up at me, his blue eyes smiling. "Of course not forever. Just for the rest of the day."

Michalina leans forward and pours tea into my cup. I purse my lips and refuse to thank her. It seems that her appalling behavior last night wasn't enough for her, and she feels the need to demonstrate her self-righteousness once again by waiting on me herself.

"Your father would like to have an intimate family discussion," Mother explains. "However, I simply cannot comprehend why Maria couldn't just wait in the kitchen until we've finished speaking. Someone will have to clean up this mess when we're done." She gestures toward the table.

I look reproachfully at my father and put a slice of hot pastry on my plate. My fork effortlessly cuts through the layers of meat and melted cheese, and I stuff a large bite into my mouth and groan with satisfaction.

"Agata, stop complaining," my father says as he stonily turns to my mother. "I've already explained to you how imperative it is that this conversation remain among just us." He folds the newspaper and puts it on the table.

A bit of pastry gets stuck in my throat, and I start to cough. Michalina rushes over to pat me on the back, and I push her hand away in annoyance. My father's brusque tone has alarmed me. He never fails to address us with respect, and his composure is seldom shaken.

"Winds of war are blowing toward us from Germany," he says quietly, his gaze wandering back and forth among us.

"Please don't tell me this conversation is about war," I lament. "I couldn't fall asleep all night because of Michalina's war talk, and I absolutely refuse to discuss such a disturbing topic on this beautiful morning." My words are partially true. I did suffer from sleeplessness, but the real reason was the rare look I earned from Michalina's suitor.

"The girl is right," Mother says as she puts down the knife and pushes the sausage plate toward the center of the table. "We are not a family of tiresome intellectuals, and I refuse to hold political conversations during breakfast time."

"Agata, keep quiet!" My father clenches his teeth and opens his eyes wide in anger.

My mother's face pales, and she shrinks back in her chair. She opens her mouth, about to protest his tone, but he clears his throat, and she goes quiet.

I expect Father to ask for forgiveness, but no apology arrives. He drums his fingers on the table, agitated and edgy.

"I assume you've heard about the problematic situation of the Jews in Germany," he resumes speaking, in a hushed tone.

I bite my tongue and try my best to not roll my eyes. He sounds exactly like Michalina, and I can't understand why he insists on ruining the mood on this gorgeous day.

"And you've seen for yourselves what terrible conditions the Jews live in, here in Poland." He continues drumming nervously on the table.

It wasn't a question, but Michalina nods in agreement. I glance over at the pictures hanging on the wall, the exhibit of artworks that my mother passionately collects from galleries across the country. I am amazed time and again by her exquisite taste. She has a keen eye and has found a way to combine her two loves when she opened the clothing boutique, which quickly became the crown jewel of the shops, according to the city's contemporary fashion enthusiasts. My eyes stray over to the foyer. The front door is just a few steps away. Maybe I should go check how my sweet little kitten fared through the night.

"Ania, are you even listening to me?" My father bangs his fist on the table.

"Umm..." I mumble and turn to face him reluctantly. He can speak to his heart's content, and I can hear without genuinely listening.

"Can you imagine what will happen if Germany decides to expand its borders?"

"They'll have more land?" I smile, answering his question with a question.

"And what if they choose to occupy Poland?"

"Why would they do something so preposterous?" my mother blurts out. "Henryk, I implore you to stop with this fear-mongering. The girls are too young for political conversations."

"Agata," he sighs and combs his hair to the side with his fingers. "If the Germans decide to invade Poland, you and the girls will be in danger."

"Us?" I recoil. "The war has nothing to do with us. War is for men in uniforms with rifles."

Michalina pats my arm and looks down.

"Father, what are you talking about?" I open my eyes wider as I ask.

"I'm talking about the fact that the political discourse has changed. There's an actual threat of German invasion, and if that occurs, the standing I currently enjoy in Poland will change."

"Henryk, I think you may be exaggerating," Mother says warily. "I'm sure our army is strong enough to defeat those despicable Germans."

The words my parents have spoken whirl around chaotically in my mind.

"But... But why did you say that *we* will be in danger?" I ask and involuntarily grasp Michalina's hand.

Father's eyes dart to the sides as if he fears we are not alone and someone might be eavesdropping on our conversation. "I said it in light of your Jewish roots," he whispers.

"I cannot believe you!" Mother stands up and throws her napkin on the table in revolt. "How can you frighten the girls over something so silly?"

Father opens his mouth to answer her, but she silences him with a wave of her hand.

"You know very well that I abandoned my parents' faith many years ago," Mother exclaims in irritation. "To imply that the girls are somehow connected to that religion is an insult to me. Once I freed myself from that suffocating community, I never looked back. We have no connection to them and never will."

So Mother really *was* a Jew? It seems that Michalina wasn't making it up, but hearing it directly from my mother shocks me profoundly. I cannot picture her living in a closed community, praying in their houses of worship, and being mocked and ridiculed. Mother is the epitome of a proud Polish woman.

"What Mother says is true," I say in support of Mother, and cast aside Michalina's hand. My sister is listening to the discussion like a spectator and doesn't utter a word. I remind myself that I don't need her assistance.

"It's not true at all," Father insists.

"It's absolutely true." Mother bobs her head vigorously. "They cannot assign that religion to us. I renounced it, and no one has any right to impose it on me and my girls." She inhales sharply and sticks out her chin. "What is the worst thing they can do to us if they find out our family history?" Mother doesn't wait for an answer. "Will they ask us to convert to Christianity? Will they ask us to renounce the Jewish religion? Let them! I have no problem wearing a cross as long as it matches my dress."

I giggle at her comment, but my laughter fades when I realize Father doesn't share in my amusement. He's rubbing his eyes and looks extremely upset.

He stands up and faces the window.

"I was able to obtain two entry visas to America," he says, not making eye contact with us. "I want the girls to leave next week."

"What?" I leap up from my seat, knocking my chair to the floor. Mother's jaw drops, and she gapes at him. Michalina bows her head, clutching the edges of the table.

"The girls need to get out of Europe as soon as possible." Father turns to us, his blue eyes forlorn. "I will send valuable possessions with them, and they can convert them into dollars there. I'll give them the name and address of my contact. He will wait for their arrival and use the money they bring him to acquire two more visas for you and me." He strides over to my mother and takes her hand. "The separation will be brief, Agata."

Suddenly the walls are spinning around me. I can hardly breathe, and I aim blindly for my chair. Michalina hurries to help me sit down. I stare blankly at my parents, like a sleepwalker trapped in a nightmare.

My mother glances at us and wrinkles her brow, frowning. She scratches her head and takes two steps back. "You've gone crazy..." she mutters, shaking her head from side to side. "Henryk, you have lost your mind."

"Maybe I have," Father answers her calmly, "but the possibility that I may be right has robbed me of my peace of mind."

"The girls aren't leaving us and aren't going anywhere," Mother interrupts snappily and sits back down in her chair. She pulls the sausage plate towards her and goes back to slicing the meat aggressively.

"Mother," Michalina utters quietly. "Father is telling the truth. Danger is waiting for us right around the corner."

"Do not interfere!" Mother waves her knife. "War, Germans, Jews... it's all poppycock. We are Polish. This is our home, and this is where we will remain."

"Father and I both hope that you are right." Michalina smiles a bit, adding, "and if you are indeed correct, we can come back home and resume our lives as they were. But..."

My heartbeat quickens, and my apprehension turns to outrage. I pound the table, and Michalina shuts up.

"I will not leave my home," I shout. "I'm staying here, in my country, in my city, with my friends, with my admirers, and living my wonderful life. This horror story you've concocted is positively absurd, and I refuse to cooperate with your plans."

Mother nods with satisfaction, and Father lets out a heavy sigh. The knowledge that I'm making my mother proud in this debate excites me. Rare is the occasion that I receive a kind word from her. Unlike Father, she's not one to embrace and encourage. She is strict and demanding and always finds fault in my decisions. The fact that we're on the same side fills me with joy.

"Maybe... Maybe try and think of it as a holiday," my father suggests. "A few months of vacation in America until the situation has improved."

"A vacation where just the voyage takes a few months?" Mother snorts mockingly. "Assuming they successfully get visas for us to join them, you'll lose your job as Deputy Manager at the bank, and I'll lose the boutique I've spent years working to expand and build a reputation for. The girls will return here as old spinsters and be forced to settle for proletarian suitors. Can you imagine our daughters marrying clerks or policemen?"

I sneak a peek at Michalina solely to amuse myself from the pale color her face has turned.

"We will have to compromise to keep the girls safe." Father crosses his arms over his chest.

"I have no intention of giving up my life here." I slam my fork on my plate. "Michalina, tell Father that we are grown women and know how to make do independently."

She doesn't react.

"Michalina!" I shoot her an angry look.

"Anushka," she sighs. "I agree with Father. I follow the news devoutly and am really worried. We have to go and get Mother and Father visas for America."

"Then you go," I reply angrily and shove my full fork into my mouth. "Your life is so boring, I can see why you want to run away, but there's no way you're dragging me along with you on this fool's errand."

"All right." She surprises me with her subdued answer. "I'll travel alone and get the additional visas."

The pastry gets stuck in my throat again just as Mother bursts out in hysterical laughter.

"Michalina, stop talking nonsense." Mother waves her hand dismissively. Then, taking a serious tone, she says, "You're not going on this journey alone. No one is going on this journey."

"Then I will go get the visas by myself." Father sits back down at the head of the table and pulls the newspaper towards him.

"He's gone mad," my mother mutters. "Girls, tell your father he's gone mad."

"I'll go with Father." Michalina pours tea into Father's mug and squeezes his hand. "I'll be allowed to complete my final year of school when we return, and this way I'll get to spend a few months with my dear Father."

He smiles back at her, but his bright blue eyes look tormented.

"Henryk," my mother moans softly, "I think that…"

"This conversation is over." He interrupts her firmly and hides his face behind the newspaper.

I pierce my fork in the pastry and shrug. I've been spared from going on this ridiculous adventure, and the thought that my self-righteous sister will finally leave me to my own devices brings joy to my heart.

I can sense Michalina's stare burning holes in the back of my neck. I feel her worries in the pit of my stomach. In all our years on earth, we've never been apart, even for one day. Every morning we meet at the breakfast table; at dusk we sit in the drawing room and share the events of the day with each other; and in the evenings, we go out together to the same places. Sometimes I feel like she knows me better than I know myself. She's incapable of seeing me sad or upset and would do anything to cheer me up. This is the first time she hasn't compromised.

I can't look at her. The thought that she's leaving me just to see if I can cope without her crosses my mind. I sip my tea and force myself to relax. She has another thing coming: When she returns from her stupid "vacation," she'll find that she's lost her only admirer and that it wasn't the Germans who captured the city, but it was *me*.

The ache in the pit of my stomach intensifies, and I find it hard to swallow my food. All of a sudden, it seems to me that the dining room is too small, and I feel like I'm suffocating.

My mother's labored breathing confirms that she's experiencing the same distress as me.

I quickly pour a glass of milk and stand up.

"I'm going to take care of Dziecko," I announce as I hold the cup to my chest.

"A baby?" All three of them ask in unison.

"My new kitten," I reply and pivot on my heel.

"Ania, don't you dare bring that vile creature into my home," Mother cries out.

"The 'creature' is in the garden." I grind my teeth. "And since my sister is abandoning me, he'll probably become my new best friend."

"I'm not abandoning you," says Michalina, her voice trembling.

"This is exactly why I prefer pets to people." I face her teary-eyed. "Pets never let me down."

"Anushka..." she says, trying to make peace. "Let's take advantage of this beautiful day and spend some time together. We'll go for a walk with Anton and..."

"Anton, Anton, Anton." I shut her up. "Do you think he'll wait for you to return from your little adventure?"

Michalina lowers her eyes in embarrassment, and Mother cranes her neck, looking at us in suspicion.

"And why exactly should the policeman wait for her?" Mother asks as she raises her eyebrows.

"Don't you see how he looks at her?" I snicker. "And how she clings to him constantly?"

"Don't talk such nonsense," my mother scolds me. "Michalina knows I would never approve of such a match."

Michalina stands up with a hurt look. "Anton is only a dear friend, and I enjoy spending time with him." She pulls her braid over her shoulder and strokes it repetitively, as she does whenever she's nervous or embarrassed.

"Ania, I forbid you to spread such harmful gossip." Mother shoots me an austere look. "Hearsay like this could dissuade worthy suitors from approaching your sister."

"Of course, Mother." I flutter my eyelashes. "Because they're just lining up to win her heart."

"Ania!" My father practically shouts my name.

"Forgive me." I feign an innocent expression. "And now, if you'll let me, I'll go care for Dziecko." I rush out of the dining room, but instead of feeling pleased that I managed to hit Michalina where it hurts, I shudder from the pain that has begun to pierce the pit of my stomach.

I hate feeling her emotions.

CHAPTER 3

The platform at Warsaw's Główna Railway Station is crowded with people. Father says that the station was supposedly designed in a modern and innovative fashion, but I don't see anything impressive about it. To me, the stone structures look cold and alienating, and the metal beams are like monuments to commemorate the construction that's been going on for years with no end in sight. It's just another place that weighs heavily on my soul. Men, women, and children run to-and-fro on the platform, and a couple of them bump into me and don't even stop to apologize.

I hold my purse to my chest and look around impatiently. I hate goodbyes.

Mother hugs Father and whispers something in his ear. The sight of them together comforts me. In the week since our family discussion, I've heard them argue countless times. As a child, I never saw or heard them quarrel and I feel relieved at the thought that their arguing will stop now.

I step back a bit and look at the station. So many people are cramming onto the platform, and everyone seems eager to board the train. A young lady clings to a man holding a suitcase. She hugs him, giggling as he strokes her hair. Next to them stands a heavy-set woman scolding two small, squabbling children. I grimace in aversion. I wouldn't want to be in her place, and I'm sure I'll always feel this way. Two men in well-pressed suits look at me and I beam at them and bat my eyelashes. These scenes are so ordinary. I have no doubt that my father's concerns are entirely disconnected from reality. I look around for Michalina and find her leaning against the wall near the ticket booth. Her luggage sits at her feet, and she's immersed in conversation with Anton, a solemn expression on her face. I knew he would come to say goodbye to her, but the unmistakable intimacy between them irritates me. He looks particularly handsome in his police uniform, and a magnetic air of rugged masculinity surrounds him. He grabs a rogue strand of hair that's escaped her braid and tucks it tenderly behind her ear. His fingers hover over her beauty mark as if he's making sure it's really her; then he gives her a smile that makes my heart skip a beat.

I groan quietly.

I have no idea if Michalina's heart also skipped a beat because of Anton's smile. She refuses to talk about him or about her intentions regarding him, and all my attempts to get her to open up are useless.

Michalina insisted on sleeping in bed with me every night since Father's announcement. I didn't object. Deep down, I don't want to part from her. The conversations we had during these last few nights were strange and different. She reminded me over and over to choose my friends with care. She listed my virtues, hailed my strengths, and begged me to restrain myself until the political situation clears up. I've trained my mind to wander to more pleasant thoughts when she begins her tiresome speeches, but the worst thing was that this time she forced me to conduct all our discussions in German.

Father had insisted on bettering us with private lessons in English and German. The English classes amused me, but the German teacher was strict and made me hate the challenging language. Even when she spoke to us about fashion, it sounded as if she was yelling at us. The fear of her harsh reactions made me master German grammar perfectly while hoping that I would never need to hear the language again.

The train's whistle awakens me from my reverie, and I stand up straight. The locomotive passes us, and the passenger cars slowly come to a stop at the platform. Suddenly I'm struck by the realization that this farewell isn't for a few days or even for a couple of weeks. Many months of separation lay ahead, and there's no way of knowing how long it will be before my father admits that the danger he fears is all in his head. How long will it be before we are reunited?

My stomach contracts painfully, and I rush over to my family. Mother pulls Michalina into a hug, but all the while her eyes remain dry. She seems worried that people around us will notice her sentiment. Anton stands next to my sister, his expression revealing no emotion, and Father pulls me into an embrace that is far too tight.

He caresses my hair. "Ania, you can still get on the train instead of me," he whispers in a tormented voice.

"Father," I try to suppress the tremor in my voice, "I'll be waiting for you right here when you get back. You know that I can't bear long journeys."

Father stands up straight and cups my chin in his hands. "Ania," he says earnestly, emphasizing my name, "you can bear much more than you think."

"Okay, okay." I chuckle uncomfortably. "Please don't make this goodbye awkward. People are staring at us."

He leans down and kisses my cheek. When he straightens up again, his gaze lingers on me and then moves to my mother, almost like he's attempting to engrave our faces in his mind. "You are in for a challenging time," he whispers. "Don't trust any of the so-called friends from our circle, but trust and believe that I'll do everything in my power to acquire two more visas."

"Henryk…" Mother says his name in a hushed voice as if reminding him to remain reserved.

Father puts his finger on her lips, signaling her to allow him to conclude his speech. "Remember that I left a large sum of money in the safe, together with the jewelry. Be prudent."

Mother nods and the heaviness weighing on my chest intensifies.

"We'll meet again soon." He bows his head in a kind of solemn promise and picks up his suitcases.

Mother gives him a kiss and clears her throat. Her face is contorted in sorrow.

Michalina stands facing me. Her eyes are pained and troubled, and I know she's doing her very best to show restraint. I stare into her face, which is completely identical to mine, slide the unruly strand of her hair behind her ear, and hover over the beauty mark that characterizes her face alone. My eyes penetrate her eyes, and it seems that all the commotion around us has faded and that there is no one on the platform other than us. Only me and my better half.

"Michalina," I say, biting my bottom lip as a wayward tear moistens my cheek. "This is the first time we'll ever be apart."

"Anushka, it's only a brief separation." She tries to smile, but her lips quiver. "Father and I will get you visas, and you'll join us in America." She fingers the gold triangle pendant hanging around her neck, and I involuntarily reach for the identical pendant hanging around mine.

"You'll come back here," I reply with confidence and wipe away the tear. "Your apocalyptic prophecies will prove to be false, and you'll return home to us exhausted from your unnecessary expedition to the land of the savages."

"I hope so." She lowers her eyes for a moment before looking up at me with endless solemnity, "Anushka, if anything happens..."

"Nothing will happen," I tell her, cutting her short.

"But if something does happen," she insists on finishing her thought, "remember that you are invincible. You always have been, and you always will be."

"Me?" A guffaw escapes my lips.

"You," she says with certainty. "You are cunning and wise and can worm yourself out of any situation. I work hard and study, but you were born with the gift of cleverness. You are the stronger of the two of us. Don't forget it."

I wrinkle my brow and ponder her compliments. We both know that the things she's saying aren't true.

She presses her lips to my ear and whispers, "If I had your courage, I wouldn't be leaving the only man who makes my heart skip a beat every time he looks at me."

My breathing stops.

"If I were a little braver, I wouldn't stutter like a child when I talk to Mother; I would tell her that he's the only man I will ever want." She sighs in anguish. "I don't think I'll ever feel this way about another person. Who knows? Maybe this trip is intended to help me find the courage to take him for myself. I've entrusted my heart to him." Her lips move away from my ear, and she fixes her eyes on mine. "Anushka, keep him safe for me."

I'm incapable of responding. Her confession has shaken me.

A small smile spreads over her face, "At least I have the comfort of knowing I'm leaving my better half in his custody."

"Michalina, we have to get on the train," my father tells her, interrupting us, and I try to catch my breath. The sound of the commotion around us abruptly reverberates in my ears again.

I pant breathlessly and stare at them as if caught in a nightmare.

Michalina stands on her tiptoes and whispers something in Anton's ear. He peeks at me and answers her with a brusque nod. This is the second time he's ever looked at me, but this time I don't find it exhilarating. The grief of the parting has dulled my senses.

Father and Michalina disappear into the passenger carriage but after a few seconds they peek through the window and wave at us.

I run to them and desperately try to reach Michalina's hand. "Write to us!" I plead.

"Of course we'll write." Michalina's voice breaks.

The train's whistle tells us that there are only a few seconds until it'll begin to move.

"Come back quickly," I holler.

"Ania, take care of your mother." The look on Father's face is one of anguish.

I nod vigorously, and the whistle sounds again. The train starts to chug on the tracks, but I continue looking at them and waving until the caboose disappears on the horizon.

Trembling, I put my hand on my heart. This send-off is too painful for me.

I spin around and race to my mother, desperate for a word of consolation.

She draws back just before I can embrace her, hiding her doleful eyes behind the lace trim of her hat.

I hug my arms to my body and sniff, choking back tears.

"I just can't understand their idiotic decision." Mother gives me an intricately embroidered white handkerchief and hooks her arm through mine. "I'm sick of fighting and arguing with your father," she says. She glances to either side and adjusts her posture, ensuring that the hat resting on her head is tilted at precisely the correct angle and that her dress isn't rumpled. "I hope this voyage will make him appreciate our fine, comfortable life and that he and your sister will stop searching for ridiculous adventures." I look back at the empty track that stole my father and sister from me and pout in sorrow. Anton assumes his place at my other side, and I wonder if he shares my turbulent emotions. His expression is closed off, revealing nothing.

We leave the station, and Anton shows us to the coachman waiting for us by the sidewalk. "Mrs. Orzeszkowa," Anton addresses my mother politely and reaches out to help her into the carriage. She scoots over to make room for me on the bench, and Anton faces me. Our eyes meet. His brown eyes see straight into my soul. "Ania," he says, bowing his head and holding out his hand to me. I take it hesitantly, and when our skin touches, I hold my breath. His hand encases mine, and against all logic, I feel his quiet intensity infiltrate me, making me feel calm and reassured. For a moment, my eyelids close, and I have a hard time letting go of his hand. Then Mother lets out a short cough, and I blink and regain my senses. When I sit down, he drops my hand, and I hurry to break eye contact with him.

"Mr. Mrożek, Anton." My mother gives him a fake smile. "Thank you for escorting us to the station. I'm sure that saying farewell to Michalina was difficult for you."

He tilts his chin to one side in a half nod.

"I've refrained from interfering in your relationship thus far," Mother smiles again, but the smile doesn't reach her eyes. "However, now I hope you understand that this goodbye isn't temporary."

"Mother," I chide her under my breath. This exchange shouldn't be taking place now and certainly not in my company.

"Ania, some things need to be said even if they are unpleasant to hear," she states calmly and decisively. "Mr. Mrożek, I'm aware that my husband, Mr. Orzeszkow, likes you, but our plans for Michalina's future do not include you. When they return from this absurd expedition, we will make sure to introduce her to suitors from our own social milieu, and your continued presence in her life may cause her confusion."

I cringe. I had no doubt that Mother would disapprove of their relationship, but I never imagined I would be forced to watch the embarrassing rejection. I sneak a peek at Anton and see that he's standing erect, not blinking an eye.

"Anton..." My mother's voice softens, and she offers him an apologetic look, "I hope you understand that I have good intentions. I'm simply encouraging you to find a suitable match for yourself while Michalina is abroad."

"Naturally, Mrs. Orzeszkowa." He nods in confirmation. He doesn't look upset or hurt; his posture is still tall and proud, and his quiet intensity still pulsates all around him. I gaze at him, and it becomes evident to me that I will never meet such an impressive man. My pain at being separated from Michalina is replaced by the fear that Mother's rejection will hinder my plans to claim him as a suitor of my own. I study his strong, serene expression and promise myself that when I reject his advances, he won't remain so reserved.

"Mother." I turn toward her while setting my shawl over my shoulders. "I have no intention of locking myself away in our house like some damsel in distress just because my sister is away." I scrunch up my nose in dismay. "Tell Anton that you want him to continue chaperoning me in the evenings as he has until now. I'm sure that you don't want me to lose my many suitors."

She ponders my statement for a moment and, at long last, nods. "I have no doubt that Mr. Mrożek will consent to escort you when you go out on the town. Isn't that right, Anton?" She stares at him. "Your friendship with our family is important to us, and I hope you won't hold this conversation against us."

"Of course not," he replies coolly. "I would be delighted to accompany Ania whenever she needs me."

"Then I suppose we'll meet again soon." Mother smiles at him, satisfied, and I can barely contain the joy I feel over receiving such unexpected aid in my schemes.

The coachman pulls away from the sidewalk and I steal one last glance at the station. I reassure myself that separation from my father and sister is only temporary. They left on their adventure, and I, too, will relish the adventures I'll create for myself. I'll utilize this time to thrive without my self-righteous half, who constantly steals all the attention of the only man capable of exciting me.

The carriage wheels screech on the cobblestones as the coachman yanks on the reins. The unhurried ride allows me to enjoy the familiar view of my beloved city: antique buildings alongside modern ones, the steady motion of the automobiles and coaches on the road, the throngs of people crowding into the tram. Sunrays tickle my face, a soft breeze ruffles my hair, and I look out at the pedestrians going in and out of the shops, and at the couples enjoying breakfast at the cafés.

The tram passing us on the boulevard spews out dozens of people at the stop and continues steadily on its way. The scenes from my window are ordinary, just like at the train station. A woman pushing a baby carriage cautiously crosses the road; an elderly couple supports each other on their morning walk; and men in suits hurry to their places of work. Just people living their lives as before.

"What a ridiculous adventure," I murmur to my mother. "When Father and Michalina return, they'll have to make up for needlessly abandoning us."

"Smooth out the creases in your dress," Mother commands quietly. "People are looking at us." She lifts her chin, staring down from her lofty perch at the passers-by as if they were subjects in her imaginary kingdom.

Her boundless confidence soon rubs off on me. My mother is a dignified and impressive woman. Father's fear that anyone would dare to bother her has no base in reality. She appears indomitable to me, and, when I'm near her, I feel the same.

I smooth the creases in my dress and mimic her perfect posture. This city belongs to us.

CHAPTER 4

I pace from the foyer to the dining room and back like a caged lion. It feels as though our massive apartment has shrunk drastically. I worked for hours on end to get ready, putting on makeup and matching my purse and jewelry to the stunning velvet dress I borrowed from my mother's boutique this morning – a masterpiece the color of red wine with a puffed, ankle-length skirt. On my hands are gloves of the same color, and a beret adorns my head. The curls in my hair are just right, and my makeup gives me a smoky-eyed, sensual look. This is the first time Anton will be escorting me out to a restaurant alone. The tingling of excitement I feel overpowers my longing for my sister and father, who left a week ago. It even helps me forget the unsettling thoughts that have preoccupied me ever since I noticed the strange stares and whispering of the women who visited Mother's boutique in the last few days. I thought I heard one of our regular customers say that Mother is an imposter.

I shake my head, banishing those pesky thoughts, and focus again on my anticipation. In her innocence, Michalina left Anton in my custody, and despite her shocking confession, I'm still determined to prove to myself that I'm capable of winning his heart.

"Maria!" I holler as I stand across from the liquor cabinet.

The maid scurries out of the kitchen. She wipes her palms on her white apron and looks at me inquisitively.

"Pour me a little brandy, please." I point to the glass cabinet.

Maria opens the glass doors with extreme care, pulls a crystal snifter off the shelf, and pours my drink.

I study her for a few moments knowing that my stare makes her uneasy. Her complexion is so pale it's practically translucent. Her hair is light-colored like mine, and her features are beautiful and delicate. If she weren't wearing her maid's uniform, she could easily be mistaken for a member of our family. I frown in revulsion at this absurd thought. The foolish girl is only here because her mother worked for us for many years until she died of some awful disease. My father took pity on the young country bumpkin and insisted that we allow her to continue earning her living with us.

She hands me the snifter, and out of the corner of my eye, I see a picture sticking out of her apron pocket. I accept my drink from her and pull out the photograph with my other hand.

The color drains from Maria's delicate-featured face.

"Naughty girl." I taunt her. "You keep a picture of your lover from the village?"

"No, no, Miss Ania," she stammers and keeps her eyes on the photo as if she's afraid I'll crumple it.

I take a sip of brandy and then pick up the picture. It's a photograph of a country family of five. A tall, rugged man lays a hand on the shoulder of a straight-backed, handsome young man. Maria stands next to them, and on her other side is a woman who looks exactly like her, and a young girl with a mischievous twinkle in her eyes.

"Your family?" I ask and study the father figure. He looks strong and proud, as does her brother.

"Yes. My family." Maria's voice quivers.

I can't hold back and needle her some more. "And your father can't provide for you?"

"My father died from an illness a few months after this picture was taken." She grabs the picture out of my hands. "My mother passed away after him, and now I help my siblings get by."

Her answer astounds me. I had no idea she'd also been orphaned from her father and that she works for us to support her siblings.

"I also had an older sister," she says in an anguished voice. "She was the first one to be struck by the illness."

"Your brother seems fit to work," I press.

"He does work." She sticks out her chin, "He works our farm. But the farm doesn't produce enough to sustain us all. I am grateful for the opportunity to work for you, so I can help support my family."

I have a fleeting urge to say something to console her, but she bows her head and sighs.

"Forgive me, Miss Ania. Here I am chatting away about my family while you are missing yours."

Suddenly I feel a searing pain in my chest. With one sentence, she was able to shift my thoughts back to my pining. I take another gulp of the brandy and groan softly. I won't allow myself to be sucked into sorrow now. Not when my moment to spend time alone with Anton and try to win his heart has finally arrived.

"I'm coping. It's just a short separation," I say as I turn away from her.

"I miss them too," she says cautiously.

I groan again and wave my hand for her to leave. I never liked her – maybe because my sister always paid so much attention to her. Michalina saw a friend in Maria, and they spent many hours in each other's company. I'm sure that Maria is saddened by my sister and father's absence, but her sadness makes me angry. The only people who should be sad are my mother and me. Maria needs to learn her place in our household and to be thankful for the living we provide for her.

The door of the house opens, and I hurry to stand up straight and smooth out the creases in my dress. I'm terribly disappointed when Mother stomps inside heavily.

I take a dainty sip of the brandy and put my glass on the table. Mother removes her fur coat, and Maria hangs it up in the foyer. Mother walks over to the table and, without saying a word, picks up my glass and takes a large gulp.

I wrinkle my brow, curious. Mother never drinks liquor.

She plops down on the armchair and rubs the back of her head. She looks tired and is slumped over. Mother never slumps over.

"Mother?" I address her, concerned.

She stares at the painting on the wall behind me and doesn't react.

"Mother?" I raise my voice.

"Ania." She shakes her head as if she's only just noticed me and moves her mouth into a strained smile. "Your murderous cat pounced on me at the entrance to the building."

"You're acting like this because Dziecko jumped on you?" I don't bother to hide my surprise.

"Baby," she snorts scornfully. "An odd name for an odd creature." She rubs the back of her neck again and inhales slowly.

"Mother, I've never seen you like this before," I say tentatively. "Are you sure it's because of the kitten?"

"Of course it's not because of the cat." She exhales sharply. "I went through an incredibly infuriating incident." She sits up straight and pulls off her gloves. "I went to your father's bank to take out money to pay the draper." She peers at me and I bob my head to assure her that I'm listening.

"I went to Wilhelm, your father's replacement. You've met him," she says viciously, "he's the mustachioed man who fawns over your father every time we see him at an event."

I nod again.

"You won't believe what he said to me." She opens her eyes wide and, without pausing, goes on, "He said that our account is frozen until Henryk returns to Poland."

"What?" I ask, baffled. "Why would he say such a stupid thing?"

"Because he's stupid," she barks at me. "He mumbled something about the account being registered under the name of a Polish citizen, so I'm not authorized to withdraw money from it."

"But... but you're also a Polish citizen, and you are married to Father. That account has always been open to you."

"I'll go back there tomorrow and meet with Jarosław." She stands up and secures an unruly lock of hair with a golden hairpin. "When the bank manager hears about this idiocy, he'll fire the idiot." She stretches her neck to one side and then the other.

"But Father said he left us money in the safe." I bite my bottom lip. "Are all the zlotys gone?"

"I deposited the cash." Mother exhales forcefully. "Why would I keep such a large sum in the safe? I'm not a thief."

I shrug. Mother knows best and always acts wisely. I have no reason to doubt her decisions.

"I'm furious with your father for leaving us at a time when my business is doing so well. To go off on a ridiculous adventure all because of rumors. Who would have thought...?" She takes another sip of the brandy when suddenly her eyes seem to darken, and she gives me a hard stare. "The day I chose to leave the Jewish faith, I knew my decision was final. They tried to pull me back in with all their might, but I stood strong in the face of all their schemes. I left them and never looked back." She grits her teeth. "We are Polish citizens with no affiliation to any religion. Don't let anyone tell you otherwise." She points her finger at me threateningly. "The Jews don't like to be forsaken, and you have to be wary of them, too. They'll use sophisticated maneuvers to ensnare you."

"We are Polish citizens with no affiliation to any religion," I repeat after her with my head held high.

She nods, appeased, and then lets out a long breath as if her speech drained the fight out of her. She puts the snifter of brandy on the table and heads down the hall.

"Mother," I call out, and she looks back at me. "Do you want me to stay in with you tonight? I can tell Anton I'm giving up on the evening's amusements."

"Don't be silly." She stifles a yawn with her hand. "You are my clever girl. You stayed here to go out, have fun, and find a worthy suitor. Who knows, maybe by the time Father and Michalina get back, we'll have thrilling news about a respectable engagement to surprise them with."

I answer her with a proud smile. I actually earned a compliment from Mother!

"Fix your makeup," she chastises me. "Lipstick in that shade of red is for promiscuous women."

Her words wipe the smile from my face, and I grab a napkin from the table and wipe the color from my lips.

She disappears down the long hall, and a moment later there are two knocks on the door.

I fight the strong desire to open it but remind myself that I should try not to look overenthusiastic.

Maria ambles over slowly and waits for my signal to open the door.

I nod, and she wipes her palms on her apron and approaches the knob at a glacial pace as if she were stalling purposely to drive me out of my mind.

She opens the door, and my heart beats wildly. Anton stands tall in front of Maria, wearing a gray three-piece suit without a tie. His light hair is combed to the side, and his deep eyes radiate serenity and confidence. He moves his lips into a warm smile that he directs at Maria, and shivers of yearning jostle my stomach. It's rare to see a smile grace his face, and I'm sorry that this spectacular grin isn't meant for me.

I clear my throat, and Anton turns to look at me. The smile no longer reaches his eyes.

"Ready?" he asks, his tone formal.

I nod my head and walk over to him with a broad smile, but the disappointment from his cold reaction echoes inside me.

Maria passes him my fur cape, and he arranges it on my shoulders. The fragrance of his cologne creeps into my nostrils, and I catch a delightful whiff of his distinctive scent. I feel encouraged by his decision to put on perfume for me, but I almost immediately realize how stupid it is to entertain such a thought.

I yank my purse off the hook, push my shoulders back, and together we leave the apartment.

Anton opens the door of the building for me, and my ginger-colored kitten pounces on me with enthusiasm. He digs his tiny nails into the lace hem of my dress, and bending down to pet his fur, I giggle. He purrs with delight.

In an authoritative voice, I say to the kitten, "Dziecko, stay here, and when I return, I'll treat you to a piece of fish."

He tries to pounce on me again, but I pick him up gently and put him down on the grass.

"Don't move!" I shake my finger disapprovingly; the cat yowls, but stays put.

I stand up straight and beam at Anton, pleased with myself. His brow is furrowed, and he stares at me with a thoughtful expression on his face. It seems like he's about to say something but regrets it and instead turns around and opens the gate for me.

We walk side by side down Jerozolimskie Avenue. All my attempts to start a conversation with him are unsuccessful. I chatter about subjects close to my heart, like the winds of innovative fashion blowing here from Paris, the beautiful designs my mother has begun selling at the boutique, and my love for the jazz that comes from America. But he appears to refuse to share in my enthusiasm. His eyes wander across the avenue, and he looks tense and troubled, barely listening to me, only nodding politely from time to time.

His silence is beginning to weigh on me, and the agonizing feeling that he is suffering from my company creeps into my heart.

He holds the restaurant door open for me, and I feel relieved. This is my natural habitat. I feel most confident when I'm surrounded by people and can exhibit my social skills. It's the only arena where I effortlessly defeat Michalina; in her absence, I'll be able to command Anton's attention and prove to him that he chose the wrong sister.

Anton takes the cape from my shoulders and hands it to the man with the tie who is standing at the entrance. I pause, waiting for the man to welcome me as he does whenever I come to the restaurant. But instead of greeting me, he looks mortified and scampers around to hang my cape in the cloakroom.

I wonder what the meaning of his behavior could be and even consider admonishing him for the rude reception, but decide to wait and speak to the restaurant manager about it instead.

The band on the stage is playing classical music. Elegantly dressed men and women sit around the round tables, and a few couples sway on the dance floor. I sneak a peek at Anton, and my heart skips a beat. He is, without a doubt, the most handsome gentleman in the entire establishment. His quiet intensity radiates toward every corner of the room, and everyone looks at him with respect. I draw my lips into a wide grin and make my way between the diners. I have a feeling that this evening is going to be a huge success.

I stop at our regular table. My friends from school, Paulina and Nina, are already seated at the table, their two boring suitors next to them. Until a few months ago, both men chased after me determinedly, sending me flowers and buying me gifts. One of them even used to send me love letters. But when they realized I'd never want them, they moved on and started courting my friends. I smile at them, and they answer with curt nods. Paulina leans over and whispers something in Nina's ear.

The air seems to thicken, and a tingling feeling of unease grows inside me.

Anton pulls out a chair for me, and after I sit down, he sits next to me. The other people at the table look at him with forced smiles.

I put my handbag on the table and clear my throat. "I don't recognize your dresses," I say to my friends. "They aren't from my mother's boutique."

Paulina slides her hands over her dress and snaps, "We thought it would be nice to buy some new dresses from the shops owned by pure-blooded Polish women."

"Excuse me?" My back stiffens.

Anton touches my arm lightly, and I look away at him in astonishment. This is the first time he's ever initiated physical contact, and a feeling of excitement bubbles inside me even though his touch was innocent, meant only to get my attention.

His aloof expression in no way conveys the same thrill that I'm feeling. "What would you like to drink?" he asks.

"Red wine would be splendid." I watch as his hand moves away from me and signals to the waiter to come over. "I'd also love a golonka." I giggle and address the rest of our table, "There's nothing like ham hocks on a chilly evening."

The waiter jots down our order in his notepad, throwing me peculiar looks all the while. I frown and glance over at the other tables. All the restaurant's occupants seem to be staring at me and whispering. I recognize almost everyone here and know what they do, what their hobbies are, and where they buy their clothes, but they seem to be looking at me as if I were a stranger.

"This place has gone bad," Nina clucks her tongue. I glimpse at her again and tell myself that the discomfort weighing on me is due to the fact that I haven't entrapped Anton in my web yet.

"You also noticed that the atmosphere here is different tonight?" I ask, gracefully flicking my hair. Anton needs to learn that he has to compete for my attention. "It's quite shocking that I've been sitting here for a few minutes, and no one has invited me to dance yet." I fix my gaze on Nina's suitor.

Nina links her arm with his and lifts her chin. "I meant that the place has gone bad because they started letting Jews in."

"Where?" I turn my head snappily right and then left.

Paulina and Nina burst out laughing, and I smile, confused.

"Tell me, Anushka." Paulina uses Michalina's nickname for me, even though she knows I loathe it. "Did your father run away with his successful daughter and leave you behind?"

I gape at her, wide-eyed in surprise. I'm used to our harmless teasing, but she's never favored Michalina over me.

"Father and Michalina went on a trip to America," I tell her, reciting the answer my father instructed me to tell people. "You know how much she loves to learn and explore." I wave my hand dismissively. "When she comes home, I'll have to listen to the tales of her thrilling adventures for hours."

"We all know that's not the real reason they ran off," Paulina interjects. "You're afraid that the Germans will come and pull off your ridiculous disguises." Her voice drips with venom, and I feel my cheeks getting pale. "Your father may be a proper and respectable Pole," she says as she combs her frizzy hair with her fingers, "but everyone knows that your mother is a Jewess."

"Watch your mouth!" I hiss through clenched teeth.

"And to think how condescending you were to us for so long," Nina sniggers, "Wearing your fancy clothes and babbling on about your suitors... Who will want you now that everyone knows you're a Żydówka?"

Uncontrollable fury rises in me, and I spring from my chair, determined to slap her across the face. But my waist is seized by a firm grip, and I'm dragged back into my seat.

"Let go of me!" I yell at Anton.

He spins me toward him and stretches his lips into a slight smile. "I believe that as your escort tonight, I am entitled to have one dance." He motions with his head towards the dance floor.

I'm trying to figure out if he's joking, but he stands and ushers me onto the dance floor.

I stand in front of him, but the conversation that just took place at the table doesn't leave my mind.

Anton puts one hand on my waist and holds my hand with the other. I'm distracted and try to remember which direction I need to move my legs. He tightens his hold on my hand, and I bow my head, signaling to him that I'm ready. I let him lead me in a slow waltz and peek at the tables around us. I'm not imagining it. The guests are staring at us and whispering.

"I don't understand what's going on here," I confide quietly, perplexed.

"I believe it's called dancing." Anton smiles at me again, but this time his brown eyes sparkle warmly. Instead of getting excited by these first signs of courtship and relishing his strong, soothing touch, a spasm jolts my stomach.

"I don't think I want to stay here," I'm silent again as he effortlessly leads me to the center of the dance floor.

"Then we'll finish our dance and leave." He stares at me. I feel completely exposed, as if his eyes are penetrating and finding all my vulnerabilities. I lower my eyes and count my dance steps. The stares and whispers are robbing me of the joy my first dance with him should have provided, and I long to run far away from here.

The song ends, and I put my arm through his and try to ignore the stares piercing my back as he leads me to our table.

I grab my purse from the table and demonstratively turn my back to its occupants.

"Anushka," Paulina addresses me loudly, "you should have run off with your pathetic twin sister and relieved us of your company."

I snarl and extend my hands, fully intending to lunge at her and scratch her flushed face.

"Paulina." Anton pronounces her name, his voice dripping with malice, and he overtakes me. He leans over her and puts his hand on the table firmly. "Say one more word, and I'll make your life a living hell. You know I can do that effortlessly."

"I don't understand why you're defending her," Paulina snaps. "She's just another Je..."

"I told you to shut up!" He slams his hand on the table, and she falls silent.

My jaw drops. I've never seen Anton lose his temper, and what's more, I hadn't imagined that he would ever come to my defense like this.

"Enjoy the rest of your evening," he says coldly to the two couples staring up at him in fear. He stands up straight, puts his hand on the small of my back, and leads me across the restaurant.

I'm still at a loss for words when he halts in front of the waiter, points at our table, and pulls out some cash. Even when he puts my fur cape on my shoulders, I don't utter a single syllable. If until now I believed him to be the most attractive man I'd ever seen, now I know that he can truly take my breath away.

We approach the exit, and he opens the door for me.

"Miss Orzeszkowa." I hear the restaurant manager's voice and turn around. "Miss Orzeszkowa," he calls my name again and stops in front of us, out of breath.

"Władyk." I feign a smile and offer him my hand.

After a moment of hesitation, he finally grabs it, shaking it briefly. I dig my teeth into my bottom lip. He always made sure to greet me with great enthusiasm, flattered me on my appearance, and treated me to exceptional dishes, compliments of the chef. His eyes used to shine brightly as he scurried around me, but now they're dull and look disconcerted.

"Miss Orzeszkowa." He straightens the tie on his button-down shirt and bows his head respectfully at Anton. "Are you leaving?"

"I'm finding the company unpleasant," I announce. "I'll come back another time."

"About that..." He averts his gaze. "I'm afraid I'm going to have to ask you to find another restaurant to dine at, at least until..."

"Until what?" I interrupt him, dismayed.

"Until your father returns from his trip." He forces himself to meet my eyes again. "I'm sorry, Ania, but your presence here is making some of my guests uncomfortable."

I try to swallow the lump that his insult has left in my throat and hug my arms to my body in an attempt to hide the fact that I'm trembling. I feel so humiliated, and the reality that Anton is standing next to me only intensifies the feeling. I have no choice but to regain my composure.

"Miss Orzeszkowa to you," I say forcefully. "Don't worry. I won't come back here even after my father returns from his trip, and I'll make sure that the rest of my family don't dine at your damned restaurant either."

"I'll accept it with understanding." He appears unshaken by my answer. "However, there is one matter we need to settle before you can leave." He pulls a note out of his jacket pocket. "There is a balance due from your previous visit. I would appreciate it if you would settle it now." He hands me the paper, and I stare at the amount owed.

"Umm... My father is responsible for our payments." I hand the note back to him. "That's how it was until now and how it will be this time."

"I'm sorry, but I cannot wait until your father returns. Please settle it now."

I hear giggling from a nearby table, and the blood drains from my cheeks. Not daring to look up, I open my handbag with quivering fingers and rummage through it irritably.

"Ania, with your permission, I'll take care of it." Anton grabs the bill from me and hands the manager some money. "Władyk, I hope no noise complaints come from the neighbors," Anton addresses him in a scathing tone. "And I should hope I won't be forced to send policemen here to search for illegal alcohol."

"There has never been a search here," Władyk answers indignantly.

"I never felt the need," Anton winks and turns his back to him. He opens the door, and I run outside and stride quickly down the avenue without looking back.

The sky looks gloomier. The old classical buildings seem so dark, and an overpowering cold penetrates my bones.

My beloved city has been stained with shades of hatred.

CHAPTER 5

Anton closes the distance between us and walks up next to me. The air is thick and foggy, and a strong wind rustles the tree branches. I pull my cape tighter and whimper softly.

"Ania, do you want to talk about what happened tonight?" Anton asks, but suddenly another incident captures his attention.

On the sidewalk in front of us, three boys block the way of a man wearing a wide-brimmed hat with long sidelocks hanging in front of his ears. He tries to walk to the left, and they move with him. He tries to break through between them, and they react by toppling his hat and laughing.

Anton walks towards them and picks the hat up from the dirty cobblestones. I can't hear what he says to the boys, but they break into a run and disappear down a nearby alley.

The man nods to him in thanks and is quickly swallowed up into the darkness of another alley. This isn't the first time I have witnessed such an incident; I just never really gave it much thought before. But suddenly I realize that the estranged treatment I received today was due to my friends associating me with the religion of this unfortunate man. A feeling of extreme rage overwhelms me. How could anyone be foolish enough to assume that I have any connection to these strange people?

Anton comes back and walks next to me, and I decide to erase the evening's events from my mind. I have no doubt that Paulina and Nina's behavior stems from jealousy. I'll make sure Mother handles it tomorrow morning. She won't allow anyone to humiliate me and won't rest until it's been dealt with.

"Ania?" Anton addresses me again, reminding me of his question.

I lift my head toward the sky, and a light breeze caresses my face, calming my anger. A sense of peace slowly envelops me again, and I remind myself that I only have a short time left to spend in his presence and that I should use it wisely.

"What happened tonight isn't worthy of our time." I look at him and grin broadly. "It was all just a series of unfortunate mistakes." I shrug. "My girlfriends will sober up and apologize, and maybe I'll even find it in my heart to forgive them."

"I think we need to talk about the changes happening in your life," he responds somberly.

"What changes are you talking about?" I huff to emphasize my vexation at his words. "You know that all their drivel is nonsense. The only true thing they said is that my sister is a coward." I bat my eyelashes and link my arm in his again. "If you were my suitor, I wouldn't dare run away from you."

His arm muscles tighten.

"Michalina is smart," he rules softly. "She recognized the impending danger and understood that she would be better off away from here."

A pang of envy rattles in my chest.

"An intelligent girl doesn't leave her country because of rumors," I counter, raising my voice. "A proud Polish woman doesn't run away from her country even if war threatens to break out. If something as terrible as that occurs, we should stay and do everything we can to defeat the enemy."

"And how exactly do you plan to defeat the enemy?" he asks sarcastically. "Will you throw your fancy dresses out the window at them? Or perhaps your hats and your purses?"

I halt in my tracks, and he stops with me. "Mr. Mrożek, are you teasing me?"

"Heaven forbid." He lets out a short laugh, and I look at him in amazement. This is the first time I've heard his laughter, and it's clear to me that there is nothing I wouldn't do to hear it again.

"Anton, I don't want the humiliation I underwent at the restaurant to be the last thing I think about before falling asleep," I pout in anguish. "The night is still young, and I would love it if you would come with me to Peter's café. I promise to be content with just one drink, and then you can walk me home."

To my great surprise, he doesn't refuse. He gestures with his head towards the street and flags down a coachman.

He helps me up onto the bench, and my mood miraculously improves. He could have easily refused, but he agreed! He chose to keep spending time with me tonight, and now that we're away from prying eyes, I can relish the nearness of our bodies. I decide to forget about the evening's events for the time being, and the scent of his cologne floods my nose again. I peer at his large hands and try to picture how it will feel when he wraps his arms around me and looks at me the way other men do. I imagine the passion burning in his eyes and how he'll long for my touch.

"We're here," Anton reports, and I touch my cold hands to my face in an attempt to pale the blush that has rushed to my cheeks.

He takes my hand as I hop down to the sidewalk and drops it as soon as he sees I've steadied myself. I peek through the café's windows and smile at the sight of the lively crowd inside.

Peter's café is the perfect place to find solace.

Anton opens the glass door, and I correct my posture and strut in like I own the place.

"Welcome, Ania!" exclaims Peter from behind the bar, his handlebar mustache curled out to the sides. Clad in a stylish suit, he looks like an island of sanity to me on this bizarre evening. I assume that he's about a decade older than me, but he's never agreed to divulge his age.

I grin at him and survey the place. Guys and girls sit around crowded tables. They aren't dressed elegantly, like I am, nor are they dining on fancy delicacies cooked by renowned chefs. Peter's café is a lower-class hangout for students and blue-collar workers looking to escape their mundane, daily routines. None of the men here are suitable suitors for me. Still, the adoring looks they throw me are just what I need to recall my feminine charms.

Anton squeezes my arm gently and leads me to a corner table newly vacated by a loud, boisterous group.

Peter approaches us with his graceful strut and pulls me to him. He embraces me and kisses me twice on each cheek.

"Dearest Ania." He examines me from head to toe. "You look like a medieval noblewoman." His gentle voice is music to my ears. "All the girls here pale in comparison to you," he tells me as he gestures toward the rest of the patrons.

I giggle with delight. Encounters with Peter are always like fuel for my self-confidence.

"I had a simply rotten evening." I bat my eyelashes and sit back in my chair. "I just wanted to hear some good music and enjoy the fine food at Władyk's restaurant, but the people there treated me terribly."

Peter pouts in mock annoyance. "You should have passed on the restaurant and come straight here. I can't offer you a delectable feast, but I can certainly offer you a drink to help you forget all the jealous fools who surround you."

I giggle again and nod.

Peter turns to look at Anton, and his eyes glaze over. He offers Anton his hand to shake; when Anton takes it, a tremor seems to move up Peter's arm. Everyone knows Peter prefers the stronger sex, but he doesn't flaunt it.

When I look at Anton's lordly pose, I can understand Peter. Many of the fairer sex lose their allure next to an impressive gentleman like Anton.

"Your evening can't be that terrible if Mr. Mrożek is your companion," Peter continues staring at Anton openly.

Anton rolls his eyes, and I clear my throat, calling Peter's attention back to me.

"My drink?" I raise my eyebrows.

"Of course, of course." Peter draws a comb from his pants pocket and slicks his hair to the side. "I'll treat you to a cocktail made for aristocrats." He turns to Anton, biting his bottom lip, "And for you, sir?"

"Slivovitz," Anton answers succinctly.

"I had a feeling you were a brandy man." Peter winks at him and pivots toward the bar.

Anton doesn't return Peter's wink. He seems uncomfortable with our host's flirtations, and his eyes wander over to those seated at the bar. I catch several girls giving him the eye and feel the urge to claim my place by his side.

I nudge my chair closer to Anton's and flash a few smiles at the men looking at me. A couple of them even raise their drinks to me. I rummage through my purse, pull out a tube of lipstick and a small mirror, and paint my lips.

"Is this your usual behavior?" Anton asks me coldly.

"What behavior?" I slip the lipstick and mirror back into my bag.

"Do you normally flirt with other men when you're out with someone?"

My hand freezes inside my purse as my heart skips a beat. Is he jealous?

"When I spend time with a suitor, I give him my undivided attention." I turn to look at him and flutter my lashes. "Are you suggesting that you're courting me?"

"No," he snorts with contempt. "But the men you're flirting with don't know that." His expression became harsh. "And when you sit with me and flirt with them, you make me look bad."

His answer angers me. "But..."

"I'm a police officer," he snaps, cutting me off. "I'm not here to watch your childish games, and I won't let you embarrass me. I agreed to escort you, so you'd better conduct yourself properly."

His final words sound threatening, and despite the impulse to retort teasingly, I know I would do well to stay silent this time.

I pout quietly and nod in thanks to Peter as he puts our drinks down on the table. I sip my cocktail and tap on the glass. Anton carefully swirls his drink, inhaling the aroma, and then takes a long sip. His eyes close for a split second, and the wrinkle between his eyebrows disappears. He seems to be enjoying a rare moment of peace. Only now do I see how much responsibility rests on his shoulders. It seems that the burden of his position doesn't give him respite for even a moment.

Suddenly I realize that I've been staring at him for a few seconds too long, and I hurry to turn my eyes to the girl making her way over to us, who is wearing a chic blue dress and an excited smile. Her black hair hangs down to her shoulders like beautiful threads of silk, and her green eyes shine from her doll-like face.

Anton spots her and stands up.

"Ida." He greets her with a broad smile and kisses her cheek.

"Anton, I'm so happy to see you here." She slides her hand across his arm.

The intimacy between them stuns me. I've never seen him in the company of a girl other than my sister, and the affectionate glances they're giving each other cause twinges of envy to shoot through my chest.

"Forgive me for my horrid manners," she says, turning her perfect smile on me. "I'm Ida Hirsch," she says while offering me her hand.

I shake it reluctantly. Her last name sounds familiar to me. Last month, music from a Jewish violinist with the same name was on the radio; I remember it because Mother told Father she was surprised that Jewish musicians were still being played.

"You're not Michalina." She studies my face with kind eyes. "So, you must be her twin. You look completely identical, and you're both gorgeous."

"Ania Orzeszkowa," I introduce myself. Despite her compliments, I'm not sure I like her. How does she know my sister, and why haven't I met her before?

"Please join us." Anton gestures to the chair across from us.

"Gladly, but I can only stay for a few minutes." She sits down felicitously on the edge of the chair. "I told my brother I was only going to say hello." She giggles. "But the truth is that I ran away from the restaurant where I was sitting with my brother, because I'm sick and tired of the friends he keeps trying to fix me up with."

Anton laughs in response to her miserable expression, and she leans forward and smacks his forearm. The rare sound of his laughter rings in my ears, and I'm angry that it's not directed at me.

I feel as if I'm intruding into their private space, and now it's crystal clear to me that I don't like her.

"Tomorrow we're celebrating Yakub's bar mitzvah," she says, removing her glove. "I'm terrified that it will be a mass matchmaking affair." Just then, Peter returns to our table, and she jumps up and embraces him warmly.

"Ida, how is it possible that you get more beautiful every time I see you?" Peter grabs her hand and twirls her around. "Mr. Mrożek, don't you agree that she's remarkably beautiful?"

I shift my gaze sharply to Anton and see that he's nodding in agreement.

"Allow me to treat you to a drink on the house." Peter kisses her hand.

"I would love a drink." She sits down. "But I'll pay for it."

He opens his mouth to protest, but she waves her hand, silencing him.

"Ida, if your father approved, I would ask you to marry me." Peter chuckles and goes back to the bar.

This time I can't restrain myself and roll my eyes. I don't like to share attention that's usually directed at me alone.

Ida bends around face Anton, but I get out in front of the situation this time and decide to question her myself.

"If you're celebrating a bar mitzvah for your brother, does that mean you're...?"

"Old?" She giggles.

"No." I shake my head. "I was going to ask if you're..."

"Jewish?" She tilts her head to the side and grins. "I am indeed Jewish. Does that bother you?"

"No," I answer, looking down. "Of course not. It's just that you don't look Jewish."

Her carefree laugh embarrasses me even more.

"You're definitely not your sister," she judges. "Michalina would never say something so ridiculous."

I lift my head. My embarrassment fades as anger wells up within me.

"Oh, Ania, I'm sorry." Ida puts her hand on her heart. "That was a rude, disrespectful thing to say." She suddenly looks sad, and her apology seems sincere.

My anger fades as quickly as it sparked, and I decide to change the direction of the conversation to a subject I'm more knowledgeable about. "Your dress is beautiful," I say, reaching out and touching the satin fabric. "The design is innovative, and the material looks to be of high quality."

"Thank you." Her eyes light up. "I see that we share a fondness for fashion." She points to my dress. "You're welcome to visit Nalewki Street. You'll discover some quality boutiques there."

I nod and feign a smile. I never frequented the Jewish shopping district before, and there's no reason for me to start doing so now.

"Michalina told me about your mother's luxurious boutique. Unfortunately, I haven't had the chance to visit yet."

I nod once more. Jews don't normally frequent the shops in our area.

Ida moves her gaze to Anton and wrinkles her nose cutely. "Excuse us." She giggles again. "I'm sure our chitchat about fashion and dresses is no fun for you."

He smiles at her in amity, and I just bite my lip, annoyed. This is the only subject I am really knowledgeable about – the only topic of conversation in which I can effortlessly hold my own.

Peter returns and puts her drink on the table. She pulls a few zlotys out of her pocketbook.

"That's far too much," Peter scolds her.

She takes a sip of her drink and beams exaggeratedly. "The amount reflects the value of the exceptional drink you created for me."

"I wish all my clients were as generous as you." He accepts the money with a huge smile. But suddenly he tenses up and frowns. "Mr. Mrożek, I hope the rumors regarding the Germans' intentions towards us are incorrect."

"Of course they're incorrect," I say, speaking out of turn. "What could the damned Germans possibly want with our Poland?"

Peter ignores me and continues piercing Anton with his stare.

"Unfortunately, I can't answer you confidently," Anton replies calmly. "One can only hope that their invasion of Czechoslovakia has satisfied their hunger for occupation and..."

"I forbid you to continue this discussion," I cut him off. "Talking about wars and invasions makes us uneasy." I peek at Ida, expecting her to agree with me. But instead, she takes another sip of her drink in silence and stands up.

"Excuse me, but I have to go." Her lips stretch into a taut smile. "I have a long, exciting day ahead of me tomorrow, and I need to get a good night's sleep."

"Of course." Anton stands up, takes her hand, and kisses it tenderly.

"Ania." She addresses me, but her smile seems forced. "Fashion lovers like us also need to open our eyes and face the world outside of the boutiques that we so greatly cherish. We women can't allow men to do the thinking for us." She raises her finger and taps her temple twice.

"Intelligent women are my weakness." Peter hugs her. Then she bows her head to me and makes her way out.

I contemplate her criticism and continue to stare at her retreating figure until the bar door shuts behind her.

"We should get going now, too." Anton puts some cash on the table and motions towards the door.

This time I don't protest. Even I understand that this night isn't going to get any better, and I have to accept that I'm not at my best.

"But the night is still young," says Peter in dismay.

"It's better to quit while you're ahead," I say with a wink and turn my back to Anton so he can put my cape on my shoulders.

Peter leans in and whispers, "I, too, would prefer to continue the evening in a more intimate setting if Anton were my escort."

I hear Anton snarl in irritation and realize that he heard Peter.

"Please come again. Promise you'll be back soon," Peter beseeches, straightening his neck, a broad smile spreading across his face. He waves enthusiastically to a short, stocky fellow walking towards the bar. The man removes his hat and combs his sandy hair with his fingers. When he reaches Peter, I notice that he fleetingly caresses his arm.

Anton takes my arm and leads us out. He drops my arm as soon as the bar door closes behind us and walks away from me to stop a coachman. I lean against a tree trunk and watch the flickering of the streetlamp. It transports me back to the evening when my sister and Anton sat on the bench, and I looked on at the quiet intimacy between them with envy. My gaze roams down the street and back to him. He's standing tall and strong at the sidewalk's edge, and I'm sorry I lack the courage to walk over to him and take his hand in mine, even for just a moment. This evening has perplexed me, and I'm desperate to tap into some of his strength.

A carriage stops near the sidewalk, and Anton signals to me to join him. He helps me up, makes sure I'm seated comfortably, and sits down next to me. I cling to him inadvertently. The knowledge that the evening is about to end weighs heavily on me. I breathe in his scent and berate myself for feeling so defeated. I make up my mind to use the last few minutes I have in his company to my advantage.

The carriage comes to a stop in front of my building, and Anton helps me out. He opens the gate and comes in after me. The cat yowls and meows at me, and I lean down to him and pet his little head until he walks away from me and paws at Anton's legs.

I wait tensely to see his reaction. My breath stops as Anton kneels down, picks the kitten up in his arms, and strokes its belly. Dziecko purrs with pleasure. The discovery of this new, soft side of Anton's personality only increases the intensity of my attraction to him.

He carefully puts the cat on the grass and orders it not to move. Dziecko obediently curls up to sleep.

If I required another sign that I need to claim Anton for myself, I just got it.

He opens the door of the building, waits for me to go in, and follows me inside. The entrance hall is dark and quiet. I stand on the first step and hold the railing. Anton is right behind me, and I turn around to face him. Our bodies are close together, and shivers of excitement tingle in my stomach.

"Was tonight as enjoyable for you as it was for me?" I whisper close to his face.

"Of course," he replies politely.

"You didn't even compliment me on the gorgeous dress I wore for you." I tilt my head sideways and look deep into his eyes.

"Your dress is very beautiful," he tells me, but his voice is cold.

I refuse to give up and flutter my lashes. "I'm certain you can improve your compliments. Or maybe you only know how to flatter a girl after seeing what's underneath her dress," I say, my cheeks reddening at my own blatant flirting.

"I suppose your drink was quite strong." Anton steps back a bit. "We'll both disregard your last comment."

His gentlemanly reaction to the opportunity I've offered him spurs me on. "I'm sure you've pictured it." I lean forward. "It's just the two of us here. No one can hear us. You can tell me the truth."

A gasp escapes my mouth as he clings to me and wraps his arms around my waist. His face is close to mine, and his lips almost kiss my own. "Is this what you want?" he asks roughly. "Should I rip off your new dress and see if I find your body enjoyable?" Being so close to him is driving me crazy. My bosom rises and falls heavily. "Do you want me to be the first man to pleasure you? The first to kiss your desperate lips?"

His attempt to humiliate me succeeds. My courage slips away, and I feel so stupid. "You won't be the first man to kiss these lips," I lie and put my hand on his chest to push him away.

He smirks, then brushes his fingers through my hair and tucks a stray lock behind my ears. His eyes linger momentarily on the skin between my cheek and my ear, and I see a twinge of regret on his face.

I realize he was looking for Michalina's beauty mark and gnash my teeth quietly. "Did you use such vulgar language because you were fantasizing that I was my sister?" I say viciously.

"On the contrary, I was just making sure that you weren't her." He smiles mockingly.

"Why did you even agree to accompany me?" I raise my voice. "Did you wait for her to leave so you could humiliate me?"

He ignores my outburst, passes me, and climbs the stairs. I hurry to follow him up. He waits for me to open the house door and then bows his head in my direction.

"I didn't choose to spend time with you." His voice is quiet and decisive. "I promised your sister I would watch out for you, and I intend to keep my promise until she returns."

Staring at his back as he walks away, I feel like I've been stabbed in the belly with a knife.

CHAPTER 6

Maria pulls back the curtains and shakes them. She only does this when I miss family breakfast. The bright rays of the sun shine into my bedroom, and I rub my eyes and grumble. I like to wake up naturally, and ever since my father and sister left for their trip, I've allowed myself to stay in bed until the late morning.

"Good morning, Miss Ania," Maria whispers.

"It's not really morning anymore," I reply sharply.

"I hope you had a good time last night." She steps toward the door. "That's why I didn't rush to wake you up."

The memory of my shameful parting from Anton comes back to me all at once, and I pull the blanket over my head. I went over last night's events again and again in my head until the wee hours of the morning, and I still couldn't understand why he humiliated me the way he did. The heaviness in my heart is joined by pangs in the pit of my stomach, and I roll over onto my side and hug my pillow. I only feel pains like these when my twin sister is troubled or distressed, and I wonder why they're attacking me now.

I get out of bed, put on my robe, and go to the bathroom, where I wash my face and repeat the motion Anton made to confirm that

I'm not the sister with the unique beauty mark. I suppose Michalina is distressed by longing – not for me but for the most horrible man in the world.

I go to the dining room and wait for Maria to pour tea into my porcelain teacup. The letter that arrived yesterday from my father is sitting on the table in front of my mother's empty chair.

I open the envelope, pull out the white stationery, and read the words for the second time.

Agata, my dear wife, and Ania, my beloved daughter,

I am sending you this letter from Czechoslovakia. A once beautiful country that is now divided, and looks extinguished and sad.

Our journey began with a pleasant train ride livened by fascinating conversations with other Poles leaving the homeland.

We decided to take a detour and skip the visit to Germany. Our plan is to continue to Austria, from there to Italy, and finally France. There, as you know, we will board a ship to America.

Our longing for you is unbearable. There is still hope in our hearts that we will soon be reunited.

Michalina sends you her love and warm regards to Mr. Mrożek.

Until we meet again.

Love,

Michalina and Henryk

I fold the letter and insert it back into the envelope.

The disappointment and fury I feel toward them outweigh how much I miss them. How could they both be so selfish and cowardly? Did Father not consider the possibility that their departure might lead to false and malicious rumors?

I shake my head, disappointed, and take a fresh apple pastry from the basket. I bite into it and feel comforted by its pleasing taste.

The door flies open, and my mother bursts in.

"Mother. I'm so glad you're here!" I tell her as I sit up straight in my chair. "You won't believe what happened to me yesterday at the restaurant. My friends made fun of me, and the owner of the restaurant said that..."

I trail off as she tosses her cape onto the bench in the foyer and tries to catch her breath. Strands of hair have slipped from her bobby pins, and her eyes are bloodshot. She looks pale and haunted.

"Mother?" I stand up in alarm. "What happened to you?"

She doesn't respond.

Maria puts the cape on a hanger, but when she notices Mother's troubling appearance, she hurriedly slips away to the kitchen.

"Mother?" I address her again and approach her cautiously.

"Ania..." she whispers my name and sighs laboriously.

I grab her arm and lead her to a chair. After she sits, I put my hand on her forehead. She has no fever, but a bit of sweat sticks to my fingers.

"Mother, what happened?" I take a harsher tone, "Are you sick?"

She looks at me, her eyes tormented. "My dear daughter, I am sick with humiliation."

"What... what happened to you?" I gnaw at my lip, concerned.

Mother rubs her eyes, smudging her makeup. I've never seen her like this before.

"I went back to the bank. I tried to go to the manager's office." She keeps rubbing her eyes. "His idiotic secretary made me wait for three hours."

I exhale in annoyance.

"Finally he agreed to speak to me – in the corridor, in front of everyone. As if I were some gypsy scum." She rubs the back of her neck. "You should have seen him standing there with his arms folded and an arrogant look on his face. He informed me that he supports his new deputy manager's decision and that until your father returns from his trip, I will be locked out of the account."

I cover my mouth with my hands.

"He raised his voice so that every single one of the bank's customers would hear his explanation. He said that at his esteemed bank, they only manage accounts for Poles, and he recommended that I try to open an account at a Jewish bank." The last two words are barely audible. "Ania, what are we going to do?"

I gape at her. Is she asking for my advice?

This time, it's Mother who has been through a humiliating experience, and I have no idea how to protect her. I lean on the table and fall into my chair wearily.

"These atrocities are happening to us because of Father!" I bang on the table. "He deserted us for no logical reason and exposed us to this false and vicious gossip. Why didn't you scream that we aren't Jewish when you were at the bank? Why didn't you insist and explain that you renounced your parents' faith?"

"I tried," says Mother, her voice trembling. "I tried several times, but to no avail."

The ache of the humiliation my mother endured crashes like waves breaking on my heart. I hurry over to her and stroke her hair. Where has the brave, strong, proud woman I know so well gone? The person sitting on the chair opposite me is a damaged, broken woman.

"Get up." I instruct and pull her to a standing position. "We won't hide at home. We have a thriving boutique to run, and we don't really have anything to worry about. We can sell some of the jewelry from the safe until Father comes home and straightens out this misunderstanding."

"Sell our jewelry?" Mother grimaces in horror. "Like panhandlers? That's your best idea?"

"I'll think of something else." I bite my lip again and again. "But we can't abandon the boutique and hide out here."

"Ania, I would prefer to retire to my bed." Mother yawns.

"We're going to the boutique," I insist. "Go fix your makeup. We'll leave the house dignified and proud like we do every day."

She retires to her bedroom, and I go to my room and put on a particularly extravagant dress in a dark crimson color. Its delicate bust is adorned with hand-embroidered decorations, and its skirts brush the floor. I have no doubt that it will attract the attention I desire.

* * *

Mother and I climb down from the carriage at the corner of Jerozolimskie Avenue and Marszałkowska Street. She fumbles around in her purse and hands some money to the coachman. Her face reveals her despair, but I'm sure that when she gets to her kingdom – her shining boutique – she'll forget the whole harrowing ordeal and return to her usual self.

"Stand up straight," I whisper the command that I'm accustomed to hearing from her.

She grumbles and corrects her posture. Arm in arm, we walk down the sidewalk, and I toss smiles in every direction.

"It can't be..." I hear my mother muttering. "It isn't possible..."

I turn my head to the direction she's looking, and the blood drains from my face.

Our store window is entirely covered by one giant word: Żyds. Whoever wrote it didn't bother to add any slurs or curses; the single word was enough.

"Go inside," I order my mother quietly. "Go inside, and I'll take care of this filth."

Mother nods, and I lead her into the boutique, where she collapses onto the chaise longue, totally depleted.

I look around, my eyes peeled; to my surprise, I see Ingrid, the longstanding saleslady, sitting huddled near the lingerie section.

"Ingrid, what are you doing?" I shout. "Go clean that filth off the display window."

She stands up and shakes her head no. "Forgive me, Miss Ania." She goes over to the main cash register and picks up her handbag. "I was very worried when I saw the writing on the store window. I had hoped that the rumors weren't true. I even tried to defend you." She peeks at my mother and bows her head. "I opened the boutique this morning out of respect for Mrs. Agata, but the seamstresses refused to stay. Not a single client has come in all morning."

"Why didn't you clean off that horrible writing?" I point to the window.

"I poured some water on it." She shrugs her shoulders. "The paint wouldn't come off."

"You need to scrub it!" I stomp my foot.

"I'm sorry, Mrs. Agata." She turns to my mother, who's staring at her as if she's stuck in a nightmare. "I cannot continue working here. I thank you for the years that you provided me with a good income, but my family won't accept the fact that I work for a Je..."

"Shut up!" I roar at her. "You ungrateful hussy. Those rumors are a heap of lies. You'll see! There will be a line of women outside begging for our forgiveness."

"I truly hope so." She nods and continues, "I would love to come back to work here when Mr. Henryk returns." She hugs her purse and scampers out of the shop.

I feel dizzy, trying to think what I should do and how I can help my mother regain her composure.

"Ania," says Mother as she stands up. "I'm going home. Today is not a good day. Tomorrow will be better."

"Mother, please," I beg her. "We can beat them. Together we can beat everyone."

"Tomorrow, Ania, tomorrow we'll start a war." She kisses my forehead and wipes the sweat from her forehead. Her hollow gaze roams about the store. "Watch my boutique and remember that we are not Jewish," she mumbles. "Don't let anyone tell you otherwise." Her shoulders droop, and she leaves the shop, her back uncharacteristically hunched over.

I curse under my breath and go to get the cleaning supplies out of the utility closet. I fill a bucket with water and head out to the sidewalk, where the stupefied passers-by stare at me. I have no doubt that they've never seen a cleaning lady in such a fancy gown. For a moment, I regret my choice of dress and the attention it's attracting. But all my thoughts turn to dust under the colossal rage that overwhelms me – rage at the family members who abandoned me, rage at the traitorous residents of this city, and rage at my mother's parents, who left us the inheritance of a religion we do not want.

I hear giggling and whispering behind my back and imagine pouring the bucket of murky water on whoever dares to be happy in my misery.

I scrub the window vigorously, transferring all the anger I have growing inside me to the rag in my hand. I swear to myself that I will take revenge on anyone who dares to humiliate us. The work is hard. The color withstands my scrubbing, and I keep battling against it. One letter is nearly erased, and I move on to the next.

"Ania." The deep voice of the man I hate most in the entire world comes from behind. I refuse to turn my head and continue fighting against the damned paint. "Leave it, and I'll make sure to have it cleaned."

"I don't need any favors from you," I reply venomously.

"Leave it," Anton commands quietly.

"Go away!" I spit out the words. "I don't need your help. I'm perfectly capable of cleaning up this filth myself."

I get a whiff of his cologne even before I feel his body lean towards me. "You don't want passers-by to see that you are forced to clean it yourself," are the hushed words that penetrate my ears.

My outrage refuses to dissipate and is now directed at him. I throw the rag at the display window and turn to face him with glossy eyes. "I feel honored that all the lowlifes around me will see me cleaning this hideous vandalism myself. I have nothing to be ashamed of. This malicious writing is all part of our competitors' propaganda against us. They need to see that I won't bow my head in defeat. I will fight for my truth."

Anton's face remains expressionless as he asks, "And what exactly is your truth, Ania?"

His question catches me off guard. I open my mouth to reply but can't think of an answer that will satisfactorily end the discussion. I turn my back on him with clenched teeth and resume scrubbing the glass. I expect to hear his footsteps receding, but instead he walks forward and leans on the stone column that separates our shop window from the window of the neighboring boutique.

His presence confuses me, but I command myself to regain my composure and go back to concentrating on my goal.

Suddenly I hear a mocking, boyish voice behind me mutter, "Dirty Jews." A growl of rage erupts from my throat and I spin around with the obvious intention of smacking the cheeky boy. But before I turn all the way around, I see the boy's scrawny body pressed against the stone wall, Anton clutching his throat. The rag falls from my hand into the bucket, and water splashes on my dress.

"Apologize to the lady," Anton barks into the boy's terrified face.

"Umm... yes... I..." The boy stutters.

"Apologize!"

"For what, Sir?" The boy coughs. "I didn't harm her or her property."

I approach the boy and slap him on the wrist. "Apologize to me for saying something so ludicrous," I practically shout. "Apologize to me for daring to insinuate that I'm Jewish and not Polish."

Anton's face is contorted in contempt. He loosens his grip around the boy's neck, and the latter breaks into a quick run and disappears down the alleyway.

"Why didn't you wait for him to apologize to me?" I pick up the rag and stick out my chin.

He shakes his head, leans back against the pillar again, pulls a pack of cigarettes out of his pants pocket and lights one.

I pointedly ignore his presence and continue scrubbing with vigor. Finally, after an agonizing hour, I throw the rag into the bucket and drop my arms in relief.

"I'll escort you home now," says Anton, standing up straight.

"I don't need an escort, and I'm not interested in your company," I tell him as I pick up the bucket.

He snatches the bucket from me, pours the water into the sewer grate, and goes inside the boutique. I stretch my lips into a fake smile directed at the saleswomen peeking out at me from the nearby boutiques and stride in after him.

Anton disappears to the upper level. I stand in front of a mirror and, in frustration, examine the stains of filthy water and paint stuck to my dress.

A mustachioed, potbellied man in a dapper suit walks in, and I hurriedly arrange a warm smile on my face and welcome him. Men don't often buy dresses for their wives here, but from time to time a man of means will come in to buy a gift for his mistress. We need such money now more than ever.

"Good evening. Where is Mrs. Orzeszkowa?" he asks politely.

"Mother isn't feeling well and has gone home," I tell him as I maintain my smile. "I'd be happy to help you in her absence."

"Then I'll wait here while you fetch the money she owes me for the fabrics." His voice no longer sounds polite.

"The... money?" I stammer. "I think..."

"The money. Now!" He raises his voice and holds out his hand.

I gulp.

"Is there a problem, sir?" Anton's authoritative voice gives me time to catch my breath.

"There is a serious problem here, officer," the man answers sharply. "The owner of this boutique has stolen fabrics from me."

His choice of words nauseates me. "My mother didn't steal anything," I snap. "She isn't feeling well and therefore isn't here. She'll pay this gentleman tomorrow."

"You heard her." Anton overtakes me and stands in front of him. "Come back tomorrow to receive your payment. And I suggest that you not be so quick to accuse the women who provide you with such a good living."

The man snickers in contempt. "I am a well-known, respected fabric merchant in this city. I should have suspected the truth when Mrs. Orzeszkowa conducted such formidable negotiations with me about the prices. Now I understand that it was because of her Jewish blood."

"Stupid little man," I shriek. "How dare you call my mother a thief!"

"It's hard to resist your nature." He smirks and shrugs his shoulders.

"You..."

"Quiet!" Anton shushes me. "I suggest the gentleman leave now and return tomorrow to collect his payment. Come at noon, and I will be here to make sure you get what you came for."

I turn pale. Could it be that Anton fears that there is truth in the merchant's words and thinks I won't keep my word?

"Many thanks, officer." The merchant twists the ends of his mustache with his fingers. "If payment is not made, I will empty this store of its merchandise." He surveys the dresses on their hangers and leaves the boutique.

I grind my teeth, and without saying a word, I grab the few bills left inside the cash register, stuff them in my wallet, and leave the shop. Anton leaves right after me. He waits for me to lock the door and starts walking next to me.

"Go away!" I bark.

"I'll get us a carriage," he says, ignoring my demand.

"I'm not taking a carriage home." I touch my wallet. "I've decided to take the tram."

Anton grins. "You intend to squeeze into a tram wearing that dress?"

"You don't dictate what I can and cannot do." I quicken my pace.

He seizes my arm, forcing me to stop. "Ania, what are you not telling me?" His eyes pierce mine, and he questioningly tilts his head to the side.

"Nothing." I play dumb. "You know everything."

He pulls me to the sidewalk with him, waves his hand, and hails a coachman. I try to protest again, but he holds my waist and lifts me onto the bench in the carriage. Being near him weakens my resolve. He hops up, takes a seat next to me, and gives the coachman my address.

"You shouldn't have done that," I whisper crossly.

"Why not?" he questions, narrowing his eyes.

"Because..." I breathe in deeply and shiver. The burden of the last few days sits heavily on my shoulders and, for an instant, a pricking feeling gnaws at the pit of my stomach. "Because..." I don't know if I can trust him. I exhale slowly and clench my jaw. "Why did you ask to be there tomorrow for the merchant's payment?" I blurt out the question that's bothering me. "Are you afraid that I won't keep my word? Or are you simply starting to believe the horrible rumors about us?"

He doesn't bat an eyelid. "I asked to be there to make sure the merchant doesn't harass your mother."

His response lessens my hatred for him. His eyes wander to the point where my cheek meets my ear, and I realize he's looking at me and thinking of her. To my surprise, I don't feel angry. We share the longing for my other half. I need her so much right now. I need her advice, her words of encouragement, her friendship. I terribly miss having her to lean on, and if Michalina trusted Anton, maybe I can, too.

"I'm afraid we're having a bit of trouble," I whisper, lowering my eyes. "I'm not sure we have enough cash to pay him."

Placing a finger under my chin, Anton forces me to look at him.

"The bank has blocked access to our account until my father returns," I explain ashamedly, "Until then, our livelihood hangs on the boutique's sales, and I'm afraid it will take some time before we'll be able to pay him."

"I understand," Anton replies.

I want to ask for his advice, but my pride prevents me from doing so. The fact that he doesn't say anything only intensifies my frustration.

The coach stops in front of my building, and Anton pays him before I have time to pull the money out of my wallet. I don't know whether to thank him or scream that I refuse to let him treat me like a charity case.

"You have to find a way to pay him," says Anton, opening the gate for me.

"And how exactly are we supposed to do that?" I sigh. "Sell our furs and jewelry like beggars?"

Dziecko runs through the grass and leaps at me in enthusiasm. I get down on my knees and hold him close to me. His excitement consoles me a bit.

"That's exactly what you will do," says Anton firmly. He kneels with one knee on the grass so that I will meet his eyes.

"Absolutely not." I bat my eyelashes. "You can help by demanding that the scheming merchant wait until my father returns."

"And when is he coming back?"

"You know I don't have an answer to that." I say, raising my voice. "If I had any way to write to him, I would insist that he return immediately."

"Ania," Anton pronounces my name clearly. "I cannot demand that a merchant wait indefinitely to receive payment for goods he's already provided."

"You could if you really wanted to." I narrow my eyes indignantly. "If Michalina were sitting here instead of me, you would do anything to help her."

"But she isn't sitting here, is she?" he retorts coldly. "She would never ask a police officer to use his rank to help her avoid payment, and she was smart enough to leave in time."

His answer infuriates me. "She's a coward!" I shout. "She ran away to America and left me here to make sure that she would have a place to come back to."

"Michalina decided to leave because she recognized the impending danger," he says through clenched teeth, his voice strained. "If you had any sense at all, you would be packing a suitcase for yourself and your mother as we speak and asking me to give you a lift to the train station." He takes a deep breath, and his tone softens, "Ania, leave Poland today and wait in France for the visas they're acquiring for you."

"You aren't responsible for us." I pet the kitten and put him down on the grass. "You have no obligation towards us, and it seems like you're trying to avoid the promise you made to Michalina."

"So stubborn..." he mutters, almost to himself. "I've never made a promise I didn't intend to keep. Therefore, I will do everything in my power to keep you safe. My suggestion that you leave comes from a place of concern for your fate."

"Then I hereby release you from your obligation to keep your promise." I stand up and face the front door. The lonely old man who lives on the first floor is sitting on the bench in the entryway. He lifts himself up laboriously when he notices us and hobbles to the staircase with the help of his cane; in his other hand he holds a basket of groceries.

I pick up my pace to pass him.

"Please let me help you, Mr. Pavlitski," Anton addresses him, taking the basket from his hand.

"Thank you very much, officer," sighs the old man.

Scowling, I continue going up the stairs. How does Anton know the name of my elderly neighbor? I've lived in this building my entire life, and it never occurred to me to ask his name.

Anton helps the old man into his apartment, and I continue skipping sprightly up to my apartment. I hope that Anton will get the hint and understand that I'm tired of his company and he'll let me have a private conversation with my mother.

I go into the apartment, slam the door behind me, and come face to face with Maria, who looks at me, shocked.

"Miss Ania, what happened to your beautiful dress?"

"I wanted to see what it would look like with spots of yellow paint," I reply impatiently. "Where is Mother?"

Maria's face is sad, and her brows are knitted in concern. "Mrs. Agata is lying in bed. She refused to let me serve her a cup of tea or a pastry and asked me not to disturb her rest."

"She's still asleep?" I throw my beret on the bench in the foyer.

"I checked on her just now, and she looks very ill."

I hear two knocks on the door, but I ignore the knocking and hurry down the hall to my mother's room.

The curtains are drawn and the room is dark. Mother is lying on her side of the large bed. I come closer to her and see that her eyes are closed, and her face is pale.

"Mother," I whisper and put the palm of my hand on her forehead. She's burning up.

"They're beating Yózef up," she says hoarsely, her head jerking from side to side. "They are so many, and he is only one."

"Who is Yózef?" I ask, alarmed.

"Leave him alone!"

"Mother?" I shake her by the shoulders.

"They can't see me. I need to hide," she whispers, coughing. "I don't want to be Jewish. I'm not Jewish. I'm not Jewish."

"You aren't Jewish, Mother." I stroke her hair. "You are a proud Polish woman."

Suddenly her eyes open, but she seems to be looking straight through me. "Ania, my beautiful daughter. Michalina will take care of you. She will know what to do." Her eyes close again, and her breathing gradually deepens.

I pull the blankets over her. Only a few hours had gone by since she returned home by herself. She'd seemed grief-stricken, but I didn't expect her condition to deteriorate so quickly.

"You're tired," I whisper encouragingly. "You'll be just like new tomorrow."

She doesn't respond.

I tiptoe out of the room, close the door, and go back down the hall. Anton is standing in the foyer next to Maria.

"Mr. Mrożek insisted on waiting for you here," Maria says apologetically.

I sigh and turn towards the parlor. They both follow me. I sit down on the armchair nearest the window and hide my hands between my knees. I'm thinking about Mother. I've never seen her lying in bed so exhausted, frail, and defeated. Mother, the strong woman who never missed a day of work at the boutique, the woman whose pride is her defining feature, the woman who has always supported me. I want to consult with her desperately, but it's clear to me that I won't be able to do so today.

"What can I get for you?" Maria asks as she heads toward the liquor cabinet.

"Brandy for me." I turn my gaze to the window and look outside. The sky has darkened, and so have my spirits. The trees planted along the street don't obscure the row of buildings behind them, and I stare at the lights flickering in their windows. I wonder if there's another girl sitting in one of the other homes who also feels that her once-stable world is falling apart.

"Brandy for me, as well. Thank you, Maria." Anton sits in the armchair on the other side of the window.

We remain silent as Maria pours our drinks and serves them to us. I swirl my drink around in its glass and taste it.

"I'll wait here in case you need anything else," Maria says as she stands by the door.

"We won't need anything else," I reply, not looking at her.

"Ms. Ania," she whispers pointedly, "I can't leave you in the parlor alone. Mr. Henryk is strict about proper etiquette and..."

"Mr. Henryk is not here," I say Father's name bitterly, "And we won't be needing anything else."

Maria bows her head in defeat and leaves the room.

"Where is Mrs. Agata?" Anton asks.

"Mother isn't feeling well," I recite my answer. "She's suffering from a nasty headache."

"Then I cannot stay here." He gets to his feet. "Maria is right. It's improper for me to stay in the parlor with you alone."

"What? Are you afraid the neighbors will gossip about my promiscuous behavior?" I snort mockingly. "Maybe it would be better if they talked about my behavior rather than spreading despicable lies about my religion."

He finishes his drink in one long gulp, puts his glass on the mantelpiece, and turns to the door. Suddenly, it dawns on me: I will have to deal with my despair alone when he goes, and the thought of it doesn't please me at all.

"Maria!" I shout, and within seconds she bursts into the room. "Mr. Mrożek has finished his drink. Please remain in the parlor."

She nods energetically and looks relieved.

Anton sits back down on the armchair, and I take another sip of brandy.

"I'm at a loss," I mumble into my glass.

"I offered you my soundest advice," he says calmly and bows in thanks when Maria hands him his drink. "You have no other choice. You have to keep your heads down until your father returns. You'll need money to pay the merchant, to pay your employee's salary, and for living expenses."

I see Maria gaping at him in astonishment. The thought of paying her salary hadn't crossed my mind for a second.

I tap my nails on my glass and ponder my options, but I don't come up with even one idea that can help us obtain money.

"I don't know anyone who would purchase jewelry from me at a fair price."

"I know someone." Anton glances at me. "On the other side of town."

"Then I'll go to him now," I say before I take another gulp of my drink, trying to blur my senses just a little.

"Ania, I will do it for you." Anton leans forward and gives my arm a light squeeze. His touch is so gentle. He's trying to reassure me but, at the same time, makes me feel helpless. I don't like it.

"All right." I stand up and put my glass on the windowsill. "But don't presume that I need you. The only reason I am accepting your offer is because Mother doesn't feel well, and I'd rather stay here and look after her."

"Of course," he answers.

I leave the parlor and go to my room. The safe is in my parents' bedroom, and I don't want to add to Mother's troubles at the moment. Instead, I look at everything in my jewelry box and choose the diamond necklace I got from Father for my graduation. I don't know how to assess its value, but I presume it's not insignificant. With great sorrow, I position it in the velvet box next to its matching bracelet, hoping that this painful concession will be the last thing I ever have to give up.

I return to the parlor, hand Anton the box with a heavy heart, and run back to my room without thanking him. I lie down on the bed – still wearing the dirty dress – and I snuggle up under the thick duvet. I wish for this nightmare to be over when I open my eyes, and I wish that the annoying burning in the pit of my stomach would fade.

"Tomorrow morning I'll get my life back," I whisper confidently to myself and sniffle. "I won't cry. Tomorrow morning, Mother will be herself again. She'll take this heavy burden off my shoulders, and I'll be able to breathe again."

I hug my pillow and order myself to calm down, but the anger inside me just intensifies. I'm angry at Father and Michalina for abandoning me, and I'm angry at Mother for getting sick – just when I need her the most.

CHAPTER 7

The yellow writing adorns the shop window like a glowing sign, advertising my humiliation. I stand in front of the boutique and try to remain composed. I'd prayed that I would wake up to the life I knew before, but Mother refused to open her eyes, and I had to eat breakfast alone.

I look down at my blue dress with its puffy sleeves. I chose a gown that would flaunt my social status, and I'm extremely happy with my choice.

The salesladies in the neighboring boutiques peek out at me, but none of them offers to lend me a hand. The very same salesladies who begged my mother to hire them are now casually watching my humiliation. I scold myself for thinking such defeatist thoughts and shake my head. As soon as I get rid of the filth on the display window, our clients will return, and I will tend to them professionally, just like Mother always does.

I unlock the door of the boutique, head straight to the utility closet, fill the bucket with water, and go out to the display window. This time I assail the glass with a rough sponge that removes the paint in no time. Within an hour, the glass is completely scratched, but the paint is gone, and I smile to myself, satisfied. When Mother returns and sees the damage, I'll explain to her that I had no choice.

I pour out the water from the bucket and go back into the boutique. I sweep the entryway, dust the shelves, and air out the dresses—the place sparkles, ready to welcome customers.

The hours tick by. I pace back and forth through the store, skipping to the upper level and back down again, fixing my hair in front of the mirror, reapplying my lipstick, and glancing toward the front door. I sit down on the chaise longue and flip through a fashion magazine that arrived by special delivery from Paris a few months ago. The fact that Anton hasn't contacted me yet worries me, and meanwhile, hunger has started to gnaw at my stomach. I look at the wall clock. Noon is approaching. I have no idea what I'll do if Anton doesn't show up before the fabric merchant arrives to collect his debt.

"Good afternoon, Ania, darling," says an ethereal female voice, and I look up from my magazine. Ida is standing at the boutique's threshold with two girls about our age at her side. They're wearing trendy, contemporary dresses, gloves, and fashionable hats.

"Ida." I look at her, bewildered. She's never come to our boutique before, and I wonder how a Jew like her dares to come to our establishment.

"I hope you're free to help us." She flashes me a beautiful, toothy smile. "I imagine that at such a prestigious boutique, it's preferable to coordinate visits in advance, but we are positively swamped with happy occasions and would love to buy some of your spectacular gowns."

I bite my bottom lip as her friends walk inside and start surveying the dresses on the hangers. Ida follows them in, and I hastily peek outside to ensure that none of the neighbors are watching what's happening.

Ida holds a dress with long velvet sleeves to her body and examines her reflection in the mirror. I walk up behind her and whisper, "I don't think you should be here."

"Do you have a meeting with another client scheduled?" She gives me an innocent look.

"No... but..."

"Ania," her voice is suddenly solemn. "Ignorance and hatred of the other are unfortunately widespread in our city."

"And what does that have to do with me?" I press.

"Soon you'll wake up and understand that you can't evade it," she says, a bit too loudly, and her friends walk over to us. "Once you've been defined as one of us, you have no choice but to adapt to your new circumstances."

"I'm not interested in such a definition," I reply contemptuously. "No one can force your religion on me, and I have no doubt that the situation will return to normal in a few days."

"Are you sure?" she asks as she squeezes my arm sympathetically.

"I'm sure that your presence in my boutique is spoiling my attempts to shake off the awful gossip that's spreading about us. Every minute you spend here distances other customers. Polish customers." I emphasize the last two words.

Ida looks at me in silence and nods. I expected her to be offended, but instead, a smile graces her face again. "We wouldn't want anything like that to happen. We'll leave right away so as not to jeopardize your livelihood." She gestures toward the door and hangs the dress back in its place.

"Ania, if you need me, you can find me at this address." She scribbles an address on a piece of paper and puts it on the counter, then adjusts the hat on her head and leaves the store with one of her companions. The other girl stands in front of me and picks some lint off the shoulder strap of my dress.

"You were blessed with pure Polish looks," she sighs. "If you leave the city now, you might be able to outrun the rumors that are being spread about you."

"I'm not planning on going anywhere." I cross my arms over my chest.

"Then, let me just say that along with the disadvantages of the Jewish blood flowing in your veins, there are also many advantages.

We always take care of our people." She nods her head brusquely and leaves the boutique.

I collapse onto the chaise longue, feeling helpless. I've been marked as a Jew on both sides of the barricade, and dark walls are closing in on me from all sides.

I stand behind the counter and tap my foot, restless. The note scrawled in Ida's handwriting peeks out at me, a horrid reminder of my sorry state, and I toss it into my bag, knowing full well that I'll never use it. The hands on the clock are moving too fast, as is my pulse. My eyes pop out in astonishment when the fabric merchant strides in, accompanied by Anton. I purse my lips and look at both of them with apprehension, albeit mingled with some hope.

"The wagon is already waiting outside," the fabric merchant announces, his tone surprised. "I was certain I wouldn't get my money today and planned to take dresses from the boutique instead."

"I'm sorry to disappoint you." Anton pats him on the back. "But Mrs. Orzeszkowa kept her promise." He hands the merchant a thick envelope.

I observe their exchange in silence.

The merchant accepts the envelope and spreads the bills out on the counter. He examines each banknote, licking his index finger as he counts them. "This isn't the full amount," he barks at me.

"Uh... I... um..."

"You are 500 zlotys short!" He bangs on the counter.

I feel the blood drain from my face. "You surely don't mean to make a fuss over such a small amount." I regain my composure and add, "A respectable merchant like you..."

I see Anton's jaw quiver as he runs his fingers through his hair. "My mistake." He walks around the counter and stands by my side. "Mrs. Orzeszkowa asked me to pay you and deposit the balance in her bank account. I must have miscalculated."

"A Polish policeman performing the chores of a wretched Jewish woman," the merchant says, and promptly spits on the floor.

"A police officer assisting a dear friend," Anton corrects him composedly. "I'll make sure to bring the rest of the money to your office."

The merchant looks around the shop and shakes his head. "I think I'll nevertheless take the rest of the debt in the form of merchandise."

I stand with the racks at my back and spread my arms to the sides to protect Mother's dresses.

He sniggers and walks up to me. "What a waste!" His eyes scan my body and he continues, "All this divine beauty will be wasted on some stinking Żyd." He reaches out and traces my arm with his finger and I immediately push him away and snarl in anger.

Anton stands next to me, his perpetually peaceful brown eyes blazing with fiery rage. "I recommend that the gentleman leave the boutique right this instant and never come back." His tone is calm, yet threatening.

"I'm a law-abiding citizen." The merchant twirls the ends of his mustache with his fingers. "You can't stop me from visiting shops on the avenue."

Anton smiles a tight smile that doesn't reach his eyes. "I did a little research on you. It seems that we've received some complaints about you regarding the way you run your business."

"Those erroneous accusations have been thrown out," the merchant replies furiously, stuffing the envelope into his jacket pocket.

"Not thrown out." Anton clutches my arm and guides me back to the counter. "They're still on file in a binder on my desk. Perhaps I'll decide it's time to follow up on the investigation."

"Your threats don't intimidate me," the merchant replies toughly, although his body language says otherwise.

"I never threaten." Anton drops my arm and moves to stand facing him. "The next time you come here and try to harass the young lady, I'll have dozens of policemen haunt your offices and make your life a living hell."

The merchant grits his teeth and throws me a piercing look. "I expect to receive the rest of my money tomorrow."

I'm dying to open my mouth and tell him exactly what I think of him, but I have no energy left for another confrontation so I merely nod my head in assent.

"A policeman who loves Żyds," the merchant snorts contemptuously. "I hope she's good enough in bed to be worth the trouble."

I turn my gaze sharply to Anton, expecting to see him attacking the vile man in defense of my dignity, but he only lifts his arm and points towards the door.

The merchant leaves, and I clench my fists and charge at Anton. I hit him on the arm and then on the chest. "How could you let that scum slander my reputation!" I swing my fist again, but my arm stops, suspended in the air. Anton wraps his hand around my fist and gives me a steely look.

"I was faced with two options," he growls. "One was to end this encounter with him leaving unscathed, just like your reputation. The other," he goes on, his expression turning grim, "was to drag him into the street, throw him on the sidewalk, and smash his head to a pulp."

I'm appalled by the violent picture he paints.

"If he'd laid a finger on you, I would have killed him without hesitation." He loosens his grip on my fist, and his fingers catch a perfect ringlet artfully resting on my face.

A blush rises on my cheeks.

He tucks the curl behind my ear, and, for a moment, his eyes burn with passion, but a split-second passes, and they appear closed off and impenetrable again.

He was just making sure that I'm not her. Not Michalina.

I bite my lip and pull away from him. The walls of the boutique are closing in on me, and I have to get out of here.

"This day has spent itself." I avoid his gaze. "I don't have any appointments scheduled with clients, so I may as well leave."

"I'll drive you," says Anton, holding the door open for me. I can't find the strength to resist his offer to escort me this time, so I join him. It takes all my might to ignore the looks the passers-by are giving me. On any other day, I would have been confident they were marveling at my appearance, but now I feel as though the yellow writing I scrubbed from the display window is emblazoned on my forehead.

I pause for Anton to hail a carriage, but he motions for me to join him and walks by my side to the street corner. He comes to a stop in front of a police car and opens the front door for me.

"I've never seen you drive such a machine." I look behind me, hoping people don't get the wrong impression when they see me getting into a police car.

"I don't often use it outside of work." He makes sure I'm seated, shuts the door, gets behind the wheel, and starts the engine.

"Am I considered work?" I put my hand over my cheek in an attempt to hide myself from the people walking past us.

"I think we can agree that you provide me with quite a lot of work." He turns the steering wheel, joining the oncoming traffic.

His answer annoys me.

"I don't remember asking for your help," I tell him as I lean towards the door.

"Too bad, because I enjoy helping you so much," he chuckles. "I'll stop in front of your house and wait outside while you bring me another piece of jewelry that we can exchange for cash to cover the rest of your debt to the fabric merchant."

"But I already gave you two pieces of jewelry," I wail.

"I'm sorry, but the amount I got for them wasn't enough to pay off the full debt."

"I'm afraid that I don't own any more valuable jewelry." In desperation, I caress the triangle pendant that is around my neck. When we celebrated our 17th birthday and Michalina began her nursing studies, we received chains with matching pendants from my father. After we put the necklaces on, Father told us, "*Only when you are together, the two triangles will turn into a star that will light your way.*"

A sudden pain stabs me in the pit of my stomach, and I shudder.

"Ania, I'm sure your mother can contribute a piece of jewelry to help cover the debt," Anton states resolutely.

"But... but I haven't told her about his demands and..."

"You're hiding such critical information from your mother?" He throws an alarmed look in my direction. "How is it possible that you haven't told her that he is threatening to empty her boutique?"

"I thought I could spare her the emotional distress." I twist a ringlet around my finger. "I gave you the only jewelry I have that..."

"You need to tell your mother what's going on," he interrupts me. "She needs to help you manage the situation and help with the additional challenges that await the two of you."

His choice of words sounds odd to my ears. These aren't challenges. These are atrocities that I cannot overcome.

"Mother doesn't feel well." I shrug.

"Your mother is an intelligent, shrewd woman. She has to acknowledge the situation and do her part to make sure you get through it together."

He parks the automobile in front of my building and walks around to open the door for me.

"I'll tell Mother and come back with another piece of jewelry." I sigh in resignation and walk through the gate. Dziecko chases after me, but I'm afraid I won't be able to find comfort in him this time.

* * *

The apartment is quiet. The only sounds come from the kitchen. I don't bother to greet Maria and rush straight to my parents' room, hoping to find Mother doing her hair and makeup in front of the chiffonier. I envision myself telling her about the events of the last few days and imagine how she'll wave her hand in dismissal, convince me that dealing with suppliers isn't my vocation, and tell me that I should go back to doing what I excel at – going out on the town, flirting, and chitchatting about my suitors.

I open the door to her room, and my heart sinks. The curtains are still drawn, the room is dark, and Mother is in a deep sleep. She looks flushed, and her forehead is clammy.

"Ms. Ania," Maria whispers behind me, "I'm very worried about your mother's condition."

I spin around to face her with an irritated humph. "Did you offer her a drink? Serve her a cup of tea? Treat her to a pastry?"

"I tried." Maria puts her hand on her heart. "Mrs. Agata won't wake up and keeps mumbling strange things. She's burning up, and I think she needs to see a doctor urgently."

"Mother is fine," I scowl. "She just has a headache."

Maria opens her mouth to answer me, but I walk into the room and shut the door in her face.

I approach my mother, stroke her burning forehead, and carefully shake her by the shoulders. She murmurs something unclear.

Maybe it's better this way, I console myself. Mother won't find out that I failed to postpone the payment. I can take a piece of her jewelry without her noticing. I'll apologize when she gets back on her feet.

I remove my parents' portrait from the wall, revealing the safe hidden behind it, and I turn the dial: Seven. Six. One. Nine. One. Nine. The seventh of June 1919. The date of Michalina's and my birthday. The safe door opens with a loud screech, and I look at Mother in trepidation.

Her eyes remain closed.

I slide my fingers wistfully over the elegant velvet boxes, then finally choose one and close the safe. I hang the painting back in its place, stroke my mother's hair, and walk out into the hall.

Maria is waiting for me at the door with the shopping basket in her hand.

"Ms. Ania, the groceries are nearly finished. I was thinking of making vegetable soup for Mrs. Agata, but I need money to go to the market."

"Money?" I echo her and swallow the lump constricting my throat.

"Master Henryk gives me money for the shopping every week," she clarifies.

"Tomorrow." I nod earnestly. "Tomorrow, I'll give you money for shopping."

"But..."

"Tomorrow!" I raise my voice, almost shouting.

Maria bows her head in submission, and I run out of the apartment.

I stand in front of Anton, panting, and hand him the velvet jewelry box. "If... if there's any money left after the debt is paid off, I would like to have it." Dodging his gaze, I continue. "I need money for food. Mother is sick, and..."

"Did you tell her?"

"Yes, yes, of course," I lie. "You know her," I fake a chuckle, "Nothing upsets her. She thanks you for your help and asks that you notify the fabric merchant that she's not interested in working with him in the future." I bat my eyelashes and smile. "She said that when her headache goes away, she'll sort everything out." I'm speaking too quickly. I take a short, shallow breath and lean down to pick up the kitten bounding at my feet. "She even mentioned that you should come and accompany me on a night out one of these evenings. She doesn't want people to think these nasty rumors are troubling us."

"Good." Anton nods. "I'm glad your mother is involved." He reaches out and gently caresses my head. "I wouldn't want you to have to navigate this situation alone."

His caress stuns me so much that Dziecko almost slips from my arms. I wriggle awkwardly to catch him and feel my cheeks turn crimson.

The building door opens, and the lonely old man clings to the railing in an attempt to steady himself. I continue hugging the kitten, and Anton rushes to help him down the stairs and then crosses the walkway with him. As the old man walks through the gate, he affectionately pats Anton on the cheek.

Anton stands in front of me again, and I give him a tiny smile. He looks so handsome in his freshly pressed blue uniform, and I long for him to caress my head once more.

"Next time your neighbor needs help, I suggest you free yourself from your oh-so-important pursuits," he points to the kitten, "and try to help him."

The smile is wiped from my face.

"No wonder Michalina was so worried about you," he adds venomously. "You're so self-absorbed that you don't see anyone but yourself."

My jaw drops in astonishment, but not even lingering long enough for me to reply, Anton shuts the gate behind him.

CHAPTER 8

I lie next to Mother in bed and close my eyes, but sleep evades me. Her breathing is ragged and hindered by troublesome wheezing. I stroke her hair, wipe her forehead, move close to her, and hug her.

"Mother, please get better," I whisper. "Please. I need you."

She doesn't respond.

My thoughts wander to Father and Michalina. I feel their absence so strongly, and I try to imagine where they are and what they're doing. Have they reached France yet? Have they boarded the ship to America? Do they also lie sleepless, their minds wandering to thoughts about Mother and me?

I have no doubt that if Father had been here, I wouldn't have endured such humiliating experiences. And I'm sure that if Michalina were here now, she would be caring for Mother and nursing her back to health. I feel another pang in my stomach. How can I possibly be feeling my sister's worries? She's so far away, so happy and carefree. I'm the one who is suffering. Why do I have to feel her childish concerns when my world is crashing down around me?

A solitary ray of sunlight shines in through a gap in the drapes, and I sit up and try to wake Mother.

"Please take a sip of water," I beg, and press the glass to her lips. The water trickles onto the blanket.

I moan morosely and lie back down next to her. Slowly but surely, fatigue overcomes me and I fall asleep.

Michalina is sitting on the armchair next to the bed and stroking Mother's head. She carefully gives her a drink of water and smiles at her affectionately. Propped up by two pillows, Mother leans back and gives Michalina a reassuring smile.

"I knew that when you came back to me, I would recover." Mother pinches Michalina's cheek. "Ania is too weak and foolish. I should have sent her with Father and insisted that you stay here with me."

Michalina shakes her head in disagreement. "Anushka is smart, Mother."

"My beloved daughter." Mother coils a golden strand of Michalina's hair around her finger. "You were blessed with two kisses. A kiss here –" she circles Michalina's beauty mark with her finger, "and a kiss here –" she taps Michalina's temple. "I'm worried about your sister."

Michalina clasps Mother's hand and kisses it. "Don't worry about Anushka. Anton will take care of her. He promised me."

"Anton?" Mother's face contorts in revulsion. "I won't have that policeman cozying up to her. He will interfere with her search for a proper match – a respectable man who will provide her with financial security."

"Anton is a dear friend," Michalina insists.

"Enough of your nonsense!" Mother waves her hand.

"He will take care of her," Michalina says in a pensive tone, "But she also knows how to take care of herself."

"I'm tired." Mother sighs. "When will your father come back to me?"

"You need to see a doctor, Mother!" Michalina screams. Mother is no longer sitting. She has slid down and is lying on the mattress, breathing heavily. "Ania! Mother needs to see a doctor!"

My eyes pop open, and I sit up in a panic. Mother is lying motionless; her chest rises and falls with difficulty, and her face is flushed and feverish.

I leap from the bed straight to the bathroom and back to the bedroom, holding a wet washcloth. Maria follows me like a shadow.

"Miss Ania, your mother needs a doctor," she whispers worriedly.

"I know," I shout and put the cold washcloth on Mother's head. "I'm not stupid!"

Maria kneels next to Mother and holds the towel. "Please, Miss Ania, go call a doctor. I'll take care of your mother."

I take a step back, my head spins and I bite my lip apprehensively. A doctor. Mother needs to see a doctor, but I will have to pay him. The few zlotys I have left in my wallet won't suffice, and I don't know how much money Anton was able to get for the jewelry I gave him.

"Miss Ania, you should go now."

"Shut up!" I roar, "Let me think in peace!"

I scratch my head and peek toward the painting that conceals the safe. I can't open it in the presence of my meddling maid. I walk from the window to Mother's dresser and back, and my eyes dart to the drawer on Father's side of the dresser. I bound over to it, pour out its contents, and sigh with relief when I glimpse a rectangular box: Father's watch.

"I'll be back soon with the doctor," I mumble and rush to my room. I pick out a lavish velvet dress, put on a matching hat, and slip on lace gloves. I'm determined to return as soon as possible with the family doctor.

* * *

I knock twice on the door of the practice before going inside. No smiling receptionist is sitting behind the counter, and the clean, well-kept lobby looks deserted.

"Doctor Boniek," I call out.

The door next to Dr. Boniek's office opens, and his insufferable son steps out.

Ludović's face lights up when he sees me. The pink, oily cheeks of my irritating admirer stretch into a nauseating smile.

"Anushka," he calls me by the nickname I detest. "What a pleasant surprise to earn a visit from you."

"I need Dr. Boniek." I don't return his smile. "Where can I find your father?"

"You look troubled." He leeringly looks me up and down. "Father is out making house calls and won't be back until late this evening."

"I must locate him. Please tell me where he went."

"That's not possible." Ludović shrugs. "He didn't leave the address list here. If you're not feeling well, I can give you a check-up myself." He gnaws on his lower lip slightly, and I shudder in repulsion.

"My mother isn't feeling well." I regain my composure and bat my eyelashes. He always had a weakness for me. "Please help me find your father."

"Mrs. Agata isn't feeling well..." He drags out each word. "I think I can spare a little time to accompany you on a house call. You know I've completed my schooling and am a qualified physician now."

"I would rather your father examine her." I tilt my head to the side and offer him a flirtatious grin.

"I don't think you're in any position to establish conditions." He looms closer to me. "Your father's clumsy escape exposed your disguise." He circles around me and whispers in my ear, "Granted, it was a very good disguise. You managed to trick me."

"I have no idea what you're talking about." I turn to face him, the smile long gone from my face.

"Father and Michalina went on a vacation to America."

"A vacation... of course..." Ludović bares his teeth in an obstinate smile.

My harmless flirting has failed me, so I decide to change my approach.

"My. Mother. Really. Isn't. Feeling. Well." I emphasize every word. "I don't have time to deal with the stupid rumors you've heard."

Ludović stares at me for a few seconds and then sighs, "I cannot ignore your plight. Please allow me to accompany you to your mother's home to provide care for her."

I wrinkle my brow and try to determine whether his compassion is genuine.

"Tell me about her symptoms." He changes his posture, leaning back on the counter.

His formal manner somewhat dispels my unease. "She hasn't gotten out of bed in three days. She's feverish, and her breathing is labored."

Ludović nods. "And do you have any way to pay me for a house call?"

"Unfortunately, I didn't have time to go to the bank this morning," I lie. "But I'm sure my father's watch will suffice in exchange for the visit and any medicine she may need." I pull the box out of my bag and hand it to him.

Ludović keenly examines the watch before finally taking it out of the box and fastening it on his wrist. "A very attractive watch indeed."

"Then please come with me now," I conclude, turning toward the door.

I don't hear Ludović's steps behind me and turn back toward him with a quizzical look.

"I'm sorry, Anushka," he says as he looks at Father's watch, feigning innocence. "I didn't notice the time and just remembered that I'm expecting another patient."

"Ludović." I widen my eyes threateningly. "I gave you the watch so you would come with me."

"I thought it was a gift," he snickers.

"Give it back to me!" I charge at him. He stretches out his arms, but instead of pushing me away, he pulls me close to him, presses his face to my neck, and inhales deeply. The smell of his sweat is nauseating.

"Get your filthy hands off me," I yell, shocked, and push him away. "When my father hears about your crude behavior, he'll..."

"He'll what?" Ludović snickers. "What exactly can he do to hurt me if he's vacationing in America?"

I breathe in short breaths to calm myself. "I understand that you're not available at the moment, so I no choice but to ask you to give the watch back." I stretch my arm forward and open my fist. "I will use it to pay a different doctor."

"The proud and arrogant Ania behaving like a beggar," he snorts mockingly. "I hope you understand that if you'd reciprocated my advances in the past, you'd now be married to a respectable Polish doctor, and no one would have dared to imply that you're a Jew."

I bite my tongue. His insult has riled me, but I command myself to relax and think of Mother, who's struggling to breathe. "It's not too late." I grin crookedly. "If you give me back the watch or keep your word and accompany me, I'm sure we can go out together later this week."

"It's too late for courting," he replies smugly. "I think that a fair exchange for a visit from a Polish doctor to a Jewish home would be for me to keep the watch for myself and for you to accompany me to the other room and show me just how much you need me."

His impropriety doesn't shock me. On the contrary, it ignites in me an indomitable rage. I let out a shriek and bombard him with my fists. I manage to punch his cheek and injure his lip, but after a split second, the tables turn, and he pushes me against the wall.

"Get out of here!" He spits out the words and licks his lips.

"Give me back the watch!" I scream.

"Stupid girl." He opens the door and pushes me into the hallway. "If you dare to come back here, I'll hit you back," he swings his fist threateningly, and I run toward the stairs.

I stand in the street, disheveled and dumbfounded. Even though Ludović didn't hit me, I still feel bruised. I fasten my hat pins, smooth out the creases in my dress, and try to regulate my breathing.

I glare at the staircase leading up to the practice and grind my teeth. There are laws in Warsaw, and a person cannot simply steal another person's property without giving them what was promised in return. The police station is not far away.

I set off at a brisk pace. I intend to show that despicable excuse for a man that he hasn't heard the last word yet.

I gain control of my breathing and walk into the police station with my head held high.

I address the first policeman I see and ask where I can file a complaint. He points to an older man sitting behind a heavy wooden desk, and I hastily stride over to him.

"Officer," I speak to him in a flurry of emotion, "I would like to file a theft complaint."

He gestures to the chair and motions for me to sit.

I remain on my feet, rocking back and forth. I don't have time to sit down. Mother needs me, and rage has blinded me.

"I would like to file a complaint against Ludović Boniek," I say assertively, clutching my purse. "He stole my father's gold watch."

"Ludović?" The policeman frowns. "The son of Doctor Boniek?"

I nod vigorously.

The policeman narrows his eyes at me in suspicion. "What's your name, Miss?"

"Miss Ania Orzeszkowa." I hold my head high. "Daughter of Mr. Henryk Orzeszkow."

The policeman opens a binder on his desk and flips through it. He passes over my father's name and stops at my name. I notice a different symbol beside my name and my sister's name. "Ah..." The officer leans back and closes the binder. "Mr. Orzeszkow's Jewish daughter."

"I'm not... I'm not..." I shake my head in frustration. "I don't have time to waste on malicious gossip. Please send the police to the doctor's office to get back the stolen watch."

"Of course," he raps on his desk. "I'll send at least 10 men."

"Now? They'll head over there right now?"

The policeman bursts out laughing, drawing the attention of the other policemen in the room. "Listen, little girl, I suggest that you go home and stop making up ridiculous stories about respectable Poles from our community."

"But…"

"Get out of here." He waves his hand.

I give him a prolonged stare but can't bring the words to leave my mouth. The law doesn't concern him. He's bought into the rumors that have been spread about us and is treating me like a nuisance. I've never felt so humiliated in my life. I open my mouth to protest.

"You're still here?" he roars.

I stifle an anguished wail and turn on my heel.

I leave the station, walking away along the sidewalk. What the hell just happened? What is happening to my world?

Suddenly two familiar figures materialize in front of me.

"Łukasz! Stanisław!" I call out their names with relief.

"Ania," they reply in unison.

"Something dreadful has just happened to me." I bat my eyelashes and fan myself, to alleviate the redness on my face. "Ludović that crook has stolen my father's watch!"

They exchange a look that I cannot decipher.

"Go on…" I beseech them. "Head over there and get me back the watch straight away."

Stanisław scratches his head, and Łukasz looks down.

"What's wrong with you?" I raise my voice. "Something valuable has been stolen from your dear friend, and you don't intend to do anything about it?"

"We'll go talk to him." Łukasz nods, avoiding my gaze. "Ahem… right after we finish our meeting with the precinct commander."

"Ahhh… yes, we've been summoned to an urgent talk with the commander." Stanisław taps on his wristwatch. "Afterwards, we'll make Ludović explain. I'm sure we'll discover that it was all just one big misunderstanding."

I close my eyes tightly. Are my friends actually refusing to help me? I stare at their embarrassed faces, hoping to see some kind of sign that will show that they're only joking.

"What's happened to you?" I whisper softly, "How can you simply erase so many long years of friendship because of a few cursed rumors?"

"Ania, we'll go over there later." Stanisław walks up to me, his eyes darting hesitantly to the sides. "We're just in a hurry to go to our meeting with the commander."

They walk past me and disappear inside the police station.

I stand frozen in place for a long time, staring at the policemen coming and going. Then I look toward the glaring sunlight and wonder if my friends have collaborated and come up with a clever plot to make me lose my mind.

I'm struck again by the image of Mother lying in her bed in agony.

"Mother..." I murmur in despair.

I drag my feet down the sidewalk and get onto the tram, feeling miserable. I push between people, careful not to make eye contact with any of them. The terrible feeling that everyone around me knows about my humiliation won't go away.

I get off at my station and walk home. My heels click on the cobblestones to the rhythm of my jittery breathing.

The walk seems longer than usual, and my long dress weighs heavily on my body. I open the gate, and Dziecko pounces at me. He rubs up against my ankles as if he senses my distress and wants to comfort me. I lean down to stroke his fur, and he purrs and lies on his back. I swallow the lump in my throat and stand up straight.

"Dziecko, what should I do?" I whisper. He rolls over again and regards me with his little eyes; even they look sad.

I stroke his chin, then go inside the building and up the stairs strenuously. I finally reach my floor and stand, staring at the door. I don't even have the strength to lift my hand to the doorknob.

"Ms. Orzeszkowa, are you all right?"

I turn and see the elderly couple who live upstairs. "Everything is perfectly all right," I reply in a huff. "Why wouldn't it be?"

They keep staring at me, and I whine under my breath and sigh with relief when Maria unexpectedly opens the door.

"Miss Ania, where's the doctor?" She peeks out into the hallway.

"He can't come," I reply in a trembling voice and go inside.

"What do you mean he can't come? Did you explain to him that your mother's condition is serious?"

"He doesn't care," I snap. "He's a thief, and now I have to find another doctor."

"But Doctor Boniek has been devotedly taking care of your family for so many years."

"He wasn't there." I yank the pins from my hat. "His lowlife son was there, and he stole F..." I fall silent, realizing I was about to reveal my disgraceful humiliation to her. I can't afford to trust her. I can't trust anyone but myself.

"What are we going to do?" she asks, and I see the worry in her eyes.

Her question intensifies my feelings of helplessness, and I feel exposed like never before.

"We? *We* won't do anything!" I shout. "My Mother is not your problem. She is *my* problem, and I don't want to see your nosy face anymore."

"Miss Ania..."

"Shut up!" I bark. "You're fired! Pack your things and go back to your pathetic little village," I pull out the few zlotys left in my wallet and throw them at her.

"Miss Ania." Her eyes well up with tears. "Don't kick me out when you need me. I'm like family. If you can't pay me now, I'll wait." She wipes her eyes on her apron. "I'll wait until Mr. Henryk returns, and in the meantime I'll help you take care of your mother."

"No." I look down my nose at her. "We don't need you." I stretch my lips into a venomous smile and announce, "I'm going to check on Mother. I expect you to be gone when I get back."

Maria bursts into tears, and I sigh, satisfied. It is much easier to be on the offense than on the defense.

I walk into my parents' bedroom, and the feeling of satisfaction fades in an instant. Mother is lying on the bed, her body shivering as she gasps for air, wheezing laboriously.

A piece of paper sits on the dresser, and I pick it up. A telegram. The stupid maid didn't even tell me that a telegram had arrived. I close my eyes for a moment and pray that the note heralds the return of my father and sister.

Our loves,
We are still in Czechoslovakia. There has been an unexpected delay, but we will update you soon.
Henryk

I read the solitary sentence over and over. A sharp twinge tugs at the pit of my stomach, and I grumble in annoyance. Father and Michalina are vacationing in Czechoslovakia. They are in Europe, so close, yet totally unaware of my helpless situation. Why don't they come back?

I collapse onto my knees and rest my head on Mother's belly.

"Mother, please recover," I plead. "You must know other doctors who could help us. You know the whole city, and they all adore you. I'm just a pale imitation of you."

Mother doesn't respond. I grimace in despair and close my eyes.

A loud knocking sound comes from the front door, and I leap up. Doctor Boniek must have heard about my visit to his practice and come quickly to compensate for his son's illicit behavior.

I run down the hall and pull the door open in anticipation.

My face falls in disappointment.

CHAPTER 9

Anton bows his head. His expression is stolid as he extends his arm forward and motions to a man in a brown suit to go inside the apartment.

"Anton, what are you doing here?" I cross my arms over my chest and block the entrance.

"Ania, say hello to Doctor Singer."

"Doctor?" I look suspiciously at the man with the tattered black leather bag in his hand. "I've never heard of a Doctor Singer."

"It's okay, girl." The man grins. "I'm afraid I've never heard of you either."

I draw back a little and gnaw on my lip nervously. I'm pretty sure Singer isn't a Polish surname.

"Ania," Anton says my name through clenched teeth. "Take the doctor to your mother."

The man steps forward, and I wonder what I should do.

"I'm Jewish," says the doctor, although I hadn't dared to ask. "I understand that this fact puts you off."

"Um..." I wrinkle my brow and weigh my answer. "My mother doesn't need a doctor. She's just suffering from a headache."

"Ania!" Anton raises his voice. "Your friends told me that you came by the station."

"Friends..." I snort in contempt, "They are most certainly not my fr..."

"We don't have time to chitchat about your social life," Anton interrupts me. "Doctor Singer agreed to come here with me and he canceled all his prior commitments to do so."

"But... But he's Jewish!" I shout back. "How could you bring my mother a quack doctor? Everyone knows they cannot be trusted. They're dangerous!"

Anton stares at me in shock, and the man twists his mouth in disdain.

"I cannot allow you to examine my mother." I shake my head. "I cannot be sure that you won't hurt her. Your people's medical practices just aren't developed enough. You use poisonous potions against Poles. I know things. You are dangerous."

"Ignorance is dangerous, too," the man nods, and instead of turning on his heel, he peeks down the hall. "Agata and I know each other. Her parents were our neighbors in the village."

His use of my mother's first name surprises me. I don't know many people who allow themselves to address her like that.

"Ania." Anton sighs. "I suggest that we stop wasting Doctor Singer's time. Call your mother over or accompany the doctor to her bedroom."

I rub my temples and consider my options. It doesn't take long for me to concede that the heathen doctor standing in front of me is my only choice. My shoulders sag in defeat.

"I'll you to Mother," I address the man but refrain from saying his title.

They follow me down the hall, and when I go in the bedroom, Anton remains outside and stands by the door.

I pull the blankets over my mother's limp body and stroke her hair.

"Move back, please," the man addresses me authoritatively. He puts his bag on the dresser and takes out a stethoscope.

I allow him to approach her, but I don't move away from the bed.

He touches her forehead and sighs.

"What? What does she have?" I cry.

"Shhh…" He silences me and presses the stethoscope to her chest. He closes his eyes in concentration.

Mother doesn't open her eyes and doesn't react. The fact that I've allowed a pseudo doctor to examine her as she lies helpless and unkempt would have caused her to hurl some very harsh words my way. I imagine her opening her eyes, sitting up, and letting out a scream – at least I hope that that's what she'll do.

To my dismay, the man touches her ribs and belly, and she still doesn't open her eyes.

"Ms. Orzeszkowa is suffering from acute pneumonia," the man announces, rearranging her blankets.

"Then we need to find her a real doctor," I reply in alarm.

"A house call from another doctor won't help her," the man answers composedly. "She has to be taken to the hospital straight away."

"I don't believe you." I rush forward and clutch Mother. "She simply needs treatment from a real doctor, and she'll bounce back to health."

Anton steps into the room. "Ania, Doctor Singer is an excellent doctor. If he recommends taking your mother to the hospital, then that's what we should do."

"Don't cooperate with him." I shake my head. "Please get her a Polish doctor."

Anton narrows his eyes in irritation, and I answer him with an identical expression.

"I can give her some medicine to ease her pain a little," the man says as he rummages through his bag and pulls out a bottle of syrup.

"She doesn't need your potions," I yell. "If you can't help, just get out of here!"

"Ania!" Anton speaks my name in a threatening tone, "Stop acting like a stupid little girl. Move aside and let the doctor give your mother the medicine."

I back away from the bed, feeling humiliated, and hiss at him, "If he poisons her, it will be your fault," before moving to stand by the window.

The man carefully gives mother the syrup – directly from the bottle – and then pats her head lightly. "Agata, you'll get through this," he whispers almost intimately. "You are too strong and too proud to allow bad people to break you."

"She's not broken," I correct him. "Nobody can break Mother."

"I hope you're right." He nods. "But I believe that distress of the soul affects our bodies directly. It seems that the recent experiences your mother has been forced to undergo have broken her spirit as well as her body."

"I'm not surprised that a heretic doctor believes in such nonsense." I sneer with contempt. "I see that the malicious gossip has reached you as well."

"In our community, everyone knows your mother's religion." He stands up straight and slips the medicine back into his bag. "The ordeals she experienced as a child made her loathe our community and the way in which we are treated in this country. Being treated like a second-class citizen by the authorities never suited her character."

Ordeals? What ordeals is he talking about? I'm almost tempted to ask him, but I remind myself of Mother's last warning. He's just another agent from their community trying to endear me to them with his schemes.

"Mother isn't part of your religion anymore." I jut out my chin. "She chose to give it up, and no one can force a religion that she isn't interested in on her, not even you."

"Young Miss Orzeszkowa," he says with a slight smile, "You have yet to learn that since the dawn of time, Jews have tried as they might to run from their religion, only to find that it is burned into the very veins of their souls." He closes his bag and heads for the door.

"Doctor Singer," Anton rushes towards him, "how much do we owe you?"

I feel myself going pale.

"Nothing." He pats Anton affectionately on the back. "In time, young Miss Orzeszkowa will understand that we always look out for our people."

His answer surprises me. Everyone knows that his people are greedy and lust after money; his refusal to accept any only intensifies my distrust. I bow my head and refuse to thank him.

"I appreciate it very much," Anton replies for me. "And I promise you we won't forget it." He leaves the room with the man, and I remain frozen in my place.

When Anton returns to the bedroom, he doesn't say anything and just pulls a suitcase out from under the bed.

"What are you doing?"

"Pack some clothes for your mother. I'm taking her to the hospital."

"You're not taking her anywhere." I grab the suitcase from him.

"I won't say it again." His voice drips with venom, "You have two minutes to pack her clothes."

"But... But..."

"I won't let her stay here and fade away until you decide to grow up and come to your senses," he tells me as he grinds his teeth.

I feel like I'm suffocating. My helplessness threatens to paralyze me. I'm so confused, and Mother's heavy breathing grates in my ears.

I pull a few dresses out of the closet and carefully put them into the suitcase. I add a pair of shoes and a bag of toiletries and top it off with a fashionable hat. Anyone looking at the suitcase might think she was going on vacation to our summer house, and I find solace in the fact that she will leave the hospital looking elegant and stylish, exactly the way she likes.

I close the suitcase, and Anton wraps the blanket around Mother and lifts her into his arms. Her body droops limply, and she seems completely helpless. It hurts me to look at her.

"Maybe I should change her clothes?" I deliberate with myself out loud, "or at least comb her hair and..."

"We're not taking her out to a restaurant." Anton dismisses me and leaves the bedroom.

I pick up the suitcase, follow him down the hallway, and slam the house door behind us.

He carefully lays Mother down in the back seat of the car, then takes the suitcase from me and puts it in the trunk.

I open the passenger seat door, but Anton shakes his head no. "It's better if I take her alone."

"No way," I answer indignantly. "I need to be with her."

Anton closes the passenger seat door and leans down to meet my eyes. "If you come with me, I might not be able to get her into the Polish hospital."

"Why not?" I peek at Mother through the window.

"Ania, you have a tendency to attract attention." He fakes a smile. "I'm not opposed to the idea of taking her to the Jewish hospital, but I have a feeling that you won't like it, and neither will your mother."

"Everyone in the city knows Mother," I say, struggling to keep my voice steady.

"She doesn't look like Mrs. Orzeszkowa at the moment." He puts his hand on my shoulder. "I have a good friend at the Polish hospital. He'll admit her and make sure to take good care of her."

"But I need to be with her," I try again.

"We don't have time to stand around and chat!" Anton replies impatiently.

I pout helplessly. Both options sound completely awful to me. Mother will be furious when she finds out I didn't come with her to the hospital. Still, I have the feeling that she'll never forgive me if she wakes up in a Jewish hospital. I wail softly and nod in consent.

"I'll come back to update you." Anton squeezes my shoulder encouragingly and hurries to sit behind the wheel. A few seconds later, the automobile and Mother disappear into the night.

I shoot a look at Dziecko, who is dozing on his grassy bed, and with heavy feet I return to the building. I go inside the house, put a chair in front of the door, sit down . . .

And wait.

CHAPTER 10

The knocking pounds in my head like punches. My eyes burn from staring at the door for so long, and I leap up from my chair and open it. A groan of disappointment escapes my lips.

"Ludović!" I spit out his name and block the entrance to the apartment with my arm.

"Father sent me," he announces frostily and licks his wounded lip. "Your lies at the police station reached his ears." He pushes my arm aside and lets himself in.

"I won't let you come into my house without an invitation." I rush past him and stand still, blocking his way. "Pathetic little thieves don't get invited into my home."

"I don't like your choice of words." He pushes arrogantly into the dining room and puts a brown leather briefcase on the table. "If my memory serves me correctly, you are the one who offered me the watch in exchange for a house call to your mother."

"And you stole the watch and refused to accompany me," I correct him, raising my voice.

"Shhh..." He waves his hand, hushing me. "You've been spreading lies throughout the city and trying to tarnish my good name. I explained to my father that it was a misunderstanding. I wasn't available to come with you when you burst into the clinic, but now I'm free to see your mother." He peers down the hallway and looks back at me in anticipation.

"You're too late!" I snap. "Mother already..." I shut my mouth. I'd better not tell him where she is. He's the last person I can trust, and if Anton did succeed in getting Mother admitted to the Polish hospital, Ludović might expose her.

"Finish your sentence!" Ludović says impatiently.

"Mother is feeling better already," is the lie that I blurt out so naturally. "She reprimanded me for my childish hysteria and went out to visit a friend. They're playing cards tonight, and she won't be back till late."

Ludović looks at me skeptically, but after a moment he shrugs. "A watch in exchange for a house call. That was your offer. I've fulfilled my part, so the watch stays with me." He twists his arm up, revealing Father's watch on his wrist.

My eyelid twitches in anger as I imagine myself ripping the watch from his arm. I blink a few times to try and calm down, remind myself that my goal is to get him out of my house, and I nod my head in accord.

Ludović bares his teeth with a triumphant smile, but two seconds later he tilts his head sideways and stares at me. "Something here smells fishy," he sniffs. "It's not like you to give up so fast."

"I'm not giving up." With great difficulty, I pick up his heavy doctor's case. "We are a respectable family that honors our agreements."

He glances at the bag but doesn't hurry to take it from me. "An honorable family would offer a respectable doctor something to drink after he's invested time and effort to make a house call." He takes the bag from me and puts it back on the table. "Call your servant over to pour me a fine drink from your father's famous collection."

I peek toward Maria's room and exhale sharply. Up until this moment, it hadn't bothered me one bit that I'd kicked her out of here, but now I would've been happy to see her nosey face peek out of the room. A feeling of loneliness weighs heavily on me.

"Maria has gone to sleep," I answer casually. "You'd better leave now. It isn't proper for us to be here alone." Before I even finish my sentence, Ludović's eyes ignite with a sly spark. He loosens the knot of his tie and removes his jacket.

"What are you doing?" I cry. "I asked you to leave."

"You look pale." He puts his jacket on the back of a chair. "Since I already made the effort to come over here, I have a medical obligation to examine you before I leave."

"Ludović, I feel perfectly fine." I step back. "My mother should be home any minute, and she'll be very angry when she finds you here."

"I thought you said she was playing cards with friends." He glances at my father's watch. "I'm sure that Mrs. Orzeszkowa would appreciate the fact that a Polish doctor risked his honor and agreed to examine her Jewish daughter."

"Her Polish daughter," I angrily correct him. "I'm no less Polish than you are!"

"Not everyone would agree with you on that," he snickers. "Even my father wanted to avoid coming here and sent me instead."

His smugness is on the verge of driving me insane. "You'll live to regret insulting me." I try to keep my voice calm. "But I have no intention of continuing to argue with you now. Please leave my apartment."

"I think I'll examine you nonetheless." Stepping forward, he quickly covers the space between us and presses the palm of his hand to my forehead.

"Get away from me," I growl and try to push him.

"You're very hot," he whispers in my ear. "And I don't need a stethoscope to hear your heartbeat."

"Ludović, get away from me!" I push him again.

Someone knocks on the door, and he pulls away from me a bit but is still standing too close for comfort. "Mrs. Orzeszkowa knocks on her own door?" He swivels his head towards the door. "Or is the pious Lady Ania waiting for another caller?"

"The door is open," I call out.

The handle turns, and the door opens. Anton steps inside, and I breathe a sigh of relief. His height and sturdy physique are a stark contrast to Ludović's doughy appearance. He stands in the foyer like a mighty boulder, and the icy expression on his face makes Ludović jump back and move away from me.

Anton's eyes shift back and forth between Ludović and me. His cheek trembles and he runs his fingers through his hair as if the motion will help him form a decision.

"Officer Mrożek," Ludović respectfully addresses Anton. "I came here to examine Mrs. Orzeszkowa."

I close my eyes tightly and hope that Anton will understand that I'm signaling to him not to reveal Mother's whereabouts. When I open them, he's giving Ludović a piercing stare.

"I don't see you examining her," says Anton, his voice so cold the room practically freezes. "Or have you finished the check-up and were just leaving?"

"I was just about to leave." Ludović says as he puts on his jacket. "And you?" He picks up his briefcase. "What is a respectable police officer doing at Miss Ania's house so late?"

Anton looks down a bit and eyes Ludović's wrists. "The young lady visited the police station today, and I came to ask if she's interested in filing an official complaint."

"A complaint?" Ludović snorts mockingly. "Is it customary for a senior police officer like you to visit the homes of common riffraff to see if they want to file a complaint?"

"Laws are laws," Anton tells him as he opens the front door wide.

"The law isn't equal for everyone." Ludović stands up straight. "It appears that your lust for her sister has gotten the best of you. Have you decided to soften the blow of her escape with nightly visits to her doppelgänger? I don't blame you. Ania's alluring appearance used to dazzle me as well."

"Shut your mouth," Anton commands sternly and locks his jaw to maintain composure. "Mr. Boniek, I suggest you leave. Now!" He points to the open door.

Ludović walks towards Anton and pauses in front of him. "It's troubling that a senior Polish police officer like you has fallen for the dubious charms of a wretched Jewess." He walks out, slamming the door behind him.

I sink into a chair and gasp for breath. The sight of the closed door immediately reignites my concern for Mother's well-being. "How is Mother? Anton, what did you do with Mother?"

"My friend is looking after her." Anton is still standing in the foyer. "He promised me that he will keep her identity a secret and that she will receive the best care."

I rest my head on the table and sigh with relief. I didn't realize how much my fear for Mother was affecting me until now. A shiver runs through my upper body, and I'm suddenly struck by a paralyzing feeling of weakness.

"Ania?" Anton approaches me.

"I'm fine." I stand up too quickly and feel slightly woozy. "I'm glad Mother is being well cared for."

My answer doesn't seem to reassure him. "I'll ask Maria to make you a cup of tea." He looks toward the kitchen.

"Maria isn't here." I defy the vertigo and trudge, exhausted, to the kitchen, with Anton at my heels.

"Where is your maid wandering about at this hour?"

"I assume she went back to her village," I reply and put a pot of water on the stove. "I fired her."

"You did *what*?" Anton seizes my arm and spins me around to face him.

"I sacked her. I kicked her out," I tell him, emphasizing every word. "I'm sick of her hanging around here meddling in my affairs."

"Maria has been working for you for so many years." He drops my arm. "What were you thinking? How could you fire her just when you need her the most?"

"I don't need her." I turn my back to him and try to light a match. "I don't need anyone." I bring the burning match closer to the stove, but it refuses to light.

"You can't even make yourself a cup of tea," he snorts contemptuously, then strikes another match and shows me how to light the stove.

"I don't like her." I take two teacups from the top cabinet. "She pokes her nose around everywhere and thinks she's part of our family."

"Michalina will be devastated when she finds out that you fired Maria." He slowly shakes his head from side to side.

I feel a sharp pain in the pit of my stomach, and I groan in annoyance. "Michalina isn't here, is she? She ran away to America and abandoned me to face the consequences of her escape." I open the lid of the teapot and shove a tea bag inside. "And how exactly did you expect me to pay Maria? Should I sell my mother's earrings to keep her on?"

Anton pulls a thin wad of paper zlotys from his pants pocket and puts it on the counter, "After I paid the fabric merchant and the hospital, there were 1,000 zlotys left."

"A thousand zlotys." I roll my eyes. "That's what Mother pays the butcher every week."

"Your mother isn't here, and you don't need that much meat." He walks to the refrigerator and opens it. We both gape at the empty shelves.

"I told you that Maria couldn't be trusted." I slam the refrigerator door. "That ignorant country bumpkin must have stolen all the groceries before she left the house."

"When was the last time you gave her money to buy groceries?" I gnaw on my lip and consider lying to him.

Anton stands up straight and folds his arms over his chest. "Ania, why did you let Ludović be in the apartment alone with you?"

His question surprises me.

"I asked him to leave."

"You must not have asked clearly and explicitly enough."

"What are you implying?" I peer at him in anger.

"I'm not implying anything. I'm saying *clearly and explicitly* that your conduct threatens to jeopardize your reputation and that of your family."

"You're alone in the apartment with me, too." I stretch my lips into a reproachful smile.

"I didn't know that was the case until this moment." He walks out of the kitchen, and I hear the house door opening. He comes back, stands at the entrance to the kitchen, and leans on the doorframe. "Ania, you need to change your behavior. You can't just keep flirting with every man you meet and believing that's how you'll get what you want. This is a time to be modest."

The fact that he doesn't believe me when I say that I tried to get rid of Ludović makes my blood boil.

"You're not my father, and you have no right to tell me what to do," I say as I pour the boiling water into the teapot. "And just so you know, I did *not* flirt with that vile man. I asked him several times, very firmly, to leave the house, but he blatantly ignored me. Both here and at the clinic, he behaved in a thoroughly inappropriate manner towards me."

Anton's jaw quivers with an almost imperceptible twitch. "I don't feel comfortable with you staying here on your own. Maybe you should pack a bag and move in with a friend until your mother is released from the hospital."

"Run away from my home?" I raise an eyebrow. "I'm not afraid to stay here alone. I know where my father hides his gun, and I won't be afraid to use it if I feel that I'm in danger."

"Don't touch the gun!" he commands firmly.

"If I feel that I'm in danger, I'll touch it – and I'll use it, too." I thrust out my chin. "I'm not afraid of anyone."

Anton combs his hair with his fingers and sighs. A small smile illuminates his face for a fleeting moment. "Your pride is dangerous. Fear is an essential survival instinct that won't diminish your dignity."

I stare at his strong, chiseled features and try to imagine how I would feel if he gave me a smile that wasn't the result of some momentary amusement.

"I won't be staying to drink the tea with you," he gestures to the additional cup. "I have to go back to the police station."

Disappointment washes over me. "If Michalina asked you to keep her company, you wouldn't refuse her."

"Michalina wouldn't ask." His eyes gravitate to my cheek. "Your sister wouldn't have fired her loyal maid, leaving herself all alone in the apartment."

"But my sister didn't stay," I raise my voice. "She's on a ship on her way to America now, dancing with handsome suitors and not thinking about those she left behind, even for a minute."

His eyes seem to darken. "We both know she's always been the smart sister." He turns on his heel, his back facing me. I shudder as the apartment door slams.

The overpowering pains throb in the pit of my stomach, and I rub it forcefully. Anger floods my body. Why do I have to feel her distress? Why can't *she* feel *mine* for once?

I pour my tea and sit in our fashionable dining room, sipping the hot drink and looking at the art works hanging on the walls. Mother picked out matching golden frames for all of them. The wooden dresser that holds the porcelain dishes is polished and shiny. The glass of the display case that contains the liquor bottles is free of dust, and the radio receiver stands on a tall dresser.

I walk into the parlor, slide my hand over the jet-black piano, and sit down in an armchair.

The silence pulsates in my ears.

I sip the tea and try to console myself. Mother is being well taken care of and it won't be long before she's back home. She'll sit up straight in the armchair in front of me, take off her high heels, and assure me that everyone who harassed me will be punished. She'll scold me for allowing a heathen doctor to examine her, and she'll express her discontent about her boutique being closed. After I apologize, she'll point to my dress with a cluck of her tongue and demand that Maria scrub it clean. Everything will be back to normal.

I long for her constant scolding now. The silence is driving me mad.

I put my teacup on the parlor table and walk quickly to the door. Skipping down the stairs, I go outside to the garden, and scoop the dozing Dziecko into my arms. He and I go back to the apartment and I pour some milk into a deep saucer for him. His purrs of pleasure break the silence a bit and calm me down.

Dziecko follows me into my parents' bedroom, where I lift up the carpet and feel around for the loose floorboard. I take out the gun and the bullets from underneath it and put them on the dresser. I have no idea how to use it, but just the fact that it exists makes me feel better. It makes me angry that I couldn't get rid of Ludović by myself; it also makes me angry that I froze when he invaded my personal space. It won't happen again. I've never before felt fear that paralyzed me. On holidays, I was always the first to jump into the river and the first to go walking in the forest. I always spoke my mind to the bullies at school. Even now, I don't feel afraid, but in light of the new reality that's been imposed upon me, I feel anger welling up inside me.

I take off my dress, throw it on an armchair, and dive into my parents' bed. Dziecko pounces onto the mattress and curls up next to me. I wince when I think of my mother's reaction if she saw him in their bed; she would surely use Father's gun.

At the moment, I would take a bullet if it meant that my mother could lie here with me, healthy and strong, and take this burden from my shoulders.

"Tomorrow I'll open the boutique," I mutter and yawn. "Tomorrow, I'll get my life back on the right track." I gently pet the cat, and my eyes close.

Mother sits on her bed in the hospital and scolds the nurse who is setting a dinner tray in front of her.

Michalina sits on a chair next to her bed and rearranges her blankets. She's wearing her nurse's uniform, and her hair is in an impeccable braid.

"She sent me to a hospital." Mother rolls her eyes. "She couldn't take care of me herself and abandoned me here all by myself."

"Anushka was worried about you," Michalina defends me. "You have acute pneumonia."

"If you were here, you would have seen to it that Dr. Boniek examined me and took care of me," Mother snorts in contempt. "Did you hear that she allowed a quack doctor into my bedroom? I know him from childhood. I wouldn't even let him examine a street dog."

"He's a certified physician." Michalina hands Mother a glass of water. "You shouldn't talk about him so disrespectfully. Ania may need him or those from his community in the future."

"She won't need him." Mother puts the glass down on the dresser with a thump. "I suffered in their pathetic community for too many years; I respected their stupid laws and worshiped their imaginary god. The moment I left, I knew I was doing so to save myself, and now I'm saving you girls, too. Their religious fanaticism will jeopardize them. I managed to escape, and I won't let Ania allow them to return to my life through the back door."

"Mother, you need to support Ania." Michalina pets her head. "You have to trust her and put your confidence in her so that you can both survive."

"I should have sent her with you," Mother sighs. "Now I can't look after her, and she's bound to get into trouble." She lies back and smiles at Michalina. "Where is your father?"

Michalina smiles back at her, but abruptly her expression becomes melancholy.

"*Where is your father? And where are you?*"

I sit up in bed and clutch my belly. The pains are intense, and I exhale forcefully.

Rays of light penetrate the gap in the drapes, and Dziecko hops into my arms. An ominous sensation envelops me.

I hear knocking at the door and hurry to hide the gun under the loose floorboard and cover myself with a robe.

Looking through the peephole, I see my neighbor – the widow who lives one floor up - and I open the door for her.

"Miss Orzeszkowa," she addresses me in a worried voice. "Do you have a radio receiver?"

"What?" I answer sleepily.

"A radio receiver," she repeats herself.

"Of course we have one," I tell her as I roll my eyes. "It's 1939, not the Middle Ages."

"Turn it on, girl," she commands hysterically. "The Germans have invaded Poland. War has broken out."

CHAPTER 11

The air raids shake the buildings on the street. Dziecko is dozing in my lap, and I'm sitting on a chair in the parlor, sipping brandy. I shudder with each bombardment, and I need to remind myself not to let fear creep in. Anton is leaning on the doorframe scratching his chin with his thumb. Even today, like every day, my appearance is flawless. My hair is arranged in impressive ringlets, I'm wearing a beautiful cobalt dress, and my make-up is immaculate. Despite everything, he doesn't look at me but straight through me.

"Ania, I'm begging you once more to go down to the shelter in the basement," he implores.

"No," I reply, as always.

"Maybe if I drag you to see all the wounded in the hospitals, it'll convince you to keep yourself safe."

"The sight of the wounded won't shock me," I reply, feigning composure. "Every time I take Dziecko out for a walk, I see dead bodies." The image of the first corpse I saw still haunts me in my sleep; a young, fair-haired girl whose lifeless blue eyes were wide open. Since then, I've seen numerous sights no less horrid. The city is collapsing piece by piece, and the falling buildings bury countless people underneath them. I could have sunk into debilitating fear, but I've resisted it with all my might.

"I haven't gotten any more telegrams." I tell him as I decide to change the subject of our conversation. "It's been such a long time."

"There's no reason to worry," Anton replies calmly. "I'm sure they're already aboard a ship on their way to America."

"They're probably sitting in a grand, first-class lounge right now." I close my eyes and envision the lounge, "and they're eating a feast fit for kings to the sound of live jazz music." I open my eyes and sigh. "Meanwhile, I'm sitting here, and the only music that reaches my ears is the sound of air raids." I put my snifter on the table. "Their horror scenario came true, and they didn't even send a telegram to say I told you so."

"I'm sure they're not celebrating," Anton tells me as he lets out an unamused chuckle. "Universities throughout Poland have closed, and the Germans are systematically murdering intellectuals, professors, writers, and bank executives."

"I'm sure some of them deserve it," I snort in contempt. "At least the damn bankers who humiliated Mother do."

"And I'm sure you don't mean that," Anton replies snappily.

Day and night, my longing for Mother doesn't fade. I'm trying to be happy for Father and Michalina for saving themselves from the madness closing in on us, but my anger is getting the best of me. They should have been here by my side.

"I wish Mother were here." I lean over and tap my glass with my fingernail. "You say she's getting better, and the damned Germans keep bombing Warsaw mercilessly. Why don't you bring her home?" I shudder as I hear another explosion.

"As I told you, she's not strong enough to take care of herself yet. And if we're already on the subject, I'm afraid you'll have to part with another piece of jewelry." His gaze wanders toward the window that he made sure to seal with hideous newspapers. "We need to transfer payment to the hospital."

"I'll take care of her." I stand up and put Dziecko down on his pillow. "We've already sold two more bracelets. Mother will go crazy when she finds out what happened to her jewelry."

"Sit!" he orders curtly, and I grumble but comply.

He pours himself a drink and sits on the armchair in front of me. Even the quiet strength that emanates from him cannot mask his concern.

"I've obtained counterfeit documents for your mother," he whispers. "I'll make sure to move her to a home in the village. She can live there under a false identity until the Germans leave us alone."

"*What?*" I ask in a whisper and then burst out laughing. "Are you nuts? A false identity? Mother living in the village?"

Anton doesn't smile. He gives me a stern look, and my laughter dies down. He's serious.

"Please stop scaring me." I wave my hand. "That's an absolutely ridiculous proposition. Mother would never agree to abandon me here and move to some wretched village. Why would you suggest something so stupid?"

"She's too feeble to resist." He sips his drink. "Schools and universities have been bombed, the Jewish hospital has been bombed, entire buildings have collapsed on top of their occupants. This building could collapse on us at any moment, and you're sitting here in your fancy dress as if everything is fine. You're not responsible enough to understand that you need to go down to the basement, so how exactly do you intend to care for your mother?"

"I'm not afraid." I sit up straight and sip my drink. "The German who can force me to sit with a bunch of old strangers in a tragic, smelly, basement air raid shelter hasn't yet been born."

Anton's cheek muscles quiver, and I understand that I've succeeded in angering him. But any response is better than the worry lines on his forehead getting deeper.

"Ania," his voice softens. "The way things stand at the moment, it doesn't look like we can beat the Germans. I have no idea what will happen to us when they get to Warsaw. It seems that they don't just want our territory, but that they're also determined to show their ruthlessness. We want to protect your mother, and right now she's too weak to protect herself."

"We'll win." I swallow the lump in my throat that threatens to choke me. "We have an army and... police." I point to him. "And it's not even their country." I clench my jaw angrily. "And I heard on the radio that Britain and France have declared war. They're strong, and they're on our side. There's no way we'll lose."

"It's reassuring to know that you're following the news," he says in a tone devoid of cynicism. "You have to understand that we're fighting a strong military. We're pitting cavalry and horses against tanks and airplanes. Warsaw's line of defense is weakening. It's only a matter of time before they occupy the city."

"And do you really expect me to be here alone when that happens, without my father, without my sister, and without my mother?"

"You haven't been alone until now." He runs his fingers through his hair like he always does when losing patience. "I've been here with you, and I'm sure you'll agree with me that it would be better for your mother to stay at a house in the village with an elderly Polish couple, who I'm sure will take care of her like she's a member of their own family for a reasonable fee."

Indeed, he hasn't left me alone, and so far, he's made sure to be by my side at every spare moment. I insisted on continuing to open the boutique every morning even after the Germans entered Poland, and he's made sure to look in on me a few times a day. He always comes at closing time to walk me home and join me for a nightcap until I go to sleep. Over the last few days, he's begged me countless times to go down to the basement with my neighbors, but I continue to refuse.

Anton has become my mainstay but hasn't tried to create any kind of intimacy with me. The air raids have failed to quell my need to prove to myself that I can win his heart. Still, unfortunately, he seems to be utterly immune to my charms. The nearness to him only strengthens my feelings of loneliness.

"My mother needs to return to me. I'm her family." I finish my brandy in one long gulp. "She should be with me."

"I won't be able to arrange for you to stay in the same village as I've arranged for her." The explosions sound closer, and he stands up. "The couple's daughter worked here in the city and was killed in the air raids. She was unmarried and around Agata's age. That's how I got her documents."

"That's not what I meant." I stand up and try to get a glimpse of what's going on outside through the newspaper-covered windows, but to no avail. "I won't surrender our home to those damned Germans, or to our covetous neighbors. I demand that you bring my mother home."

I'm thrown backward by the force of another barrage and my back presses against Anton's body. I seek comfort in his protective touch and to my astonishment, he doesn't push me away from him.

"Ania, please trust me," he whispers. "The Germans are unpredictable. No one knows their military goal in occupying Poland, but there's one thing that I'm sure of; When they attack Warsaw, the situation of the Jews in the city will only get worse."

I spin around and stick out my chin.

"We. Are. Not. Jews."

"In that case, Agata can come back home as soon as we both feel that you are safe here."

"But..."

"Trust me."

I gaze at him to the chilling background music of the bombings. For days on end, I insisted on opening the boutique on time. I sat there alone and waited for customers who never came. I cleaned the dust off the shelves and smiled at passers-by looking back and forth, their eyes haunted. The air raids put a spoke in my wheels. My optimistic belief that the city's residents would stop their absurd boycott of our shop has been superseded by despair and horror at the sight of the dead bodies piling up in the streets. The face of my classic, beautiful city has changed. Today I stayed home. I preferred to stay away from the general hysteria currently reigning in the streets.

I twirl a curl around my finger and bite my lip. The possibility that we might lose to the Germans hadn't occurred to me. I keep the radio on constantly to fill the silence, and I listen to it religiously. Polish cities are falling like dominos, one after another. The eastern part of the country has been occupied by the Russians and the western by the Germans, as if Poland were a wuzetka cake that they're sharing. Still, fortified Warsaw continues to fight resolutely for its freedom. Anton's words make my heart beat wildly. I haven't entertained the possibility that the Germans could invade the city while I'm here, all alone. I haven't emotionally prepared for such an event. And what will happen if Mother's condition deteriorates? How will I care for her? Who will come to my aid?

I want to keep insisting, but eventually I bow my head in defeat and breathe out in consent.

"You've made the right decision. A courageous decision." Anton approaches me and puts a hand on my arm encouragingly. Cautiously, he strokes my hair. I lift my head towards his and stare at him with wide eyes. His comforting touch has kindled in me a fierce longing for more from him. I crave another caress, another touch. More kind words. More reassurance.

"I'll try to organize a similar arrangement for you." He slides his thumb over the border between my cheek and my ear and then abruptly drops his hand. "I'll try to get you out of the city before we have the chance to find out just how brutal the Germans can be."

I feel that my heart is on fire. Anton is here with me, but he's thinking about her. "Don't bother," I turn to the window again, tear off a piece of the newspaper and look out over the ruins of my city. "I'm telling you that I won't leave no matter what. Even if the Germans do succeed in invading the city, they'll occupy it only temporarily. It's none of my business if they decide to be cruel to the Jews. The Poles can try to impose a religion that isn't mine upon me, and the Jews can celebrate my misfortune, too, but let the Germans make no mistake; If they ask me to, I'll gladly announce in the town square that it's not my religion."

I turn around, walk into my parents' bedroom, open the safe, and return to the parlor with a diamond necklace in a black velvet box. "I'll wear a cross if it'll satisfy the Germans." I hand Anton the box. "I'm sure they're not stupid. Anyone with eyes can see that I don't belong in that community. I'll stay here, in my house, until Father and Michalina come home."

"As you wish," Anton replies coldly and turns his back to me.

"Wait!" I grab his arm. "Promise me that you'll bring my mother back to me as soon as possible. Promise me that in a month from now, she'll come back to me."

"I don't make promises that I'm not sure I can keep."

I drop his arm. His answer is like a strong blow to my abdomen. He doesn't turn back around. Instead, he keeps walking until I hear the house door slam, and I'm alone again.

I pour myself another drink and sit on the armchair. Dziecko crawls into my lap and rubs up against my hands in an attempt to cheer me up. I stroke his fur and quietly listen to the sounds of war closing in on me from all sides.

* * *

Strong hands shake my shoulders, and I open my eyes in alarm. Dziecko yowls in annoyance and leaps to the floor.

"What's the matter?" I ask Anton, and I peek behind me toward the window. Through the torn newspaper, all I can see is darkness. I must have fallen asleep in the armchair.

"I knocked on the door, and you didn't answer." He clutches my chin tightly. "I almost broke down the door. Why didn't you answer?"

"You're hurting me." I shake him off and glance at the wall clock. It's a little after midnight. "What are you doing here at this hour? Did something happen to Mother?" I feel short of breath.

"Your mother is fine." He backs away but continues looking at me, his eyes worried. "A shell hit the roof of your building. I came here as soon as I heard and knocked like a madman. I thought that..."

"You thought that I was hurt," I tell him, completing his sentence.

He closes his eyes in agreement. "I want to be mad at you for leaving the door unlocked, but instead, I'm thanking God that I was able to get inside to make sure you weren't hurt." He runs his fingers through his hair and picks up the glass I left on the table. He scrutinizes it for a moment, then takes a gulp of the brandy and shakes his head as if he's just made a decision.

"I didn't think you were the type to thank God." I get up and refill his glass. "Which god did you thank?" I raise an eyebrow in amusement. "And be careful how you answer, lest someone suspect that your god is the God of the Jews."

"Every time I think you might have knocked a tiny bit of sense into your head, you prove me otherwise." He shakes his head in disappointment.

"What did I say that sounded stupid to you this time?" I don't try to hide the fact that he's hurt my feelings. "I was only joking."

"I'm sorry that I'm not in the mood for jokes right now." He walks to the window and pulls the curtains closed. "I've arranged transportation to the village for your mother. I paid the hosts a handsome amount of money and promised to transfer a hefty addition when the situation in the country stabilizes, allowing her to leave the shelter of their home."

"Do you trust them?" I bite my lip, "That they'll provide her with food and medicine and that they won't extort money from you and force her to work for them like a servant?"

"I trust them as much as possible, given the circumstances." His answer doesn't reassure me at all. "They seem like fair, honest people. They need money, and they know I'll find them if they don't give her proper care."

I scratch my forehead and sigh. "Do you think she's mad at me?" I shudder as an explosion sounds directly above my head. "Do you think she's disappointed and angry that I didn't come to visit her in the hospital?"

"She's too weak to be angry and disappointed." Anton drags the two armchairs to the middle of the parlor. "I explained to her that you wanted to come and that I prevented you from doing so." He motions for me to sit on the empty armchair. "I explained to her that she needs to live under a false identity for a while, and I promised her that I would take care of you."

"Did she ask about me?" I sit down and look him in the eyes. "Is she worried about me?"

"Of course." He sits down, avoiding my gaze. "Right after she made sure you were all right, she asked if the boutique had been hit in the air raids."

"She asked about the boutique?" I ask as I feel all the blood drain from my face. "I hope she doesn't know that our customers have abandoned us. I didn't even go there today."

"Ania, we are at war." He puts his hand on mine. "That's the last thing you should be worried about."

"So, what exactly should I be worried about?" My eyes stray to his large hand shielding mine.

"I hope this won't worry you, but I need to leave early in the morning and join the Resistance."

"What?" I involuntarily move my hand over his and squeeze it tightly.

"Every person who can use a weapon is needed to reinforce our line of defense."

"But... But you're a police officer! You need to stay here." Just hours ago, he assured me that I wasn't alone. That he was here with me. Taking care of me.

"I know that I said you're not alone," he says, as if reading my thoughts. He suddenly pats my hair. "But I need to fight for my country. Knowing that I'm leaving you alone troubles me very much."

The sound of the bombs echoes in my head, and I cannot speak a word. I was able to bear the incessant noise and the vibrations of the building because I knew I wasn't alone. I want to demand that he keep his promise, but the fact that I've become so dependent on him makes me angry.

"Do you miss her?" I ask, without daring to look at him. "Do you miss my sister?"

"Yes."

"Me too." Tears cloud my vision. "I'm sure that if Michalina were here with me, you wouldn't leave us."

"Ania..."

"You promised to take care of me, and you're breaking your promise." I pull my hands away from him and spread out on the armchair. "I'll take care of myself. I don't need you. I don't need anyone."

"Ania." Anton sighs and pulls my hand back. "I'm joining the army to ensure your safety. Believe me, I don't want to go but I have no choice."

"Then go already!" I snap. "You'll soon find out that I can get along just fine without you."

"I have no doubt that you'll get along fine without me." The smile he offers doesn't hide the concern in his eyes. "Michalina was right when she said that you know no fear; it's a trait that will help you in the near future."

The fact that he misses her too does nothing to comfort me, but the way he says her name, practically in a whisper, irritates me. And the way his eyes are always searching for her beauty mark drives me insane.

"You can leave now." I get up from my armchair. "Don't waste your time on me. I would prefer that you went to fight the Germans."

"As you wish." He stands up and comes over to me. "I want you to know that I'll do everything in my power to return and keep my promise," he tells me while pulling me into a tight embrace.

He's hugging me.

His massive arms are wrapped around my back, and I'm sheltered between them. The tension that has built up in my shoulders dissipates, and I relax the muscles in my back and rest my head on his chest. The sounds of the air raids fade, and the floor beneath me feels stable and unmoving. His arms encircle me like the walls of a fortress, and I close my eyes and slide my hands up his broad back. My heart pounds hard and fast, my bosom trembles, and I feel a hot blush appearing on my cheeks. I'm terrified by my thirst for his touch, and terrified by the sudden spurt of desire that has flared up in me.

I exhale into his chest and hear him exhale sharply in response. Does he feel the same thirst that I do? Or is it just misplaced longing for the sister he really wants? A sharp pain punches me in my gut, and I push myself back and rub my eyes.

"Try not to die," I mumble and bite my lip.

"I'll certainly try." He stretches his mouth into a perfect, genuine smile. "In exchange, you try to wait here for me – safe and sound yourself." He winks at me and walks out of the parlor.

I want to run after him and ask him to stay with me for just a few more hours. I want to beg him to hug me just one more time, even if he's imagining that he's hugging her. But my feet stay implanted on the floor, and the door slams shut behind him.

I head into my parents' bedroom, snuggle up in bed, and close my eyes. The realization that he's leaving creeps in. Maybe I should have told him that I would pray for him. Maybe I should have told him that I lied. That I *do* need him. And what will I do if he doesn't come back? The very thought chokes me with fear. Dziecko leaps into the bed and curls up in my arms. He rubs up against my face, a partner in my plight.

   He's the only one I have left.

CHAPTER 12

The Germans march into the city in what appears to be a never-ending procession. The black boots of the gray-uniformed soldiers stomp on the road in a constant rhythm, and the soldiers on horseback look down at us with haughty expressions. An orchestra of deafening drums accompanies this march of praise for their Führer, who, with a "Sieg Heil" salute, looks down at the city that has become his. This is what a strong, conquering, proud, and invincible army looks like.

The fifth of October. I commit the date to memory, although I'm sure I will never forget what happened on this day until the day I die. I lean against a lamp post on the avenue and slip my fingers into my lace gloves. I'm wearing a long skirt and matching fitted jacket. Delicate makeup is painted on my face, and a dapper hat sits on my head. Mother used to tell the customers who frequented her boutique how important it is for a woman to maintain an elegant and respectable appearance even in times of mourning. My emotions of the past few days have moved back and forth between overwhelming sadness and addictive hope. I'm constantly plagued with concern for the well-being of my mother, who is staying in an unknown village. Meanwhile, Anton's absence has ignited in me an intense fear that he may not return. I,

Ania, who've never known fear, haven't stopped feeling it from the moment Anton closed the door to my house behind him.

The clicking of the soldiers' boots rings in my ears, and I stare at them and wonder if maybe one of them shot the man who still hasn't kept his promise to come back to me. The thought upsets me, and I correct my posture and look straight at the conquerors marching into our city as if it were theirs.

The city's residents are crowded on the sidewalks, looking at the horrifying parade with weary, sorrowful eyes. The death toll is inconceivable. Almost every single person has lost someone dear to them in an air raid or in battle.

My gaze wanders away from the procession towards the view of our surroundings. The Germans are marching through a ghost town. It is a broken, shattered city, much of which lies in ruins. Aside from the many souls that were lost, too many people have lost their source of income, and many more are experiencing the plight of hunger for the first time in their lives.

I involuntarily pat my abdomen. So far, I've managed to survive, thanks to the groceries that Anton left for me. When everything runs out, I'll find out whether I'm really capable of taking care of myself.

The woman standing next to me spits on the ground and whispers, "Stinking Germans."

"They've completely destroyed the city," sadly answers the elderly man holding her arm.

I hug my handbag and sigh. "At least the air raids have stopped. Now they'll rebuild our city."

The woman snorts mockingly, "They'll rebuild? We'll rebuild it. Yeah, even you in your fancy outfit."

I scowl and try to understand what could have possessed her to make such a stupid comment. How am I, a girl whose only skill is reading fashion magazines, supposed to repair the devastation they've caused here?

A young woman bumps into me and mumbles an apology. When she lifts her head to look at me, I open my eyes wide in astonishment.

"Paulina?" I eye her wrinkled dress.

"Ania." Her eyes seem to darken, and she studies me in the same manner that I'm studying her. "I see that you're celebrating the German invasion," she taunts me.

"Of course I'm not celebrating," I hug my handbag. "I'm just trying to take solace in the fact that the fighting is over, and we can finally get back to normal." It's been a long time since I've seen a friend, and I'm happy to run into her. The sight of her in front of me helps blur the memory of our last, unpleasant meeting. I yearn to talk to her. "Where's Nina?" I ask as I look around. The two of them are never apart.

"She's grieving the death of her fiancé. He served in the defense force," Paulina retorts, her voice dripping with venom. "While you were putting on your makeup and spraying on your perfume, she was visiting his grave."

"I'm so sorry to hear that," I answer sincerely.

"The only sorrow you're capable of feeling is for yourself," she scowls. "Sorrow that you're being deprived of your nights out and your suitors. You've only ever cared about yourself."

"I'm going through a hard time, too," I blurt out. "Father and Michalina aren't here, and Mother..." I pause in an attempt to choose my words wisely.

"And your mother will finish putting on all her jewelry soon and join you?"

"No," I shake my head. "She left a long time ago; she joined Father and Michalina."

Paulina looks at me in suspicion. "They left you here all alone?"

"Not all alone." I feel myself perspiring in discomfort. "Anton makes sure I don't lack for anything."

"So where is he?" She peers out at the crowd around us.

"He... He joined the army."

Paulina sighs and stretches her lips into a thin smile. "Then maybe instead of wasting your time in front of the mirror, you should go visit the hospitals. There are still many unidentified bodies."

"Anton hasn't been killed!" I practically shout at her.

"This time, I actually hope you're right." She pins her woolen hat on her head. "There aren't many quality Polish men left. Maybe he was spared but would just rather not see you."

I open my mouth to answer her, but no words come out. The possibility hadn't occurred to me.

"Princess Ania has fallen from greatness," Paulina sneers. "No family, no suitors, and no friends."

Her insult forces me to regain my composure, so I stand up straight and say with a smile, "It looks to me like I'm still wearing the crown while you appear to have just stepped out of a nightmare."

Instead of just looking down and leaving me alone, she walks so close to me that her face is almost touching mine. "Everyone knows what the Germans think of you Jews." Drops of her spittle dampen my face. "It's only a matter of time until your crown becomes a noose around your neck."

"I'm not Jewish!" The cry escapes my mouth, and when she walks away snickering, I realize that everyone within earshot is staring at me.

Paulina is quickly swallowed up by the crowd, and I grit my teeth and push my way toward home. I cross the park but stop short when a truck brakes on the road without warning. Suddenly, soldiers holding sticks leap out of the truck and hit two men who were innocently walking along the sidewalk and push them into the back of the truck. I stand frozen in place and cannot move my legs. The German soldiers then notice three Jewish boys, and I hear one of them shouting orders. The boys disappear down an alley, and the soldiers chase after them.

I force myself to move and hide behind a tree trunk. A few minutes later, I hear shouts and pleas for mercy, followed by the sound of the truck's wheels. I wait a little while longer and then peek out at the road. The truck is gone, and the street is silent.

That horrible feeling of fear tries to creep in again, but I fight it. These kidnappings aren't random. The Germans only kidnap communists or Jews. They are fighting their enemies, and I am not their enemy.

Walking quickly, I head down a narrow alley. My torso shakes as the sound of gunshots pierces the air. I console myself with a reminder that it has nothing to do with me, and I pick up my pace.

When I see my building up ahead, I walk faster, and my heart fills with relief as the gate finally closes behind me. I lean back on it and try to catch my breath; when I open my eyes, I see the old couple who lives upstairs peeking out of the doorway in alarm.

"Miss Orzeszkowa," the old lady addresses me in a whisper. "What's going on out there? We heard gunshots."

"I have no idea," I stammer and hurry into the building.

"Do you... Do you maybe have some milk or cream to share with us?" She grabs my arm. "We haven't left the basement for several days and are afraid to leave the premises."

I stare at her, bewildered. Does she really expect me to share what little I have left with them?

"I have nothing left," I lie and shake her off.

"If we manage to get some, we'll share it with you," the man says, talking to my back.

I don't even bother turning around to thank him and walk up the stairs as quickly as I can.

Dziecko greets me, jumping enthusiastically, and I pour him some milk and put the few groceries I have left on the kitchen table. I boil two potatoes and fry some bacon. When the food is ready, I sit down to eat alone. The food calms my hunger but not the storm of emotions I'm experiencing. The air raids, which had become the constant background music of my life, stopped as soon as the Germans broke through the line of defense. I found comfort in them because I knew that as long as the Germans bombed us, Anton was still fighting. The silence that reigns now in my apartment makes me restless because it could mean that Anton didn't survive the battle, or that Paulina was right, that he did survive but decided to abandon me.

I turn on the radio and flip through the stations. The Polish radio stations stopped broadcasting a while ago, but up until now, I could still pick up the BBC broadcasts from time to time. Now, the only thing emanating from the speakers is a harsh grating noise, so I switch it off. I don't know what I expected to hear. After all, the news about the man I'm waiting for won't be broadcast on the radio. I'm overwhelmed with unbearable frustration.

I move to the parlor and sit down at the piano. I press the keys gently at first and then forcefully before slamming the lid down in irritation. If Michalina were here, she would be playing a cheerful tune to try and reassure me. I, on the other hand, have never been able to concentrate on sheet music long enough to produce a melody that is pleasing to the ear. The pains in the pit of my stomach have come back to torment me, and I groan and curse under my breath. I feel her distress, and it angers me. She's probably unhappy with the dessert they were served at some gourmet meal, or God forbid maybe she can't find an unwrinkled dress to wear to the ball on the ship. Either way, her silly distress annoys me, and I hope she's writhing in pain from my real, warranted anguish.

I leave the parlor and wander around the rooms. The clouds of dust that have gathered make the house feel stuffy, so I draw back the curtains, tear off the newspapers, and open the windows. If Maria were here right now, she would be running around and scouring every corner of the house. Mother would scold her loudly for allowing our beautiful apartment to fall into such positively criminal neglect, and I would demand that she air out all the dresses in the closets. But Maria isn't here, and Mother is so far away from me.

I stick my head out the window and stare at the ruins of the buildings across the park. My street is quiet and empty. The conversation I had with Paulina runs through my head, and my heart sinks. How has my life changed so drastically? Where have the friends who surrounded me my entire life gone? Why am I all alone?

I coil a curl around my forefinger, and Ida's image pops into my head. Is she currently surrounded by friends and family? Is she safe, or have the Germans already raided her street?

The thought that she's in danger troubles me, and I don't know why, but for several minutes I can think only of her. Maybe she's heard from Anton? Yes! That's why I have to see her.

I return to the foyer and pull the crumpled note with her address out of my bag. She lives in the Old City. Logic tells me to stay home and wait until the chaos in the streets is over, but my loneliness threatens to make me lose my mind.

I open the door and dash down the stairs – knowing full well that I'm making the wrong decision.

* * *

After a long, excruciating walk in high heels, I spot the crowded alleys that lead to the Old City. Every so often, I pass by distraught people walking hastily, staying close to the buildings. Beggars pop up here and there and entire families who've lost their homes have settled in the parks. Poverty is evident on every street corner. Only a few weeks have gone by since the war broke out, and the whole world has gone crazy.

I cross the alley that leads to the street I'm looking for. The street Ida wrote on the note is supposed to be between the market square and the wall. I look around. The Old City didn't escape the air raids and considerable destruction was sown here as well. I cross another alley and look at the unique buildings with interest; they all have intriguing architectural elements. It's as if every structure is telling a story that I don't understand. I'm sad that Michalina isn't here with me. She would appreciate this uniqueness, and she would probably know all about each building. I turn onto a particularly narrow alley, and the silence diminishes, replaced by sounds of life. Two women pushing baby carriages nearly collide with me, and a group of bearded men in black suits walk briskly, conversing in a foreign language. They look at me with curiosity but don't address me. I'm in the heart of the Jewish district, and my mother's voice echoes in my head, urging me to leave immediately.

I stand on the street corner, looking out over the square and trying to understand which way I should turn. An elderly man with curly sidelocks dangling down in front of each ear pushes a wheeled vegetable cart as several women crowd around him. If it weren't for their frightened expressions, I would think they were unaware that the Germans have occupied the city.

I recheck the address on the note and scratch my chin. What on earth am I doing here?

A youthful voice addresses me in a foreign language, and I notice a black-haired boy. His shabby pants barely reach his ankles, and his shirt is stained.

"I can't understand what you're saying." I pout.

"Are you lost?" he asks in Polish.

"I'm afraid so," I sigh, "Maybe I should just go home."

"Who are you looking for?" He stares at me with innocent, jet-black eyes.

"It seems I'm not destined to find her," I say as I turn on my heel. "I made a mistake coming here."

"What's her name?" The boy won't let it go.

"Ida. Ida Hirsch." I walk away from him with two quick steps.

"Miss, I know where you can find her," he shouts after me.

I stop and draw in a quick breath. I have to see her to find out if she's heard from Anton. That's the only reason I'm here. I'll ask her just one question, and then I'll go home.

I stand up straighter and turn back to the boy. His face lights up with a proud smile, and he motions with his hand for me to join him. He breaks into a run, and I pick up my pace and follow him. He turns again and again down a maze of alleys. It seems that with each alley, the number of people multiplies, and I slither among them, trying to catch up. Suddenly I can't see the boy; panicked, I look left and right.

"Over here, Miss," the boy shouts, pointing to a flight of stairs that leads to a well-maintained building. "Ms. Hirsch lives on the first floor." He waves goodbye and disappears into the throng.

I stare at the men and women who pass by me with their heads bowed. The men are all wearing suits and hats, and the women are dressed in modest frocks, with scarves covering their hair, each of them surrounded by a group of toddlers. I suspect the crafty boy led me into a trap, and I feel the crowd closing in on me. I look around in distress. I have no idea how to get out of this place. Troubled, I approach the building that he pointed to.

I open the door of the building and stand in the vestibule. It is brightly lit and looks renovated and modern. There's a bench against the wall with two tall urns next to it. I turn my eyes to the door of the apartment on my right and then to the door across the hall. My chest rises and falls with labored breaths, and the hall seems to become darker in front of my eyes. This is the last place in the world I should be.

I proceed carefully to the stairs, grab the railing, and climb to the first floor. There is only one door in front of me. Without further delay, I knock twice.

I hear the click-clacking of heels, and the door opens.

"Ania?" Ida's eyes widen in surprise.

I push her inside and close the door behind me.

"Ania, is everything all right?" She looks at me, concerned. "Has something happened to Anton?"

Her question implies that I won't be getting the answer I was hoping for from her, and a feeling of disappointment shoots through my abdomen. Suddenly, I'm overwhelmed with frustration and despair, and I bury my head in my hands and burst into tears.

"What happened?" Ida asks in horror.

"Nothing happened." I dry my tears and blow my nose. "I must be losing my mind."

"So… So, is Anton back? Have you seen him?"

"I haven't seen him!" I lash out in frustration. "I was hoping that you'd heard from him. I was hoping he hadn't come to visit me because he wasn't interested in seeing me. Now I know he hasn't come back from the battlefront."

"He'll come back." Ida exhales sharply and wipes her face with her hands. "My brother will also come back. They'll both come back." She steps back, and I notice dark circles under her eyes. She's wearing a long pencil skirt and a white button-down shirt and seems reserved, yet the expression on her face reveals that she's going through a difficult time. "I'm glad you're here." She puts a smile on her face. "I thought about you. I worried about you. But I couldn't convince myself to leave the apartment. I'm waiting for my brother." She turns around and crosses the foyer. I follow her, studying the apartment. It is massive and very tastefully designed. Unlike my mother's eye-popping interior design style, this apartment is modest, but every item somehow contributes to the warm atmosphere that prevails inside. Ida leads me to the sitting room, furnished with big leather sofas and brown wooden credenzas. A pot of tea and a plate of cookies sit on the coffee table. A large family portrait hangs over the fireplace depicting a man and woman in elegant apparel. Beside them, on an armchair, sits a little girl holding the hands of her brothers, one of whom is a toddler and the other a young boy.

"My family," she explains with a loud sigh. "Mother and Father left for Switzerland with Yakub right after his bar mitzvah celebration." She takes two teacups out of the sideboard.

"So, you were also left on your own?" I ask, and sit down on the sofa.

"I stayed here with my older brother." Her hand trembles as she tries to pour the tea. "We were supposed to travel to the Holy Land, but my brother decided he had to beat the Germans first."

"You must feel very lonely." I bite my lip.

"It's hard to feel lonely when you live in the heart of the Jewish district." She flashes me a lopsided smile. "I have a lot of visitors."

I lower my eyes and hope she doesn't ask me if I feel lonely. I haven't been visited by anyone except Anton.

"I'm glad you're here." She hands me a teacup and sits next to me. "You're welcome to come and stay here with me."

I shake my head no. "I won't be staying long. I have to get back home. I can't risk anyone suspecting that I belong to your community."

"Ania, we're not lepers." The corners of her mouth turn upward in a reluctant smile. "If you allow yourself to open your heart and mind, you'll find that some of us are really nice."

"You're nice." I nod. "And you don't look anything like the people walking around outside. Now that the Germans have invaded Warsaw, maybe you should leave the Old City and deny that you're Jewish."

Ida chuckles hoarsely and rolls her eyes. "I'm a proud Jew. No one can make me forsake my religion."

I peer at her hands. "How is it that you're not married? You're a beautiful young woman."

"Thanks for the compliment." She takes a sip of her tea and puts the cup on the coffee table. "I think I dreamed of marrying a yeshiva student ever since I was a little girl, but we have a clear social hierarchy here."

"You don't look poor." I look around the sitting room again.

"Classes are different for us than for the gentiles. The non-Jews, I mean." She hands me the plate of cookies, and I select one. "My father is not ultra-Orthodox – not religiously conservative. He chose to become a jeweler instead of studying our Holy Bible, the Torah, so I'm not worthy of a talmid hacham. That's what we call a full-time student of the Torah."

"You want to marry a student?" I grimace. "How will he support you? How will he provide you with a comfortable life?"

She opens her mouth to answer me but turns pale when we hear loud noises from the street – wheels screeching, engines growling, shouting in German, and footsteps running.

She moves closer to me and grabs my hand.

"I have to go now." I pull my hand away and stand up. "They might think I'm one of you."

I run out the door and head down the stairs but stop short at the sight of three Germans banging on the door of one of the ground-floor apartments. Another higher-ranking soldier is leaning against the doorframe at the entrance to the building.

I hear Ida panting behind me and start looking for an escape route.

The Germans break down the door with a kick, and seconds later, leave the apartment dragging a young boy behind them. An elderly man and woman hang on to the boy, refusing to release him into the hands of the Germans. They cry out, begging and sobbing, and the soldiers beat them with their clubs.

"What are they doing?" Ida whimpers behind me. "He's just a kid. What good is he to them?"

"Shhh..." I try to hush her, but she sidesteps me and runs down the stairs.

"What are you doing?" Ida yells at the Germans in Polish. "His family needs him."

The lieutenant leaning on the door frame straightens up and walks over to her. I gasp as he swings his arm and slaps her cheek with such force that she falls backward onto her behind.

"He... He's just a boy who helps take care of his grandparents," Ida stutters, rubbing her cheek.

"You dirty Jew," the lieutenant barks in German and pulls out his pistol.

My breath stops. The lieutenant points his gun at Ida.

"I... I..." Ida is unable to finish her sentence and covers her face with her hands.

The lieutenant looms over her and presses the barrel of the gun to her head.

This can't be happening. There's no way this despicable officer really intends to harm the kind, goodhearted Ida. The lieutenant cocks his weapon, and I shriek in alarm and push myself forward. I almost trip down the stairs but quickly regain my footing and command myself to act composed.

"What a commotion," I proclaim in German and hold my head high. The lieutenant looks up at me, and I realize that I've gained a few invaluable seconds. If I play my cards right, I might be able to save Ida. "I've been walking from building to building for hours and can't find my way out of this dreadful neighborhood."

The lieutenant wrinkles his brow but continues to point his gun at Ida. I ignore the lamentations of the elderly couple and the sight of the boy writhing in the soldier's grip. Only Ida matters right now.

"I was told I could find buttons for a dress in the Old City," I flutter my eyelashes and walk down the last few steps, "And instead, I found myself in a maze." I wrinkle my nose in distress. "I was so glad when I heard you. No one here agreed to show me the way out."

"Are you German?" The lieutenant moves his weapon away from Ida, and I suppress a sigh of relief.

"I'm sorry to say I'm not." I shrug. "I'm just a Pole who admires the Führer."

"Heil Hitler!" all three soldiers proclaim, raising their hands in the Nazi salute.

"Yes… Umm… Heil." I raise my arm clumsily. "Lieutenant, I'm sure your soldiers can handle this Jewboy while you show me the way out." I concentrate on gazing into the soldier's cold eyes.

He studies me for a few moments and then looks at his soldiers. I use the distraction to kick Ida's leg, and she crawls backward. He turns to look at me again, and his gaze softens.

"A Pole who supports the Führer?" He tilts his head sideways. "I could have sworn you were of pure Aryan blood."

"It's not the first time I've heard that." I fake a giggle and lightly touch his arm.

"Load him into the vehicle and bring me five more," he commands his soldiers, then clicks his heels and gestures for me to join him. The elderly couple's wails of misery and the boy's pleas pierce my hard shell, and a lump sticks in my throat when I see the merciless soldiers push the elderly couple to the floor. I don't risk turning around to check on Ida, but I hope with all my heart that she's run back to her apartment.

I step outside to the empty street with the lieutenant. The shutters are closed in all the surrounding buildings, and a mournful silence prevails.

"Where do you live, Frau…?"

"Frau Paulina," I use the first name that comes to mind. "And I live in the city center."

The lieutenant turns us down a narrow alley and keeps sneaking looks at me. "I can't escort you any further." He halts, taking my hand. "At the next alley, turn toward the square. From there, walk toward the wall until you reach Jerozolimskie Avenue." He kisses my hand and gives me a slight smile. He's a handsome man, and I shudder at the thought that in another reality, I might have responded to his advances without knowing what cruelty resides within him.

"I thank you for your help from the bottom of my heart." I force my lips into a broad smile.

"Frau Paulina, you should avoid the streets of those stinking Jews. They are like leeches; their filth sticks to you." He shakes his finger, warning me, "The next time you socialize with them, you might encounter soldiers less sensitive than me."

"Of course." I nod vigorously. "I'll never go near their neighborhoods again."

"Heil Hitler," he declares with a salute and clicks his heels.

I bow my head and walk away quickly without looking back. My heart is beating wildly, and the simple act of breathing hurts my chest. Only when I reach the wide boulevard do I bend down and rest my hands on my knees. I'm worried about Ida's fate, and all my attempts to convince myself that it has nothing to do with me are in vain. The fear that creeps in now is poignant and overpowering. Anton is missing, and I have no idea whether or not I succeeded in saving Ida.

CHAPTER 13

I go into the apartment and pull the pins from my hat. Dziecko jumps at my feet, and I bend down and take him into my arms. For three days now, I've been going from hospital to hospital, from dawn until dusk. I searched all the regular hospitals as well as the underground ones, and I scanned every ward without skipping a single bed. But there's no trace of Anton. The fact that he's not among the many injured doesn't cheer me up. Terrible thoughts run through my head, and my tears flow on their own. Anton is gone, and so is Ida. I haven't dared to return to the Old City, and I haven't heard a word from her.

I go to the parlor, pour myself a drink, and put a Bing Crosby record on the gramophone. I remember the day Father brought us Big Band and Bing Crosby records from America. Michalina and I tried to imitate a pair of dancers who'd performed the night before at the restaurant and Mother was aghast, claiming that the words that accompanied the melody were too vulgar for her gentle ears.

The sun is beginning to set, so I switch on the table lamp and turn my armchair to face the window. I stare at the bombed-out buildings and listen intently to the lyrics. Crosby's voice is deep and soothing. He confesses his feelings and his longing for his lover and asks her to let him call her "sweetheart." The words are beautiful and moving, and make me wonder if I'll ever get the chance to experience such love in my life.

The record ends, and the gramophone needle comes to a screeching stop. I want to get up, turn the record over, and let the music calm my nerves, but my thoughts wander to the last time I saw Anton. I ponder his surprising display of affection, and my cheeks flush when I recall the warm feeling that flashed through me when I felt his body so close to mine. My concern for his fate threatens to paralyze me. I didn't actually realize that my feelings for him were genuine until he left me, and I shudder at the thought that the embrace he gave me was goodbye and that I'll never see him again. I swear to myself that I'd be willing to surrender his affection at this very moment just to know that he's alive.

I close the window and walk to the bathroom, my heart aching. The thought that I'll never see him again bombards me cruelly, but I stubbornly push it away. I soap myself up quickly and rinse my body with cold water. There is no one to heat the water since Maria left. My hair dripping with water, I cover myself with a bathrobe and return to the parlor. I stare at the fireplace and then at the split logs arranged in a perfect tower in the alcove. I should have tried to start a fire before bathing.

I crank the gramophone's handle and adjust the tonearm. The music banishes the silence, and I push two pieces of wood into the fireplace and throw a lit match between them. The match goes out immediately.

I get down on my knees, move the logs, and soon my fingers are black with soot.

I light another match and cautiously carry it closer to one of the logs. A few seconds later, my fingers are burned, but the wood still refuses to catch fire. Annoyed, I push my hair away from my face and light another match.

"You have to learn to lock the door," says a familiar low voice, and I gasp for breath. I toss the match and stand up, my heart pounding.

His perfect smile lights up the room.

"Anton!" I shout his name and run toward him. I wrap my arms around his neck, and my feet fly into the air as he grabs my waist and spins me around. I have never felt such happiness.

"I see that you've missed me," he says with a laughs as he puts me down.

"I've been so worried about you." I let go of him and slide my hands over his chest. He's wearing a dusty flannel shirt with black suspenders, and the hat on his head is tilted to the side. His face is covered with stubble, and his hair has grown wild, but despite everything, I've never seen a more handsome man.

Dziecko meows and rubs against my ankles but I push him away. This perfect moment is mine. Only mine.

"I promised you I'd try not to die." Anton winks at me and strokes my hair.

"I didn't know what to think." I bite my lip. "The Germans invaded the city and..."

"They won." The smile continues to adorn his face, but it no longer reaches his eyes. Releasing one arm from my waist, he wipes the soot from my face with the edge of his sleeve. The closeness of our bodies excites me.

"I must look terrible." I giggle nervously. "I was trying to light a fire to warm up the house."

"You are the loveliest sight a man could possibly hope to see after coming home from a crushing defeat." As he slides his hand over my hair, his eyes remain fixed on the intersection between my cheek and my ear. His gaze lingers there for a second too long. The warmth that enveloped me dissipates, and my body feels frigid. Even if he'd poured a bucket of ice over my head, I wouldn't feel colder than this.

I free myself from his grasp and step back.

His eyes dart directly to the deep cleavage of my bathrobe, and he quickly looks away.

"Forgive me," he says, embarrassed. "I didn't notice that you weren't dressed. I should have waited outside the parlor."

A blush rises on my cheeks, and I tighten my robe. My face goes hot with disappointment. He doesn't feel the excitement that I do. For him, I'm just a living, breathing copy of my other half. I'm like a permanent image constantly reminding him of his longing for the woman who left him.

"Help yourself to a drink." I point to the liquor cabinet. "I'll be right back."

In my bedroom, I take off my robe, put on a simple house dress, and wrap my hair into a tight bun at the back of my head. Now my cheeks are completely exposed. This way, he won't confuse us.

When I come back, there's a fire burning in the fireplace, and the parlor is flooded with warm light. Anton is by the window, holding a drink, and I go to the gramophone and lift the tonearm. The room is plunged into silence.

"It's nice to be back in a sane place." He turns to stare at the burning and crackling logs. "Nothing can prepare a person for the images of battle."

"Things weren't exactly pleasant here either." I sit down on the armchair and cross my ankles.

"I'm sure." He nods and sits down on the armchair across from me. "I'm sorry I didn't return sooner. The Germans broke through our line of defense, and many of our soldiers were captured or murdered in cold blood; others were sent to labor camps. As soon as I could, I returned to the city and came straight here."

The knowledge that he came straight to me doesn't cheer me up.

"Why didn't you go visit your family first?" I ask as I pat my knees, and Dziecko pounces up into my lap.

Anton furrows his brows and looks at me in wonder. "I've never met my father. My mother and I moved here from Germany when I was eight years old, but she died more than 10 years ago. She never remarried, and I have no brothers or sisters."

I open my eyes in surprise.

"Does that mean you're German?" I ask him in German.

This time he's the one who looks surprised. "It's nice to discover that you speak the language, but I have no ties to Germany," he replies in German before continuing in Polish, "Ever since we moved here, I see myself exclusively as Polish."

I peer at him and study him at length.

"Is this the moment that you realize you've never asked me a personal question?" he chuckles.

"You've never asked me anything either." I stick my chin out defiantly. "You know nothing about me other than my lineage."

"I think I know more than enough." He gets up and refills his glass. Instead of taking a sip, he hands the glass to me. "I know who your parents are and who your sister is." He pours another glass and sits back down opposite me. "I know you love fashion and that you invest too much time in your appearance."

I don't like his teasing, but I don't say a word.

"I know that you like to go out and that you're thirsty for attention, and I know that you enjoy the attention of many suitors but that you still haven't found the man who can make you settle down."

I look down and clench my teeth. He's summed up my entire life in just a few sentences – sentences that sound so shallow and uninspired. He made only one mistake. I have found a man who makes all other men pale compared to him, a man who makes me want to settle down, but his heart belongs to my sister, and he's utterly immune to my charms.

"Ania," he speaks my name softly.

I refuse to look up at him.

"I also know that you're resourceful, fearless, and proud. Too proud for a time like this."

"And I know that you're quick to judge me," I say, forcing myself to look into his eyes. "I was worried about you, and I missed you. For three days, I searched for you in all the hospitals. I was afraid that my behavior had made you hate me, that you'd returned already, but you'd decided not to come back to me."

"You looked for me in all the hospitals?" he asks in astonishment.

"Yes." I dab a wayward tear. "I hate being scared, but I was so terrified for you. I feared the worst."

"I'm sorry." He takes my hand and kisses it tenderly. "I want you to know that we both shared the same fear. Before I opened the door, I prayed that I would find you here. The thought that I would return and discover that something terrible had happened to you drove me crazy."

"Because... Because you promised her that you'd take care of me?" I say as I wrinkle my nose.

"Because you're important to me." He squeezes my hand. "And it turns out that I'm important to you as well. The entire time bullets were flying over my head, all I could think about was how I had to continue fighting so I could get back here and take care of you." He won't meet my gaze. "It's true that we have our differences, and it's true that we seem to have nothing in common, but you are my anchor in these chaotic times." His jaw trembles, and he meets my gaze again with a look so penetrating and intense that it makes my heart pound faster in my chest. "I'm not sure anyone else would have spent the time to look for me in all the hospitals."

"Would you have looked for me?" I raise an eyebrow threateningly.

"Do you doubt it?" He laughs.

The cat sits up at the sound of Anton's laughter and leaps onto his knees.

Anton pets Dziecko's fur and looks at me with a smile. "Ania, you're just like your cat. Proud and spoiled, but for some reason, being near you is addictive."

I don't like his choice of words. "Addiction is something you don't want and that you'll try to get rid of."

"I meant it as a compliment," he says in a conciliatory tone.

The realization that I'm thirsty for his compliments and the feeling that I'm dependent on him irritates me. "I want you to know that although I did miss you, I managed just fine without you, and I don't need you."

"It comforts me to hear that." He puts Dziecko down on the floor and stands up. "I'll have to disappear for a few days until I find out the Germans' plans for me. I assume they intend to use the Polish police force that preserved order here before the war, but they're unpredictable, and I don't intend to get inside one of the trucks taking men to labor camps."

"You're too pessimistic." I wave my hand, dismissing his words. "They wanted Poland, and they got Poland. Now they'll rebuild it so they can take advantage of its resources." I scoop the kitten up into my lap, "You'll see very soon that the horror scenario materializing before our eyes will be nothing more than a passing episode for the Germans. We'll be the ones taking advantage of them." I smile. "They'll rebuild the country and then retreat with their tails between their legs when France and Britain defeat them."

Anton combs his hair with his fingers and sighs. "You have no idea, Ania. You have no idea how ruthless they are."

"That's legitimate on the battlefield." I roll my eyes. "If we had fought with the same ruthlessness, maybe we'd now be celebrating a victory instead of a defeat. But there's a big difference between brutality on the battlefield and brutality directed at innocent civilians. The Germans are civilized people. The only people who will be harmed by the Germans are the Jews." I look down at my feet. "Have you seen Ida since you came back?"

"Why are you asking? To make sure I came to see you before visiting my *Jewish* girlfriend?" His tone is angry.

"No... Um... I'm asking because..."

"Where were you when German soldiers stormed the streets, kidnapping and abusing innocent civilians?"

"It's understandable that they won't tolerate provocations from civilians," I groan in irritation and decide not to tell him about my visit to the Jewish Quarter.

Anton sets his mouth in a straight line and bows his head curtly.

"I'd better leave now." He puts the glass on the table.

Leave? He's leaving me again?

"Stay." I jump out of my chair, and the cat yowls, landing on the carpet. "You can hide out here."

"I won't put you in danger," he answers firmly and rubs his face with his hands. "I'll come back as soon as I know it's safe for you, but promise me that you'll try to keep a low profile until the situation clears up."

"What do you mean 'keep a low profile?'" I scowl. "You expect me to hide here, too, until you realize that your imagined scenarios aren't going to come true?"

"It means I expect you to stop walking around the city as if the citizens are your subjects," he blurts out. "Stop dressing like you're going to a ball, and don't cause any trouble. Behave modestly, like your sister would."

His last sentence makes my stomach churn.

"My sister isn't here. I'm here. And I'll navigate these new circumstances as I see fit."

Anton closes his eyes and shakes his head in frustration. "Ania, I wish that, for once, you would prove to me that you have just a little of her intelligence."

He leaves the parlor, and seconds later, I hear the door to the apartment slam shut.

I pick up the glass he'd put down on the table and throw it against the wall.

I hate my sister, and I hate the man who worships her.

* * *

The mattress I'm lying on sags, and I sit up in a panic and wave my arms around in the dark.

"Ania, it's me." Anton turns on the lamp on the bedside table, and I pull my blankets up to my neck. He's sitting on my parents' bed in the middle of the night.

"What are you doing here?" I rub my eyes.

"I saw Ida's brother." He brings his hand to my head and strokes my hair. "He told me about your visit with her."

"Is she all right?" I ask apprehensively.

"Thanks to you, she is." His lips stretch into a slight smile.

"I only went there to see if she'd heard from you." I avoid his incandescent gaze. He's so near; his touch makes me feel all warm inside. "I don't hang out around there by choice."

"But you intervened when she was in danger." He slides his palm over my cheek, and I gulp, not daring to breathe.

"I had no choice." I close my eyes for a moment. "The lieutenant, he... he wanted..."

"Why didn't you tell me?" He stares deep into my eyes. "Why did you let me ridicule you instead of telling me that you risked your life for someone I care about?"

"I had no idea what happened to her after I left." I look down. "The lieutenant hit her and then pointed his pistol at her. I thought he was going to kill her." Recalling the memory is painful for me, and my eyes fill with tears. "At that second, I didn't think about myself at all. I was afraid for her."

"I apologize for coming into your bedroom." He wipes away the tear running down my cheek with his thumb. "And I beg you to learn to lock your door."

I nod and tilt my cheek toward his hand.

"But I couldn't wait till my next visit to tell you how proud I am of you."

My entire body trembles and I'm incapable of articulating a single word.

"I'm glad I saw him. Hearing about what happened helped me understand why my feelings for you…" He stops, and I wait anxiously for him to finish the sentence.

"I meant it when I said you're addictive." He drops his hand and stands up.

I gape at him. The pains in the pit of my stomach are unrelenting, and in my head, I hear my mother's voice berating me and nudging me to rebuff his dangerous compliments.

"Anton," I say softly, "it's important to me that you understand that my visit there was a mistake. I'm not one of them. I don't belong to their community, and I'll do everything in my power to make sure no one suspects I have anything to do with them." I wait a moment and then say in a loud and clear voice, "I'm. Not. Jewish."

"And somehow, you've managed to ruin this beautiful moment, too," he sighs, turning the corners of his mouth up into a lopsided smile. "Ania, lock the door," he says and waves his finger at me threateningly.

I nod, he flashes me a disappointed smile and leaves the bedroom.

CHAPTER 14

The tram stops on the corner of Jerozolimskie Avenue and Marszałkowska Street, and I get off and walk towards the boutique in my tailored suit and fur coat, with my head held high. Almost a month has gone by since the Führer invaded Warsaw and his chilling regal parade marched through our streets. The German soldiers strut through the streets like lords, instilling fear in the citizens. Much of the city has been demolished by the bombings, and what's left of it is decorated with red flags bearing swastikas. The cafés are full of Wehrmacht and SS soldiers, and the city's residents look terrified and dejected.

I go to the boutique every morning, sweep the floor, dust the shelves, and change the dresses on display. Many of the city's shops haven't bothered to reopen after the air raids. The people of Poland are licking their wounds and having a hard time recovering from defeat.

The doorbell rings and I turn around expectantly. I haven't seen Anton since that night, and I have no idea where he is. Two German soldiers walk inside the boutique. They walk between the shelves, crudely pull a dress from its hanger and leave it crumpled on the floor; then one of them nods at me, and they go back out into the street.

They'll probably be the only people to come into the store today. I haven't sold a single dress since the Germans entered Warsaw. The Poles no longer have a reason to celebrate, only to mourn. And mourners don't treat themselves to fancy new dresses.

I sit on the chaise longue, leafing through old magazines and waiting for the time to pass. I'm hungry. Hunger has become a constant nuisance. I settle for one modest meal a day. Soon I'll run out of money and will have to come up with a way to provide for myself without selling property, like my neighbors have done. People who were once proud and established now walk the streets, offering to sell items such as paintings and chairs to passers-by.

I lean on the door frame and look at the café across the street. Two Polish waitresses serve the soldiers who sit around the tables that are scattered all along the sidewalk. The waitresses grin and giggle, using their feminine charms to make their loathsome customers like them.

A bearded man with glasses nears the café and scurries off the sidewalk onto the cobblestone street. His clothes are slightly worn, and he's carrying a sack on his back.

The waitress taps one of the soldiers on the shoulder, then steps into the street and mimics the man's stooped walk. The soldiers seem amused by her imitation. Abruptly she approaches the man and pulls the sack from his shoulders; when he turns around to her, she pulls the glasses off his nose and spits at his feet.

The soldiers burst out laughing as the man stares silently at the contents of his sack scattered all over the road. He leans down to pick up his glasses, and the waitress spits on his back to the sound of the soldiers' applause.

A snarl escapes my lips, and I clench my fists and head back inside the store. It has nothing to do with me, I repeat to myself as my heart pounds. It has nothing to do with me. At times like this, it's every man for himself.

The tram ride home seems longer than usual, and I can't help but listen to the conversation between the two women standing next to me. One of them says that the gypsies and the Jews are to blame for everything that's happening, and her friend giggles and proudly recounts how her son and his friends broke into Żyd shops and brought home quite a haul. I lose interest in their conversation and slip my fingers into my gloves. The knowledge that I'm going to spend another tedious evening all alone casts a shadow over my mood.

I climb the stairs, go into the apartment, and am instantly consoled by Dziecko's attention. He no longer looks like a defenseless kitten. He's fast and energetic, and his long nails leave marks on Mother's expensive furniture.

I heat some porridge on the stove, divide it into two bowls, and put one on the floor for him. Dining in restaurants seems like a distant memory.

I hear a tentative knocking at the door, and my heart thumps in my chest. It's Anton. It has to be Anton. No one else comes to visit me.

I fling the door open with excitement, and my face falls when I see that it's Ida.

"It's you," I say, hunching my shoulders.

"It's me," she says as she smiles her beautiful smile. "It's taken me far too long to come and thank you." She pulls me into a tight hug. "Ania, what you did... What you did for me..."

"It's nothing." I break out of her embrace. "In truth, I just did what I had to do to save myself."

She nods but continues beaming at me excitedly, "Were you expecting a visit from someone else?"

"No," I lie.

"Maybe from Anton?" she asks cautiously.

"Why should I be expecting Anton?" I reply angrily. "I don't know where he is. I haven't seen him since..."

"He asked me to come here."

"What?" I swallow the insulted lump that is building up in my throat. He went to visit her but couldn't find the time for me?

"I apologize for stopping by uninvited," she says, ignoring my flurry of emotions. "May I come in?"

"Did anyone see you come in the building?"

"I don't think so," she replies, confused.

"Good." I yank her inside and shut the door. "I don't want my neighbors to get the impression that I fraternize with your kind of people."

Ida stares at me in shock, but after a few seconds, she blinks and composes herself. She looks at the dusty foyer and the dirty dishes piled up on the table and then pulls up a chair and sits down.

It's been so long since I've hosted anyone besides Anton, and I can't think what would be appropriate to offer her.

"We can have a cup of tea together," she suggests with a smile.

"Of course." I go to the kitchen and put the kettle on. Until now, the persistent disorder in the apartment hasn't bothered me, but now, with Ida sitting in her elegant clothes in the filthy dining room, I feel that I have failed at housekeeping. I put the teapot and two teacups on a tray and ask her to join me in the parlor.

"You have a beautiful home," Ida says politely. "It looks as if each piece was carefully selected."

"Mother designed it herself," I say with pride and nod towards the armchair.

Ida sits down and crosses her legs. She nods in thanks when I hand her the cup and puts it down on the table.

"Anton has joined the Blue Police," she says and pulls off her gloves, finger by finger. "The Germans have assigned many tasks to them, and he believes that visiting your apartment could put you in danger."

"And how do you know all this?" I ask as I sit down across from her and swing my legs restlessly. "Wouldn't a visit to your apartment endanger you as well?"

"My older brother saw him," she sighs. "Anton has been passing him information about which houses the Germans plan to raid."

"Why is Anton passing him such sensitive information? Won't that put him in danger?"

"Ania, sometimes I don't know whether you're serious or whether you just have a really peculiar sense of humor." She picks up her cup and sips carefully. "He asked me to tell you that your name, your mother's name, and your sister's name are all included in our census."

"The census of Warsaw?"

"The census of the Jewish community."

I leap up and a few drops of boiling hot tea spill onto my dress. I groan in annoyance and put my cup on the table. "Who authorized you to do such a thing? Who authorized you to force us to belong to your community? I demand that you remove our names from that horrible list immediately!"

"Please, calm down." Ida hands me an embroidered white handkerchief. "Your names have always been listed as Jewish in the Polish records. Still, you need to understand that these lists have now been passed from the Jewish Council to the Germans' Central Headquarters." When she realizes that I have no intention of taking the handkerchief she's trying to hand me, she tucks it back into her handbag. "You're all alone here in this big apartment. Anton is worried about your safety. I would be happy if you would agree to come and stay with us for a while. I know you don't have pleasant memories from your last visit to my home, but they could break in here at any second, and we should be together when that happens."

My eyes turn to slits and I gawk at her for some time. What she's saying is absurd, but it looks like she's not joking, and her expression remains solemn and concerned.

"My mother warned me about you people." I smooth out the creases in my dress and sit back down. "She said you would use creative tricks to try and lure me into your community. You're trying to scare me by portraying the situation inaccurately to make me believe my fate is sealed. I'm smarter than that, and I won't let you fool me. I'm. Not. Jewish."

"I already told you that my parents and my younger brother left for Switzerland," she says sadly.

"Good for them." I reach out to pet Dziecko, but he jumps into Ida's lap and rubs against her hands as if she's the one who needs consolation.

"And that Leib and I were supposed to go to the Holy Land, but he decided to join the Resistance, and now it's too late." She strokes Dziecko's woolly fur.

She's repeating herself, and I'm losing my patience. "At least you have a brother who stayed with you," I snort disdainfully. "My sister abandoned me."

"I just wish he were somewhere safe." She puts her hand on her heart. "I wish I only had to worry about myself. Worrying about a beloved family member is much harder than worrying about me."

"Stop whining. Things are much easier when you have someone to share your hardships and this awful loneliness with."

"Ania, you don't have to be lonely." She gives me a lopsided smile. "I know why your mother left our community, and I don't judge her for it."

I long to hear the story but am afraid it's just another crafty scheme, so I purse my lips and say nothing.

"Life in our community also has its advantages. We don't abandon our people. We'll take care of you, reassure you, and stand by your side when you need a comforting hug."

She's saying everything I long to hear – but not from her. I need my real family members and the man who ignores my very existence. I will not fall into the trap she's setting for me.

"I think it's time for you to go." I don't smile as I say this. "I'm not one of you. Anyone who can see me knows that I'm the epitome of Polish womanhood."

"Ania, the Germans want to move all the Jews to a closed compound. They..."

"That has nothing to do with me."

Ida pets Dziecko before carefully putting him down on the carpet and standing up. I can see that she's fighting the urge to keep trying to convince me, but when I cross my arms over my chest, she bows her head and sighs. "You know where I live. If you need me, don't hesitate to stop by – even uninvited."

"I won't be visiting you again. And tell the leaders of your community to stay away from me. And to remove my name from all their lists!" I add, and wave my finger threateningly.

She slips her fingers back into her gloves and leaves the parlor.

I stretch out on my armchair and nod with satisfaction. Mother will be proud of me when I tell her how I drove away the scheming Jews.

CHAPTER 15

The floor shines. The furniture is dustless, and the dishes in the cabinet are polished. I have begun to enjoy taking care of the house, and I've discovered that I like to cook. The many hours I spend alone allow me to do things I've never done before, like arranging the family photo albums and even reading a little poetry from Michalina's extensive library.

I boil water on the stove and throw the apron into Maria's room. I still haven't successfully met the challenge of doing the laundry. I pour the boiling water into the teapot and bring the tea with me into the dining room. I am wearing an elegant velvet dress in shades of earthy brown. Mother would shriek in horror if she saw me wearing it while cleaning the house.

Suddenly, a loud knocking shakes the apartment.

I peek at the mirror, make sure that every curl is in place, and rush to answer the door before the thunderous knocks break it down.

I open the door, and my eyes light up with excitement at the sight of Anton standing in front of me. He's wearing a perfectly ironed blue uniform, his hair is combed to the side, and he's clean-shaven. I clench my fists and remind myself that jumping on men standing on your doorstep isn't proper.

"Close the door." He pushes me inside.

"What... What happened?"

"Open the safe," he barks at me.

"Is this how you greet me after all this time?" I pout miserably.

"Ania, open the fucking safe!" He grabs my arm and drags me into my parents' bedroom.

I don't think I've ever heard him curse, and the painful way he's gripping my arm is starting to scare me.

He pushes me forward, takes the painting off the wall, and gives me a stern look.

"Do you need more money for Mother?" I ask hesitantly and turn the dial with trembling fingers. My first attempt fails, and Anton snarls in annoyance. I force myself to concentrate and turn the dial according to my date of birth. The safe clicks open, and Anton pushes me aside.

He takes out the velvet boxes that contain the expensive necklaces from the top shelf.

"Bring me a big paper bag or a box," he orders.

I pull out a box with a wide-brimmed hat from the closet and hand it to him. He tosses the hat on the bed and throws the velvet jewelry boxes inside. Then he moves on to the bottom shelf of the safe and takes out the smaller boxes that are full of bracelets, earrings, and rings.

"Leave these in the safe." He points to the few boxes left inside, slams the safe shut, and puts the painting back in its place.

"Where are you taking everything?" I look at the hat box in shock. "I need them. Mother will go mad when..."

"Where do you keep the money?" He interrupts me and closes the lid of the hat box.

"In a jar in the kitchen." Taking the hat box with him, he drags me down the hall to the kitchen.

"Take the money out."

I open the cookie jar and put all the zlotys on the counter.

"Is that all you have?" His eyes dart from bill to bill as he counts them.

"It's all I have left. I thought..."

"Put it back in the jar." He waves his hand impatiently and leaves the kitchen.

"Where are you going?" I run after him. "Where are you taking all my jewelry?"

He snarls softly and leans toward me. With his face close to mine, he says, "You have no jewelry. The only jewelry you have left is in the safe. Your parents left with Michalina, and you stayed here alone. And you don't speak German. Understood?"

"Are you stealing my jewelry?" I gasp for air.

"Understood?" He raises his voice in a hushed shout.

"Understood!"

"Put on a wool hat and change out of that stupid dress into something more modest," he mutters angrily and leaves the apartment.

I stare at the open door and breathe laboriously. What just happened? Did Anton actually just steal all of my valuables? Did he deceive me all this time just to rob me of what I had left? Has he become one of *them*?

I close the door, fall back, and land heavily on a chair in the dining room. I can't figure out why he behaved like a bully.

Dziecko comes out of the kitchen, walking slowly, and stretches his front legs. I wait for him to leap into my lap and when he does, I stroke his fur mechanically like I'm trapped in a nightmare. He rolls over onto his back and rubs against my hands, but I refuse to be consoled.

I hear booming sounds coming from downstairs. Shouting in German. Heavy footsteps shake the stairs, and then there are loud knocks on my door.

I'm incapable of getting up from my chair.

"Open up!" someone yells in German, and a split second later, the door is torn from its hinges.

"The door was unlocked," I mutter in Polish. "You didn't have to break it down."

They don't seem to understand me, or maybe they just don't care. Two soldiers in gray uniforms with swastikas burst inside, and I count another ten who push in immediately after them. They line up in pairs, some carrying cardboard boxes. Each pair rushes in a different direction.

Dziecko jumps off my lap and hops onto the leg of one of the soldiers. The soldier kicks him hard, and the cat lets out a horrifying screech. He rolls himself into a ball and curls up motionless under the bench in the foyer.

I hold the armrests and lean forward but still can't seem to get up off my chair.

I hear smashing sounds from the parlor and the bedrooms. Jars break in the kitchen, and the last pair of soldiers in the foyer move into the dining room and start taking the paintings off the walls.

I imagine my mother sitting next to me and scolding me. I hear her horrified voice say *"Ania, are you crazy? How can you just sit there while those goddamned Germans destroy my home?"*

I have to stop them.

I stand resolutely and exhale sharply. I open my mouth to address them in their own language, but suddenly Anton's warning echoes in my head.

"What are you doing?" I shout in Polish at the Germans who are taking the paintings out of the apartment. "Those paintings don't belong to you."

I pull on the arm of one of the soldiers, and he shakes me off and aggressively pushes me back into the mirror that hangs in the foyer. The glass shatters, and I feel stabbing pains in my back. I get ready to rush at him again, but at that exact second, a Scharführer strides into the apartment with his arms crossed and Anton at his side. The Scharführer's uniform is decorated with numerous badges and insignias, and around his neck is a necklace with a swastika.

I look at Anton with tears in my eyes and point toward the stairwell, "They're stealing Mother's paintings."

Anton looks at me with a blank expression and addresses the Scharführer in German, "Scharführer, this woman claims that the paintings are worthless."

I want to correct him, but he shoots me a cold, threatening look.

"Herr Goering will decide that," the Scharführer replies indifferently and he walks into the apartment as if it's his.

I rub my hands together and resolve to change my approach.

"Tell your commander there's nothing for him in this Polish woman's house," I flutter my eyelashes and smile at the Scharführer.

Anton does not translate my words.

"Tell him that I submissively accept the German occupation," I say, practically whispering, and twist a curl around my finger.

Anton doesn't say anything.

The Scharführer looks me up and down and then snorts with contempt. He looks to the left and then to the right, clicks his heels, and gestures with his head for Anton to join him.

Anton sneaks a terrifying look at me and growls quietly.

I inhale deeply and follow them. The parlor looks like it's survived an air raid. Father's liquor bottles are packed in boxes, the gramophone has been thrown on the floor next to piles of broken records, and the beautiful crystal goblets have been set out on the table like merchandise for sale.

"Where is the jewelry?" The Scharführer directs the question at the soldier packing the bottles.

"We couldn't find any jewelry," the soldier answers apologetically.

I breathe a sigh of relief, and the Scharführer's venomous gaze pivots sharply to me.

He pulls a note out of his pants pocket and then stretches his lips into a poisonous smile, "Miss Orzeszkowa?" He asks in broken Polish.

"Yes. I'm Miss Ania Orzeszkowa," I reply in Polish and jerk my chin up.

"Ask her where her cowardly family members are hiding," he says to Anton in German.

"How dare he call them cowards," I mutter angrily through clenched teeth. "They worked for their possessions, unlike this despicable thief."

"She says that her parents and sister left Poland before the war," Anton replies calmly.

"And left the Fräulein here all alone?" He raises an eyebrow in amusement.

"Why did they leave you here alone?" Anton questions me in Polish.

"Because someone had to stay here to guard the house against thieves," I snarl.

"She was supposed to join them after completing her studies, but the war interrupted her plans." Anton once again distorts my answer.

"The jewelry?" the Scharführer barks. "Where's the jewelry?"

"The Scharführer wants to know where the jewelry is," Anton directs the question at me.

"You stole it," I snort mockingly. "Why don't you tell him that you robbed me of all my expensive jewelry?"

"It's in the safe in her parents' bedroom," Anton points down the hall, and before I can bombard him with a heaping dose of hateful words, he tugs my arm and leads me to the bedroom. He points to my parents' portrait, and the soldiers hurry to pull it off the wall.

"Fräulein," the Scharführer points to the safe.

I clench my fists, and my whole body shakes. Anton has betrayed me. The hatred I feel for him overpowers my hatred for the Germans.

"Open it!" The Scharführer barks into my face.

I take a deep breath, and turn the dial. This time the safe clicks open on the first try.

The Scharführer pushes me back and takes the velvet boxes out of the safe. One by one, he examines their contents, nods with satisfaction, and passes them to another soldier, who carefully puts them in a cardboard box.

The earrings that Father gave to Mother for their first wedding anniversary are now buried in the cardboard box, as is the ring he bought for her when we vacationed at our summer house five years ago. The bracelet and pearl necklace she received from him at the grand opening of her boutique are next. I cannot look. My family's treasures are being stolen in broad daylight, and Anton is entirely complicit in the dreadful crime.

"I suspect that the Fräulein is hiding more jewelry," the Scharführer says to Anton.

"Do you have any other jewelry?" Anton translates his accusation.

Before I have the chance to answer, the Scharführer grabs my neck and lifts me up in the air. He shoves my back against the wall and jerks my body around. I gasp for air.

"Where is the rest of the jewelry?" He barks into my face.

Anton stands behind him, and I detect a slight tremor in his jaw, yet he doesn't utter a single word.

"Tell him you stole it all," I cough and shake my head.

"Her parents took everything else with them," says Anton in a quiet but forceful tone. "She's just a frightened girl. She wouldn't lie."

His grip loosens, and I land on my feet and clutch my neck.

"Look at this Frau." The Scharführer chuckles and pulls my hair until my back arches and my chin sticks out. "This is what the most dangerous ones look like." He pulls a gun from his holster and presses it to the underside of my chin. I force myself to look up at the man standing next to him, watching me endure such humiliation in silence. The gun doesn't intimidate me, and I wonder if it's because my rage is overpowering my other feelings, or if maybe I'm simply terrified to the point of complete numbness.

"She looks like one of our own." He slides the barrel of the gun down my neck. "She looks like she was born to the most superior race." The gun slides down to the bodice of my dress. "She wears beautiful clothes and makeup, she smiles, and she could seduce any one of us." He snickers and pulls my hair harder. "Her deceptive disguise is dangerous because underneath it is the sensual body of a woman who will trap you in her web and then bewitch you with her feminine charms and contaminate your pure blood." He pushes the barrel into my cleavage, and suddenly Anton's face is no longer expressionless. His eyes seem to darken, and his jaw quivers. "Do you want to see what she looks like without her costume?"

Anton clenches his fists and grunts. "Scharführer," he says, "I can hear the tenants upstairs. I'm afraid they'll destroy their artwork before we get to them."

The Scharführer pushes me against the wall and whistles sharply. Clicking his heels, he leaves the room, his soldiers hurrying along in his wake.

My eyes remain fixed on the carpet, and I bite my lip. My gun is close at hand. I take one step in its direction and fall flat on my face as a large foot trips me.

I lift my head and meet Anton's angry eyes.

"Don't you dare," he whispers and leaves the room.

I remain rooted in place for a long time and then go over and take the gun out of its hiding spot. I sit under the window with my back to the wall and listen to the commotion going on upstairs. I hear shouting and the clicking of boots. I also hear glass breaking and voices pleading and crying. Then I hear a gunshot. I shudder and tighten my grip on the gun. Dziecko limps into the room and sits on my lap. He doesn't even meow, just rests his head on my thigh and closes his eyes.

After an hour that seemed like an eternity, the ceiling finally stops thumping, and loud footsteps shake the stairwell. After that, a deafening silence sets in and surrounds me.

I reach for the blanket that lies discarded on the floor and cover myself. I slide the palm of my hand over my neck, and my fingers tremble over the thin chain and stop at the triangle hidden deep in my cleavage. I breathe a sigh of relief. The bastard of a German didn't notice my pendant. He didn't rob me of the only jewelry I have that ties me to my sister.

I close my eyes. The minutes tick by and turn into hours, and complete darkness shrouds the room and swallows me up.

* * *

The apartment door creaks, and I straighten up and hold the gun with both hands. My arms shake as my finger grips the trigger. A tall figure steps inside, and I close my eyes and pull.

"Is that how you planned to take out the Scharführer?" Anton asks. He doesn't sound amused.

I open my eyes and stare at his silhouette approaching me in the darkness.

"You forgot that a gun needs bullets." He pulls out a pack of cigarettes and lights one. The tiny glare of the lighter illuminates his face for a split second, and rage erupts inside me, hitting me like a punch in the belly.

I pull the trigger again and again and again, and a moan of frustration escapes my mouth.

Anton tosses his cigarette on the floor and walks toward me with broad steps. Leaning in front of me on his knees, he wraps his palms around my hands and carefully takes the gun from me.

"I hate you," I whisper, depleted. "You're a filthy traitor, and I hate you."

"That's okay. I don't particularly like myself right now either," he sighs.

"How dare you come back here after robbing me of all my possessions?" I clench my hand into a fist and punch his shoulder.

"Ania, I didn't steal anything from you," he replies, his voice soft.

The cat yowls and climbs off my lap. He doesn't pounce onto Anton but instead limps to the corner of the room and curls up.

"Look what they did to Dziecko!" I point to the cat and punch Anton again. "Who behaves like that? Who harms the helpless?"

Anton puts the gun down and sits down next to me with his back against the wall. I raise my arm to hit him again, but he seizes my fist and clutches it to his chest.

"Have you finally woken up?" he asks quietly. "Do you finally understand who we're up against?"

"We?" I spit the word out disdainfully. "You're worse than them."

He closes his eyes and shakes his head in dismay. "Do you truly not understand why I rushed here and asked you to give me your jewelry?"

"So that you could steal it before the Germans did?"

"Ania." He holds my fist between both his hands and holds it close to his chest. "I took your jewelry and hid it so that I could keep it safe for you."

I open my eyes wide in astonishment, and he bows his head and looks into my soul. "When he held the gun to your chin, I felt as if he was holding it to my head." He pulls my hand to his lips and kisses it tenderly. "When I realized that he was going to strip you down in front of his soldiers, I knew that if I didn't do something, rage would overcome me."

His lips kiss my hand again, and my entire body quivers.

"And yet you did nothing." I try to pull my hand away, but he won't let go.

"Yes, I did. I did something terrible." He lowers his eyes, tormented. "I didn't care about anything but getting them away from you." He pulls my hand back to his chest as if trying to draw comfort from it. "I led them upstairs to the apartment of your elderly neighbors, who weren't even on their list. They trashed their house, beat them brutally, and robbed them of what little possessions they had left. I led them to your neighbors to protect you, and now I'll have to live with it forever."

"And the gunshot?" I swallow the lump that is choking my throat. "The gunshot I heard?"

"The Scharführer fired into the air," Anton squeezes my hand.

"But he could just as easily have shot you or one of them in the head."

"I'm not afraid of them." I pull my hand away and bury it between my legs. "If you hadn't tripped me, I would have put bullets in the gun and shot them."

"Ania," Anton sighs and smooths out the sleeves of his uniform. His fingers quiver over the smooth spot where our nation's flag was once embroidered. "What frightens me most of all is your lack of fear. You need to be afraid of them. Only fear can protect you from their cruelty."

"Well, that's not going to happen." Trying to stand up, I cry out in pain.

"Are you hurt?" Anton rotates me toward him and checks my arms, as if searching for an injury.

"I think my back was hurt," I mumble and again try to stand up.

Anton grabs my shoulders and swivels me around to see my back. "Fragments from the mirror's glass tore your dress and cut your skin."

"Mother will be furious when she finds out this dress was ruined." I let out a short laugh, and my eyes fill up with tears of longing.

"Your mother will be even more furious when she finds out that you tried to provoke the German soldiers who broke into your house." He strokes my hair. "I've been on dozens of home raids with them, and I didn't come across one person whose pride overshadowed their fear – until now." He stands up, picks up a lamp that they'd tossed onto the floor, and turns it on. Our eyes roam around the room, which looks like a war zone.

Anton puts the mattress back on the bed and then begins rummaging through the dresser drawers.

"The first aid kit is in the bathroom," I say, groaning in pain.

He leaves the bedroom, and I stare at Dziecko, my face downcast. His silence saddens me.

Anton comes back and sits behind me. He brings the lamp closer to us and carefully unclasps the dress hooks on my back. I let out a whimper as the hooks chafe against me and cut into my skin.

"Just cut it off!" I gasp in pain.

He takes the scissors out of the first aid kit and cuts the material slowly and carefully. The pain only intensifies.

"Anton, please get it over with," I beg. He drops the scissors and tears the dress off me using both hands. The chiffon fabric of the slip scratches against my skin like sandpaper. My shoulders tremble as he rips it from my body. My bare back is exposed to him, and I hug my bosom in embarrassment. With just the two of us in the room, sitting so close, I feel acutely aware of my nakedness.

"If you'd rather I go find a doctor to do it instead of me, just say so." Anton moves his fingers away from my back.

"I'd rather you just get it over with." I rest my head on my knees and close my eyes.

"I'm sorry." He picks up the tweezers and pulls out one of the slivers of glass. "I'm so sorry I couldn't protect you."

"Why do you cooperate with them?" I ask, hoping our conversation will distract me from the terrible pain.

"I couldn't believe that this was what they would demand of us." He pulls out another shard of glass and rubs the sore spot with his thumb. "I thought they needed us for normal police work." He pulls out another shard and immediately presses his thumb to the wound. "I can still leave and escape into the woods to join the resistance."

"But you want a respectable salary. And you want a share of the confiscated property and the power and respect you gain from being a police officer." I regret my words as soon as I hear them come out of my mouth.

"I wish you could see me in a more flattering light." He pulls out another shard and presses on the spot to dull the pain. "The reason I'm staying in this position is information."

"Information?"

"If I'm with them long enough, they'll get used to my presence, and the information that reaches me will be of higher quality and more useful."

"Is that how you found out they were planning to come to my house?"

"Yes. I have access to the lists." He yanks out a piece of glass, and this time caresses my head. "Many good Polish people live among us, but unfortunately, there are also some less good Poles. There's a constant stream of whistle-blowing, and the Germans are determined to leave us with nothing. They take everything. Art, jewelry, even drinks," he snorts in contempt. "But what they want most is to rob us of our self-respect and our national dignity." He falls silent as he continues pulling out more glass, and I ponder his words.

"I thought you'd betrayed me," I whisper.

"Did you really believe I could betray you?" He dips a cotton pad into the antiseptic and carefully dabs it on my back.

"I didn't know what to think," I wail, struck by the sensation that my back is going up in flames.

"One of the reasons I decided to stay with the Blue Police is you." He blows cool air on my back. "You may be annoying, arrogant, and childish," he laughs dryly, "but you're all I have left."

"Really?" I ask in surprise and turn my head to look at him.

"Really." He strokes my hair and tucks an unruly ringlet behind my ear. "The other important people in my life didn't stay here."

His eyes linger on the intersection between my cheek and my ear, and he hurriedly looks up and smiles at me.

His gesture hits me in the pit of my stomach. I seem to have gotten used to it but my need for support overshadows my disappointment. I have no energy left to taunt him at the moment, and I decide to tell the truth.

"I also have nothing left here but you." I blink and try to fight back the tears that well up in my eyes. "My entire life I was surrounded by family, friends, and suitors. And during the greatest crisis to ever befall me, they all disappeared. I feel like no one can see me, as if I don't exist."

"I see you." He wipes the tear running down my cheek with his thumb. "You're not alone. But maybe when you realize that you're not the only one in this crisis, then you'll be able to see the pain and suffering of the people around you, and they'll see you too."

I am overwhelmed with unpleasant feelings by his words. He's trying to encourage me, but in the same breath, he's criticizing my conduct. He doesn't really see me. He sees her in me.

"Your friend Ida was here," I scowl. "She tried to convince me to come and stay with her. She tried to convince me that I could be one of them, but Mother warned me about their tricks. She said *they* would try to entrap me in their net and pull me into their community. I explained that my visit to her was a mistake that I won't be repeating."

Anton clenches his jaw, and I see a tremor in his cheeks. He's angry, and I have no idea why.

"Who are *they* exactly?" he asks, his tone restrained. "The smart and kind-hearted Ida? Or perhaps her brother, who fought by my side in the line of defense?"

"*They* are the J..."

"How do you fail to notice that your attitude towards them is so similar to the Nazi officer's attitude towards you? That the words you use to describe them are almost identical to the words that he used to describe you?"

"We aren't similar at all! He was cruel and tried to humiliate me." I grit my teeth.

"Hatred of the 'other' always stems from ignorance." He closes the first aid kit and stands up. "People are afraid of what they don't know, and their fear fills them with hatred. Try to be more like your sister." He lights a cigarette and looks down at me. "She asked, researched, and learned about her roots. She wasn't afraid of Ida. She learned to appreciate her and the tremendous benefits her community has to offer. *Your* community."

"It's not my community!" I stand up, clutching the ribbed material of my dress to my chest. "Don't be like that! Don't conspire against me with them."

"You'll wise up." He nods to himself. "Even if it takes a while, eventually you'll wise up." He sticks his cigarette between his teeth and lifts the lamp onto the dresser. "I'm sorry I cannot stay and help you straighten up the house. But I better go now." He looks up at the ceiling and combs his hair to the side. "I won't be able to visit you in the near future. You can relay messages to me through Ida if necessary. Her brother knows how to reach me."

He's leaving me again. My confession wasn't enough to make him stay.

"Or I could just come down to the police station." I roll my eyes.

Anton draws near to me and clasps my chin in his hand. "Do not come to the police station under any circumstances. Right now, the Germans need me, but if the circumstances change, I don't want them to know that you're important to me." He runs his finger along my jaw line, "Understood?"

His explanation makes sense but does nothing to alleviate my frustration.

"I understand," I answer angrily.

"And please, Ania, don't attract unnecessary attention," he pleads.

He's leaving me, and I have no idea when I'll see him again.

I look down and say nothing.

CHAPTER 16

The year 1939 is nearing its end. The month of December has arrived, but the city isn't decorated with colored lights, and there's no hint of the festive ambiance that usually characterizes this time of year. A few stores have hung the traditional Christmas decorations, but the depressed faces of the citizens attest to the grief that prevails far and wide. Many local businesses have remained closed, and numerous others have changed owners. No one is renovating the ruins. The Germans strut around the city like they own it, while the Poles scurry about like frightened mice.

I trot down Jerozolimskie Avenue and remember the excitement that used to grip me during the holiday season in the past. I would walk from shop to shop, buy dozens of gifts, and wait enthusiastically for the moment when I would get the chance to unwrap the presents my family and friends got for me. I finger the triangle pendant hanging around my neck and wonder how Father and Michalina are celebrating. Maybe they're still on the ship, strolling leisurely on the upper deck, looking out over the clear water and chitchatting with the other passengers. Or maybe they've already docked in America and are presently roaming through crowded markets, purchasing gifts for new friends and preparing to welcome in the new year with a sumptuous meal at a luxurious hotel.

The pains in the pit of my stomach make me groan softly, and I roll my eyes in irritation. There is no way that Michalina is actually troubled right now. After all, if she were a little less absorbed with herself and her festivities, she undoubtedly would have found a way to communicate with me by now. No letters or telegrams have arrived, not to mention the visas they promised to obtain – if not for me, at least for Mother. And how is Mother celebrating the holiday? The thought of her in a remote village, with only the company of two strangers, gives me no respite.

I peek into a store that a few weeks ago was defaced with a large, painted inscription. The writing is gone, but there are still remnants of the paint. Different women are standing behind the cash register than before, women who don't have yellow armbands on the sleeves of their dresses. The Germans' new mandate – forcing Jews to mark their clothing – has made them stand out as if illuminated by a bright flashlight, precisely at a time when I assume they would have preferred to be invisible. Whenever I walk to or from work, I see German soldiers and ordinary Poles brutally abusing people wearing the yellow armbands. I'm often amazed to see armbands on the sleeves of men and women who don't look Jewish at all. I constantly remind myself that these stupid yellow markers have nothing to do with me.

I tie the belt of my coat and tighten my hat pins. My hair is done up impeccably, and my makeup is flawless. I make sure to wear a beautiful dress, put on makeup, and spray on my perfume before opening the boutique at the exact same hour every morning. This week I celebrated a victory! A German soldier came in with a Polish girl and bought her a dress. I refrained from asking about the nature of their relationship. I suppose her path to survival is through the bedroom, and I don't judge her for it. From the second the Germans invaded our country, all Poles have had to look out for themselves. Anton doesn't come to see me, so the boutique and my faithful cat are the only things keeping me sane. The loneliness is complex and challenging, and it only intensifies as time goes by, but I won't let it dampen my spirits.

Two soldiers in gray uniforms stop in front of me. They click their heels and nod their heads in greeting. I respond with a slight nod. I can't stand them, but I've learned to live with them. The Germans haven't harassed me again since the day they broke into my apartment and stole all my valuables. I watch silently from the sidelines when they bully other people. I remind myself again and again that it has nothing to do with me.

Two teenage boys wearing armbands on their coat sleeves pass by me, and I hear the soldiers barking at them. I don't bother to turn around and watch them be humiliated. A vision of the elegant, smiling Ida receiving the same humiliating treatment frequently appears in my dreams. I shake my head and command myself to remember that none of it has anything to do with me.

I stop short in front of the boutique and open my eyes wide in horror. The door has been forced open, and my mother's two seamstresses are standing behind the cash register.

"What happened?" I run inside. "Was there a break-in? Has anything been stolen?"

They exchange a look but don't respond.

"I don't understand..." I scan the boutique quickly. All the dresses seem to be hanging in their places. "What are you doing here? Have you decided to come back to work?"

Olga puts on a thin smile. "Mrs. Agata forgot to pay us for our final month working for her."

"My mother joined my Father and Michalina on their travels," I tell them, reciting the familiar lie.

"It's none of our concern where Mrs. Agata has decided to travel." Olga continues smiling.

"Is that why you broke into the boutique?" I shake my head in confusion. "I'm here every day. Why didn't you just ask me to settle the payment?"

Paula comes out from behind the counter and stands in front of me. She's almost a full head taller than me, and I need to crane my neck to look at her. "The spoiled little girl should've taken care of her mother's obligations, tsk-tsk," she clucks her tongue. "We've checked our rights. Since you failed to pay us, we have every right to claim the boutique for ourselves."

"What?" I step back. "I've never heard anything so stupid in my life." I burst out laughing. "How much do I owe you? Five hundred zloty? Seven hundred zloty? Come tomorrow morning, and I'll pay you."

"It's too late for that," Olga comes over to stand next to Paula. "We've received confirmation from the Reich stating that the ownership of the boutique is being transferred to us." She pulls a folded piece of paper out of her bag and hands it to me. It's written in German.

"Pathetic imbeciles," I throw the page at her. "Did you really think you could bring me a phony document, and I'd just hand Mother's boutique over to you? Get out of here immediately!"

"Why don't you try to kick us out and see what happens?" Paula crosses her arms over her chest.

I clutch my handbag and clench my fists. What should I do? What would my mother do in a situation like this? She certainly wouldn't hand the boutique over to them without a fight.

I go out into the street and rush over to the two German soldiers whom I passed a few minutes earlier.

"They broke into my store," I wail in German. "Bad women and..." I'm too frustrated to recall the rich vocabulary I learned from my German tutor. I point at the boutique and pull on the sleeve of one of the soldiers.

"Calm down, Fräulein." The soldier pulls his arm away, and I throw him a pleading look and continue pointing at the boutique.

They click their heels and walk towards the boutique. They'll fix everything, I reassure myself. They'll get those awful women out of Mother's boutique.

Paula and Olga stand at the entrance to the boutique and bow their heads in respect.

"Kennkarta. Identification," the soldier barks at them, and they pull their identity documents out of their handbags.

The soldiers pass the documents back and forth and eventually return them to Paula and Olga.

"They're stealing my shop," I say in broken German. "These idiots broke into my shop."

"Get out of here," the other soldier barks at them.

I sigh with relief. I made the right decision.

"No, no," Olga shakes her head, and I gape at her in dismay. Is it possible that this pathetic woman isn't afraid of the German soldiers? "Documents. Documents," she repeats and hands him the piece of paper she showed me before.

The soldier's eyes flit over the document, and suddenly he scowls in contempt. "Juden?" He spits out the word.

"No," I shake my head. "Not Jewish."

"Kennkarta!" This time he roars into my face.

I take my identity documents out of my bag and hand them to him. It looks as if he's comparing my name to the name on the German document Olga gave him.

"Juden!" He flings my documents onto the floor and pulls out his club.

"I'm not Jewish," I shout. "Just look at me, and you'll be able to see that I'm not Jewish." I stand up straight.

In my panic, I've been shouting in Polish instead of German, and it seems I've managed to make him angry. The other soldier also pulls out his club.

Regain your composure, Ania! I admonish myself.

"I'm not Jewish," I repeat in eloquent German. "I don't want to be Jewish. You cannot force me."

"Juden, where is your armband?" The first soldier pulls on my sleeve, ripping the top seam.

"I'm. Not. Jewish."

He hoists the club into the air, and I close my eyes and shield my head with my arms.

"Her armband fell off!" I hear a shout in Polish and open my eyes. A dark-haired man with bright green eyes stands between me and the soldiers. He has an armband in his hand, and he ties it around my arm.

The club lands on his back, and his face is contorted in pain but he doesn't make a sound. The other soldier's club hits him in the shoulder, and he groans softly and grabs my hand. "This girl is crazy," he winds his finger around next to his temple to demonstrate his point, and I stare at him like a sleepwalker, entranced. On his arm, he wears an armband identical to the one he tied around my arm.

The soldiers start kicking his legs.

"She put on band," he says in broken German, pulling me along as the soldiers continue to beat him with their sticks.

"Dirty Jews!" shouts one of the soldiers, as the stranger grabs my hand and, sprinting, drags me away. My high heels strike the cobblestones, and my lungs cry out for air. Abruptly, he pushes me into an alley and peeks out at the avenue.

"They're not chasing after us." He lets out a sigh of relief and then turns toward me and throws me a reassuring smile.

I study the band that was tied around my arm. Then I look up again and meet the man's eyes. I try to speak, but my voice has gone mute.

"I'll walk you home." He gestures down the alley with his head.

With great difficulty, I move my head from side to side. My breathing is irregular, and my chest is rapidly rising and falling.

"Come with me," he implores. "Don't worry, I won't hurt you."

"I... I..." I look at the armband he tied on me again and try to tear it off my sleeve.

"Don't do that." The man puts his hand on mine.

His touch is so gentle.

"Don't touch me." I pull my arm away from him and walk away. My head is spinning with all kinds of thoughts. "The boutique," I mumble. "My mother and... the boutique."

"I'm sure it's unpleasant to have your property taken away from you," the man says in earnest. "But keeping your life is more important."

"The boutique *is* my life." My whole body is shaking. "It's all I have left."

"I find that hard to believe." He smiles again and nods toward the end of the alley.

I understand that I can't hide in the alley forever, but I can't seem to force my legs to move forward.

"Ania, please let me walk you home."

I open my mouth in shock. How does this strange man know my name?

"Leib Hirsch." He tips his hat and gently clasps my arm.

"Leib Hirsch..." I repeat after him. "Hirsch... Are you...?"

"Ida's older brother." He winks at me.

I nod and stare at him like I'm stuck in a never-ending nightmare. My heart is pounding and my legs fail as he leads me out of the alley. I pull him towards a bench and collapse onto it, exhausted.

"Get up," he requests softly and pulls me into a standing position.

"I need to sit down," I moan. "Please, let's just sit on the bench for a few minutes so I can catch my breath."

"We're not allowed to sit on public benches," he whispers and tightens his grip on my arm in order to steady me. "And you're not allowed to go to public parks or take public transportation, and you're not allowed..."

"Shhh..." I hush him. "You're confused. *You're* not allowed to do all those things, but I'm not supposed to be wearing this armband, and I don't have to obey all the decrees they imposed on you."

"Keep your documents safe." He grabs my handbag and stuffs my papers inside. "Maybe, if you weren't so well known in the city, you could continue strolling around the parks and sitting on benches. But if just one person points you out, next time, the Germans will point their guns at you instead of their clubs, just like you saw them do to my sister."

His attempts at intimidation don't scare me. I'm still numb from the earthshaking experience I just had, and I'm taking advantage of the time to study him. He's wearing gray tailored trousers and a vest of the same color, and the hat atop his head is tilted to the side. He reminds me of a young Ronald Colman, the star of the Hollywood film "Lost Horizon" that I saw in the theater before the war broke out.

"I would like to take this opportunity to thank you for helping my sister," he says as he bows his head in thanks.

"Stop thanking me," I huff. "All I did was save myself."

"That's not what I heard." He winks at me.

I scowl.

"Soon, the Germans plan to issue us new documents," Leib explains as we cross the street, and it seems that everyone we pass eyes the armband I'm wearing with distaste, or maybe I'm just imagining it. Usually Polish people bow their heads and warily attempt not to make eye contact with anyone.

"What reason could they possibly have to issue new documents for you?" I throw him a questioning look. "Aren't the armbands a sufficiently noticeable indicator?"

"Not only the Jews will receive new documents," he explains, steering me to a side street. "Ania, from now on, try not to take the main roads where all the soldiers are."

"All this talk about what I am and am not allowed to do is driving me crazy," I groan. "Why can't anyone seem to comprehend that I'm not Jewish? I shouldn't be punished because of my mother's ancestry. She renounced it herself. Surely I have the right to choose my own religion."

"I suppose you're right," Leib chuckles but doesn't really sound amused. "In a perfect world, you should be able to choose your own religion. But unfortunately, the Germans disagree."

"But someone will realize there's been a mistake, won't they?" I look at him, wide-eyed. "Because my mother doesn't allow me to be Jewish. I promised her I wouldn't let it happen, and I..." I can't bring myself to finish the sentence and, drained, I let my shoulders droop. My head aches from all the oppressive thoughts spinning around in it, and I just want some peace and quiet.

"Everything will be fine," Leib answers and looks down as we pass by a couple standing in the street. "If it were up to me, Miss Orzeszkowa, I would let you be anything you want, Christian, gypsy, or whatever your heart desires."

"But I just want to remain Polish," I tell him as a tear runs down my cheek. "I don't want to be Jewish," I whine and stomp my feet.

"Please don't cry." He seems alarmed. "I promise that if you let me, I'll prove to you that it's nice to be part of our community." He looks helpless up against the tears streaming down my cheeks.

I sniffle and move through the alleys at a faster pace. I scold myself for showing him such vulnerability. Why have I allowed this Jewish man to walk me home? Have I gone insane?

"Let me try to cheer you up." He stops and flashes me a toothy smile as beautiful as his sister's.

I shrug. He can try, but there's no way he'll succeed.

He drums his fingers on his lips with a thoughtful expression and then nods as if he's decided what to share with me. "Listen, the people of our community constantly stick their noses into everyone else's business. It's impossible to keep anything a secret with us." He sneaks a peek at me to make sure I'm listening. "In order to be considered a good Jew, you have to follow a million rules, most of which no one understands. And at every event, regardless of whether you're rejoicing or mourning, you have to kiss and hug dozens of pesky aunts, some of whom you aren't even related to." He laughs, and the sound of his laughter manages to slightly calm the ache in my head. "We don't really need newspapers or radios. If you want to spread information, one prayer service is enough, and the hundreds of thousands of Jews in Warsaw will have heard it by the time the next prayer service rolls around."

"It doesn't sound all that tempting." I giggle dutifully.

"You're right. I'm not doing a very good job of selling it." He nods and laughs again. "But you should know that with us, there's no such thing as loneliness unless you choose it and insist upon it. If you're mourning, people will bring you pots of food. If you're celebrating, the whole neighborhood will celebrate with you, and if you're in need, everyone will rally to help you." He pulls me to a stop, letting a group of Polish youths pass us, and then gestures for me to keep walking. "I'm proud to have friends who would do anything to encourage and console me – friends who would stand by my side through thick and through thin and even risk their lives for me, just as I did for you earlier."

I tense up. He really did that. He really did risk his life for me.

"You bore the blows of the clubs that were meant for me." I look at him in a new light. "You don't even know me, and you stood between me and them like I was really important to you."

"First of all, if I'm not mistaken, you risked your life for my sister. But in any case, you're really important to my dear friend, and therefore you're important to me as well." He shrugs. "When he asked me to keep an eye on you, I had no doubt that he meant I should also endure beatings instead of you if necessary."

"Anton?" I ask in astonishment. "He asked you to watch over me?"

"The very same."

My eyes tear up again, and I sniffle. I don't know if this news consoles me or saddens me. I haven't seen Anton in such a long time. He hasn't even walked past the boutique to hint that he's thinking of me. I've respected his request that I keep my distance, but I don't understand how he can just go on with his life while I feel so lonely without him.

"I believe we have arrived at your building, my lady." Leib flourishes with his hand dramatically and bends down in a comically exaggerated regal bow.

I wipe my tears and smile at him. He's the first person who has made me laugh and cry at the same time, and I find that I feel an unexpected closeness with him.

"May I thank you with a cup of tea?" I ask cautiously.

"I would be glad to accept your invitation. Truly." He puts a hand on his heart. "But I don't think our mutual friend would be very pleased if I spent time with you alone in your apartment."

"I didn't mean to suggest that..." I blush.

"Of course not." Leib waves his hand, dismissing my embarrassment. "I'll take you up on your invitation to visit if you'll allow me to come with my sister."

The thought of seeing him again comforts me, and I nod in agreement.

"Well then, I'll see you again soon." He takes my hand and kisses it tenderly.

I open the gate of the building and then turn around and watch him walk away. Mother would go mad if she knew I invited a charming Jewish man into our home. I sigh and climb the stairs to my giant apartment, where no one awaits me but my faithful cat, who tries with all his might to console me.

But today, unlike most other days, I don't feel so lonely.

CHAPTER 17

The house is spic and span. The rooms are admittedly less impressive without the beautiful paintings and expensive works of art that adorned them before, but since I learned to light a fire in the grate by myself, the parlor is warm and cozy. I sit on the armchair, thread a needle, and begin mending the tear that the German ripped in my coat. It's late, but I'm not ready to go to bed yet. I know that as soon as I get under the covers, I'll remember how lonely I am, and the day's events will start to haunt my thoughts. As long as I keep busy, I can direct my thoughts to the new friend I made today and suppress any thoughts about the man I so long to see.

The front door creaks, breaking the silence, and I jump to my feet, my eyes darting around for the gun. It's in my parents' bedroom.

Footsteps echo in the hall, and I try to estimate how long it will take me to get to the bedroom.

"Damn it, Ania, your door is wide open," a loud voice scolds me from the threshold.

I open and close my mouth like a fish. My heart threatens to burst out of my chest. His quiet intensity floods the room around me, making me feel safe and secure, and my intense anguish forms a suffocating lump in my throat that grows, wrapping itself around my neck. I fall into the armchair, bury my head in my hands, and burst into tears.

"Ania," Anton calls my name softly and rushes to me. He kneels down and caresses my head. "I'm sorry that the first thing I did was criticize you."

"I'm not crying about that." I sniffle and wipe my eyes with the partially mended coat sleeve. "I haven't seen you in such a long time, and suddenly, when you entered the room, I realized that I can only really breathe when you're here with me."

Wiping my tears dry with his thumb, he sighs heavily. "I wish I could stay with you and take care of you." He gets up and takes a seat in the armchair opposite me. "The things I have to do every day make me feel so dirty." He looks up at the ceiling and then looks back at me, his eyes pained. "I try to make things easier for the citizens, try to warn whoever I can, try to find food for the elderly and for people who've lost their source of income, and try to temper the Germans' visits to the homes of people whose only sin is that they dared publish a book or write a newspaper article." He lights a cigarette, and I go to the cabinet and put an ashtray down in front of him. "My successes are like specks of sand on a vast shore. The cruelty of the Germans is inconceivable."

I want to tell him about the cruelty I experienced today, but Leib's words echo in my head. Words about true friendship and solidarity. For the first time in my life, I understand that at this moment, I need to console him in his pain and not pile my own pain on top. For the first time in my life, I'm not acting selfishly. I long to comfort him with all my heart.

"Anton." I bite my lip in embarrassment. "I want to be a good friend to you."

He stares at me like he's seeing me for the first time.

"Maybe... maybe you were right, and I was too self-absorbed."

I gasp as Anton jumps out of his armchair and cups my chin in his hands. He tucks my hair behind my ears, and his eyes flit to the intersection between my cheek and my ear. I shut my eyes and purse my lips. It would have hurt less if he'd slapped me.

"You thought I was her." I don't hide the disdain in my voice.

"You managed to confuse me for a minute," he replies contemplatively and slides his finger over the missing mark.

"Because there's no way I can be as good as her?" I push his hand away. I don't feel a need to comfort him anymore. I'm angry with him. Angry that he's breaking my heart yet again.

Anton returns to his armchair, and I clench my teeth and shout, "You have no idea what I went through today!"

"I have some idea, actually." He sighs.

"No, you don't." I raise my voice. "They stole my boutique, humiliated me, screamed at me, called me a dirty Jew, and tried to beat me with clubs. And you sit here feeling sorry for yourself."

His jaw quivers, and I understand that I've managed to irritate him. I don't really care. I'm just getting started.

"You promised to take care of me, you promised to protect me, and instead, you hang out with Germans and loot innocent people's houses, leaving me to face the hostility of the soldiers alone."

He puts out his cigarette and lights another one.

I drum my fingers on my knees, chew on the inside of my cheek, and try to think of what else I can hurl at him.

Anton exhales a thin trail of smoke, and suddenly the corners of his mouth curve up, and he bursts out laughing.

My jaw drops, and I stare at him, not comprehending.

"It took you exactly three minutes to go back to your old self." He glances at his watch and chuckles. "For a second I was afraid that the club hit you in the head and caused irreparable damage."

"Are you laughing at me?" I ask, shocked. "I just told you about the terrible ordeal I went through today, and you're sitting here and laughing at me"

"I'm sorry." He puts his hand on his heart and stifles a laugh. "I'm sorry about what you experienced today, but frankly, you caused me more concern when you started acting so out of character. Your selfishness is an inseparable part of who you are."

His cheeky response provokes a shriek from me, causing me to brandish the only weapon I have in my hands and charge at him, enraged. I stab his shoulder with my sewing needle over and over, but instead of writhing in pain, he laughs and tosses his cigarette into the ashtray. He seizes my wrists, and I sway and fall onto his knees. I try to free my arms to stab him again, but he holds my hands to his chest, and I cannot move.

"You're an idiot with no manners," I yell in his face.

"An idiot with no manners who really missed you," he replies with a dazzling smile.

"You should know that I didn't miss you at all." I try to get up, but he won't let go of my hands. Our improper nearness makes my breath quicken, and I feel his heart beating beneath my hands. A pleasant warmth flows through my body, and a crimson blush rises on my cheeks.

"You're lying," he whispers. "Admit that you missed me."

My eyes are fixed on his succulent lips, and I involuntarily lick my own and murmur, "I... I..." A warm sensation climbs up between my legs, and my upper body arches as if suddenly possessed with its own will.

"Ania," he utters my name softly, "I'm very sorry I couldn't be by your side today." He keeps my hands pressed against his chest and wraps his arms around me.

"Every time you come to see me, I dread the moment you'll have to leave." I look up at him and see that his gaze is locked on my lips. His hands stroke my back, and the rhythms of our breath blend together in perfect harmony. The pleasant warmth spreads to my upper body, and with each caress, it only intensifies. I close my eyes, and a weak moan escapes my parted lips.

His hands slide to my backside, and I open my eyes when I hear his husky moan. His lips are so close to mine, and I have a fierce need to feel his touch. Suddenly, an intense pain jolts in the pit of my stomach, and I push myself back and leap up. Michalina. I spin around, and then walk to the window, and look out at the dark street. Is she mad at me? Disappointed in me? Does she feel my forbidden thirst for her man? It was *she* who abandoned *me*. I scowl in irritation. It was *she* who abandoned *him*. I try to break free of the guilt that overwhelms me.

I feel Anton's substantial frame behind me, and I tense up, frozen in place.

"I'm sorry," he whispers, putting his big hands on my shoulders. "Every time I see you, I get all confused by my feelings." His palms slide down my arms, stroking them tenderly.

I want to tell him that I'm not confused at all – that every time he touches me, I just want him more, that I feel his every caress in my heart – but the twinges of pain in my belly return, and I exhale in frustration.

"I think the constant worry I feel for you is messing with my reasoning," he says, sounding tormented. "Just because I promised to take care of you doesn't make you mine. There is no way for me to justify my indecent conduct."

I muster up the courage and turn towards him. My gaze locks on the buttons of his shirt, and I can easily picture myself opening them and clinging to his bare torso.

"It probably also stems from my longing for..."

I groan and cover his mouth with my hand, forbidding him to continue the sentence. At this moment, despite the guilt that I feel, I'm desperate to hold onto his beautiful words. Words dedicated to me alone.

"You are my only friend, and you will remain my friend," I tell him as I conclude our conversation and return to my armchair. "It's a shame I don't have any fine spirits to drink to our good health."

"I'll try to bring something on my next visit." The understanding that he is about to leave terrifies me. "I put a basket with groceries and two thousand zlotys on the dining room table." He combs his hair to the side and lights a cigarette, "But I'm still mad that you left the door open."

"And what exactly will they steal?" I giggle nervously. "The Germans took all the valuables."

"You are the most precious thing of all," he tells me while giving me a piercing stare.

My heart again feels like it's ready to explode. My whole body yearns to sit back on his knees, but I can't allow myself to get confused again. "The door is open because even when I really try, I can't close it." I shrug. "The Germans knocked it off the upper hinge."

Anton furrows his brows and then frowns apologetically. "I'm an idiot. Forgive me. It didn't even occur to me that it was because of that. I'll have someone come to fix it tomorrow."

I nod and put the torn coat back on my lap.

"I would do it myself if I didn't have to sneak in and out of here like a thief." He blows out his smoke angrily. "I'll make sure Leib comes here tomorrow."

"I'd love for him to come." My face breaks into a broad smile.

Anton takes a drag on his cigarette and slowly blows out the white smoke. He tilts his head to the side, and his jaw trembles with resentment. "Leib told me about your encounter today. I hope you thanked him for risking his life for you."

I finger the tear in my coat sleeve and try to remember if I thanked him. "I invited him up to come up here," I say as I nod proudly.

"You did *what?*" Anton straightens up.

"Oh... I didn't mean that the way it sounds." I blush. "I invited him to come for a cup of tea. He risked his life for me."

"You invited a strange man into your apartment where you live alone?" His tone is venomous.

"I was being polite," I reply, offended. "And besides, Leib's not a strange man. He's Ida's brother and your friend."

"He's a stranger to you." Anton mutilates his cigarette as he extinguishes it in the ashtray.

"I didn't feel that way," I tell him, biting my lip. "I felt like he was my friend, too. He comforted me, reassured me, and made sure I got home safely."

"Did you bat your eyelashes at him a lot?" He glowers at me. "Did you tell him how helpless you are and that he's the only man who can save you? I'm simply trying to understand exactly how you charmed him."

"I cried, and then I laughed." I direct an angry look at Anton. "He made me laugh, and it's been so long since I heard myself laugh. He was there for me when you weren't!"

"I'll send someone else to fix your door," Anton concludes and stands up. "I don't want you to drive him crazy like you do with your poor pathetic suitors."

"I don't want you to send someone else." I throw the coat on the floor and stand in front of him with my fists clenched. "He didn't agree to come upstairs to my apartment when I was here alone. He behaved chivalrously, which can't be said about you."

"What happened tonight will never happen again." Anton turns his back to me. "The only reason for my behavior is my longing for your other half."

The spasms in my stomach make me double over and groan in pain.

Anton slides his hand into the pocket of his pants and takes out the earrings that Father gave Mother on their first wedding anniversary, the earrings that the Germans deprived me of. He puts them down on the sideboard. "This is the compensation I got from the haul the Germans stole from you," he says without glancing in my direction. "I thought you'd be happy to have them back, but you had better hide them." He goes out into the hall, and I collapse on the armchair as I hear his heavy footsteps clomping down the stairs, away from me.

My eyes fill with tears, and I groan in frustration.

"Dziecko, come here," I say and pat my knees.

Yowling, he limps towards me. I lift him onto my lap and let him lick my hands. He tries to console me, but my poor heart is bleeding.

The spasms in the pit of my stomach send a shock through my body, and I cry out, "Michalina, stop it already." I hit my stomach. "I don't care about the nonsense that's bothering you. I hate you!"

I hate her, and I hate her man. I won't let my damned emotions confuse me again.

CHAPTER 18

The groceries that Anton brought are arranged in the pantry. The dinner dishes have been washed, and the cat is lying on his blanket, watching me with a bored look. I definitely share his feelings of boredom. I haven't left the house all day. I have nowhere to go. I toyed with the idea of going back to the boutique and kicking the damn seamstresses out. But regretfully, I conceded that it's a struggle I'm bound to lose.

I sit down in the dining room. The coat is on the table in front of me, and I examine the perfect seam that I sewed with my own two hands. Even my mother wouldn't be able to detect that there'd been a tear. The armband lies next to the coat like a glaring symbol of my humiliation.

I look at the earrings, put them in the palm of my hand, and touch the delicate diamonds. I remember that one evening Mother hosted her friends for dinner and a game of cards. They sat in the dining room, elegantly dressed, made up and perfumed, each one wearing her very best jewelry. Mother wore a beautiful gold bracelet and these earrings.

My eyes dart to the door swinging on its hinges, and I realize that I had better hide my little treasure.

I fold the earrings in my fist and walk around the house. Hiding them in the safe is out of the question. Putting them in a hat box is too risky. There's no corner of the house that the Germans didn't taint. Even the gun's hiding spot doesn't seem secure to me anymore.

I drum on the dining room table with my fingers. My eyes find the perfect seam that I stitched, and in a spur-of-the-moment decision, I undo the stitches, push my fingers into the lining and bury one of the earrings in the down filling. I feel both sides of the coat and smile with satisfaction.

A knock on the door startles me, and I put the coat on top of the other earring.

I go to the door, which swings on its broken hinge and opens of its own accord.

A smile lights up my face when I see Leib standing in front of me and Ida at his side.

"Now that's a smile worth taking a beating for," Leib says as he winks at me.

I laugh and invite them in. I need this visit so much.

"Ania, it's nice to see you again." Ida kisses my cheeks as if we're old friends.

"It's nice to see you two as well," I reply honestly.

Leib puts his toolbox on the bench in the foyer and rolls up his shirt sleeves. His black hair is tousled and unruly, his green eyes sparkle, and the yellow band tied around his arm emphasizes his muscles. His simple workingman's clothes only contribute to his electrifying masculine appearance. I admit to myself that he's the most handsome man I've ever met, save for the man who keeps breaking my heart over and over.

Ida's shoulder bumps against mine and she giggles.

I blush when I realize she was watching me while I shamelessly gazed at her brother.

"Let's let Leib work in peace." She puts her arm in mine and walks with me to the kitchen. "I'm afraid if you keep looking at him like that, he'll nail himself to the door instead of fixing it."

"I didn't mean to..." My cheeks are burning.

"Don't be embarrassed," she giggles again. "He has that effect on women."

"I'll make a pot of tea," I tell her as I disentangle myself from her arm and stand in front of the stove.

"I heard about what you went through yesterday." She pats my back sympathetically. "I'm sorry you had to experience such criminality. I know how dear the boutique is to your heart."

I grit my teeth and force myself to maintain control. Could she be gloating over my misfortune?

"I'm sure we can find another job for you, so that you can support yourself and maintain your sanity. We talked about it with our community and..."

"I don't need your help." I turn to her. "I'm doing very well with what I have, and as soon as I regain my strength, I'll return to the boutique and demand it back."

Ida bites her lip and doesn't respond.

I pour the boiling water into the teapot, arrange the teacups on a tray and add a plate with the few cookies that I have left. Ida picks up the teapot and follows me into the dining room. I put the tray on the table and look at the modest refreshments I have to offer them, embarrassed.

Leib has already dismantled the hinges and is now screwing them back into place. He's engrossed in his work and doesn't join us.

Ida hangs her coat on the back of her chair and smooths out the wrinkles in her dress as she sits down. I pour the tea into two cups and push the plate of cookies toward her.

She carefully sips from her teacup without touching the cookies and lights a cigarette.

"You smoke?" I ask in astonishment. "My mother says that only promiscuous women..." I stop mid-sentence and blanch.

Ida rolls her eyes and giggles. "It's my little rebellion. Every woman needs to rebel once in a while."

I nod and smile. I want to hate her, but I'm having a really tough time doing so. She's elegant, pleasant, and friendly, and the fact that she came here again after my rude behavior suggests that there are sides to her that I would like – if I got to know her.

I go to the parlor, bring the ashtray that's full of Anton's cigarette butts, and put it in front of her.

"Oh, I'm so sorry I didn't offer you a cigarette as well." She hands me the pack. "I should've asked if you wanted one."

"I don't smoke."

"Then who used this ashtray?" She raises an eyebrow.

Leib puts down the screwdriver and looks at us.

"An annoying, rude police officer." I cross my arms over my chest.

"Ah, of course. Anton." Ida shakes her head and laughs as if her question had been stupid. Leib grins as well and goes back to screwing on the hinges.

I don't share in their amusement.

Ida's laughter dies down when she detects the angry expression on my face. She wrinkles her nose apologetically and puts out her cigarette in the ashtray. "This coat is beautiful." She picks it up.

"Leave it," I yell and yank it away from her. The tear at the shoulder widens, and Ida drops the coat in alarm.

"Oh, no! I'm so sorry," she says as she covers her mouth with her hand.

I huff in exasperation, but when Leib pricks up to see what all the commotion is about, I suddenly feel embarrassed for overreacting.

"It's not you who tore it." I push my fingers into the down filling and pull the earring out.

Ida's eyebrows rise in surprise.

"I was trying to find a safe place to hide my mother's earrings," I whisper, "But when the Germans were here, they got into every hole. I'm surprised they didn't peel the plaster off the walls."

Ida nods and continues to look at the slit in the coat.

"I don't think they'll undo the seams of this coat." I thread the needle and sew two precise stitches. "See?" I show her. "When I finish sewing this up, no one will suspect that I'm hiding earrings in my coat."

"That's a fantastic idea." Ida's eyes light up. "Leib! Come see what the talented Ania is doing."

He puts down his screwdriver and comes over to us. He leans over the back of my chair and watches intently as I bury the second earring in the filling and tighten another stitch.

"Very good." He pats my shoulder, and I blush. "It's a shame Ida doesn't know how to do anything but smoke." He pulls a cigarette out of her pack, positions it between his lips, and goes back to fixing the hinges.

"Big brothers are the worst." She giggles, looking at him fondly. "But he's right. I know how to write beautiful poems, I know how to bake delicious cakes, and I'm a delightful conversationalist, but even if they put a gun to my head, I wouldn't be able to sew to save my life. I should have learned to sew instead of wasting my time teaching."

"You're a teacher?" I ask in surprise and realize that I don't know anything about her.

"Yes," she replies with pride. "I'm trying to teach dozens of naughty children to love beautiful literature."

"Children?" I grimace in aversion.

"I'm in love with my job." She nods. "And I'll keep teaching until I have children of my own."

Leib chuckles. "And how does my dear sister expect to have children if she refuses to let me fix her up with a decent gentleman?"

"I won't refuse when you find the right man for me." Ida sticks out her chin.

Her reaction makes me like her even more.

"If you have jewelry, I can do this for you, too," I suggest, immediately regretting it. Why would I take on such a chore? I might be too busy – after all, I plan to demand my boutique back.

"I wouldn't want to trouble you." Ida waves her hand, brushing off my proposal. "I'm sure the seamstresses in our neighborhood would be happy to do it for a reasonable fee."

"A fee?" I prick my finger and suck the droplet of blood that has appeared.

"Naturally, for a fee." She applauds proudly as Leib opens and closes the door, and the hinges work soundlessly.

I smile at him in thanks and he winks at me and wipes his hands on a rag.

He sits down next to Ida, and she pours him a cup of tea and pushes away the plate of cookies.

"I apologize that I don't have any other drinks to serve you." I flash an angry look at the empty liquor cabinet. "If you had come to visit me a few months ago, I could have offered you something from my father's lavish collection."

"Fine company is more important than fine drinks." Leib raises his glass and mumbles something that sounds like a prayer under his breath before taking a sip. "And I have the feeling that we wouldn't have been such welcome guests a few months ago."

I look down in embarrassment.

"I'm not judging you," he hurries to apologize. "In our community, we are also reluctant to accept strangers."

"I thank you for trying to smooth things over." I hang the coat on the back of the chair next to me and push away the yellow armband. "I'm not ashamed that I didn't want any connection with members of your religion, and I still don't understand why the Germans won't allow me to choose my own religion." I sip my tea and scowl. "Maybe if I walk around wearing a swastika, they'll understand that I'm secular."

"I wouldn't do that," Ida blurts out in alarm.

"Unless you desperately want a bullet to tear a hole in your beautiful face." Leib chuckles, albeit bitterly. "You are listed as a Jew.

The only way to get off the Germans' list is in a burial shroud."

His description startles me, and I bite my lip nervously. "So, what will I have to do to get Mother's boutique back?"

"There's nothing to be done," Leib replies calmly. "The Germans are seizing Jewish businesses. Businesses that they deem useful they take for themselves. Dress boutiques don't interest them at all. But there's no way they'll go back on their decision and take a store from a Pole and transfer it to a Jew. You won't get your boutique back."

"That's it?" I stand up and bang my fist on the table. "Is that how you were raised? To give up everything you worked so long and hard for, just because someone else decides that it no longer belongs to you?"

Ida shifts uncomfortably, and Leib leans back in his chair and smiles at me.

"Your fighting spirit is impressive but naïve." He lights a cigarette and blows smoke rings into the air. "If you go to the boutique and stir up trouble, they'll kill you. If you try to approach senior German officials and demand the boutique back, they'll kill you. Truth be told, they might even kill you just for walking around the streets without your armband." He falls silent.

I crumple up the armband and throw it at them, "I refuse to wear this stupid thing! No one can force me to wear it, and no one can force your religion on me."

Ida straightens up in her chair as if planning to say something, but Leib puts his hand on hers, and she remains silent.

"So what's your plan?" Leib asks, and for the first time there's no trace of humor in his eyes. "Do you want to go out without the armband and gamble with your life? Is your distaste for a stupid piece of cloth stronger than your will to live?"

I fall into my chair and blink, trying to prevent tears from coming into my eyes. The happiness their visit filled me with has morphed into despair.

"Look what you've done." Ida pummels Leib's arm. "You've made her cry."

"I'd rather she cry now than we cry over her tomorrow," he argues defiantly.

"Ania," she addresses me tenderly. "What are you going to do?"

"I'll stay home." I pull the coat towards me and try my best to concentrate on sewing another stitch, but the tears flowing down my cheeks make it difficult to do so. "If I have to wear that armband outside, I simply won't leave the house."

"How long will you hole up here?" She stands up and walks over to me. "A day? Two days? A month? Two months? The war could last for years."

"Stop talking nonsense," I sniffle. "The French and the British will kick them out of here in no time."

"Sister, that's our cue to leave." Leib leans on the edge of the table and stands up. "We'll come back for another visit when Ania stops feeling sorry for herself. Or maybe when she comes to her senses and stops hating us."

His words anger me.

"You aren't welcome back at all," I shout.

It seems that my yelling has amused him because he bursts out laughing. "Anton didn't describe you very well. He said you were spoiled and had a quick temper, but he left out the fact that you're as stubborn as a little girl. I have no doubt that if you'd fought alongside us, the Germans would have given up and run away."

Ida lets out a quick laugh and then tightens her lips in an attempt to maintain a serious expression.

"Why are you still here?" I pierce them with my stare and cross my arms over my chest.

"We're leaving." Leib laughs again and puts his arm over Ida's shoulders. He swivels her toward the door and picks up his toolbox.

"And don't come back!" I yell.

"We can't make any promises." Leib opens the door and shuts it behind them.

I stick the needle into the coat's fabric and curse under my breath. Why does every visit to my home end with an abrupt exit? Dziecko limps over to me and sits down at the foot of my chair. He rubs up against my ankles, a companion in my misery.

CHAPTER 19

I powder my nose in front of the mirror and nod in satisfaction. I stick two hat pins into my elegant fascinator, adjust its lace netting, and then stand and study myself in the mirror. My puffy dress reaches the middle of my calves, and garters secure transparent pantyhose on my thighs. I slip on black pumps and twirl my petticoats. The perfect look for an exciting night out.

I open the drawer, pick out a pair of lace gloves, and head to the parlor. The clicking of my heels echoes through the room as I make my way to the armchair. I sit down and swing my legs restlessly back and forth. That sums up my "night out."

It's been 10 days since the visit of my most recent guests – Leib and Ida – and my tiresome routine continues as scheduled. I eat breakfast, clean what's already clean, change my dress, fix my makeup, and sit on the armchair staring at the hands of the clock in anticipation of the hour when I can go to sleep again. The loneliness is killing me. The only thing that helps me maintain my sanity is the vivid dreams that descend upon me at night. In my dreams, I'm surrounded by my family. We vacation together at our summer house or in picturesque towns far away from here – swimming, dining, chatting, and laughing. An idyll of the life that was once mine. But when I open my eyes every morning, the first thing I feel is the searing pain in my stomach.

It's already afternoon, and I try to decide whether now's a good time to make dinner. The groceries that Anton brought are nearly gone. The eggs, milk, and cheese are long gone. The only thing left is a little rice and peas. I know I have to go shopping so I won't starve, but the days go by, and I can't bring myself to put the damn armband on.

Suddenly, I hear three raps on the door.

I straighten up, alert.

Two more raps.

The cat yowls, vexed by the disturbance, and curls back up on his blanket.

I walk hesitantly to the door.

It's not the Germans. They would have broken the door down by now.

I turn the key, pull down the handle, and meet Leib's dumbfounded stare.

"Good God, Ania. You're breathtaking." He looks me up and down.

I could say the same about him. I have no doubt that he turns the head of every young lady on the street. He's wearing a gray vest and tailored trousers, and the top buttons of his shirt are open, giving him a naughty, charming appearance.

I smile at him and try to remember why I kicked him out of here during his last visit.

"So..." He tilts his head to the side. "Are you finished feeling sorry for yourself?"

The smile fades from my face, and I remember.

"No, no, no." He waves his hand. "I refuse to upset you every time we see each other. Do you want me to compliment you again?"

A tickle jiggles in my chest, and I start to laugh. Really laugh.

"This is a delightful sight, indeed." He leans against the doorframe with ease.

My smile is so wide that it practically hurts my cheeks, and I know I can't let him leave.

"Can I invite you in for a cup of tea?" I ask cautiously, even though I know what his answer will be.

"Unfortunately, Ida went on a condolence visit and couldn't join me." He picks a basket up off the floor. "But she asked that I bring you this."

"What is it?" I pull a gray wool coat out of the basket.

"You'll find two bracelets and your payment in the pocket," he whispers. "She'll come over to pick it up in a few days."

"Of course." I turn around and put the basket on the table in the dining room. "Are you sure you don't want a cup of tea or even just a glass of water?" The thought of him leaving makes me sad.

"I don't want to keep you." He points to my dress. "Were you invited to some special event? Or are you hosting?" He peeks into the apartment.

"I'm not going anywhere." I shrug. "And no one ever comes to visit me."

"That's odd." He raises an eyebrow. "After all, you're such a cordial host."

I scowl in annoyance, but when he chuckles, the smile returns to my face.

"Have a good evening." He tips his hat and pulls it back on his head.

"Wait," I exclaim, "maybe I could give you some money to buy groceries for me? I would love to treat Dziecko to a nice piece of fish." Upon hearing his name, the cat yowls from the parlor.

"Why don't you go yourself?" He looks at me suspiciously. "If you're afraid to go to the markets alone, I'd be happy to accompany you."

"I'm not afraid of anything." I cross my arms over my chest. "I'd just prefer that you buy the groceries for me."

"Ania," he asks, giving me a stern look, "have you stayed inside your apartment since the incident with the German soldiers? It's been over two weeks. Haven't you left the house?"

"I thought it's only been 10 days," I mumble.

"I should have known." He looks distraught. "I should have offered to go with you before..."

"I have no interest in an escort," I interrupt him. "I don't want to go out because I'm happy here at home. Please, just buy the groceries for me."

"No," he replies calmly. "You'll come with me."

"I will not come with you!" I snap. "I refuse to leave the house with that ugly armband on my sleeve."

"Ah..." Leib shakes his head. "I should have guessed it was because of that."

"Good." I nod. "Now that you know, will you buy the groceries for me?"

"No." He grins. "You'll put on a coat, we'll tie on the armband, and you'll join me on a pleasant walk to the markets."

"No I won't!" I stamp my foot. "I will not walk around with a mark of shame on my forehead."

"Not on your forehead, on your arm," he corrects me and chuckles again. "And it's not a mark of shame. It's a sign that you're one of the Chosen People."

"Why chosen?" I grumble.

"Chosen to survive terrible plagues, for not only one enemy has risen up against us to destroy us. In each and every generation, they rise up to destroy us." He recites this in a strange sing-song and then grins again. "I told you I'm not very good at selling our religion. If you want a more serious answer, I can refer you to a scholar wiser than myself."

"You're confusing me." I straighten the lace fastener over my forehead.

"Ania." He says my name in a conciliatory tone, "Let's take a short walk to the market, and I promise that the second you feel uncomfortable, I'll bring you back home immediately." He takes my long coat off the hanger, and I automatically turn my back to him and slip my arms into the sleeves.

"Can I leave off the armband today?" I wrinkle my nose miserably. "Just for today?"

"If you don't mind getting beaten up." He shrugs. "Or making me take a beating for you again."

"I'd rather not." I exhale in exasperation and give him the crumpled armband. He ties it around my arm and holds the door open for me.

I take an empty basket, slip some money into my handbag, and go with him.

As soon as my foot hits the first step outside the building's door, I raise my face to the sky and inhale the crisp air deep into my lungs. The sun is beginning to set, and I'm suddenly sorry that our time together will be so brief.

"Stop a coachman," I tell Leib with a smile.

"We'll go to the Jewish market on foot." He puts his hand on the small of my back.

"I know a shortcut." I turn towards the park and motion for him to come with me.

"Ania," Leib sighs and pulls my arm, "we're not allowed to use public transportation, and we're not allowed to go through the park."

"The Germans expect me to walk to the market in these heels?" I wail.

"It seems to me they'd rather we didn't walk at all," he replies coldly and then shakes his head and says, "Think about the benefits of going by foot. The fresh air and the pleasant company." He points to himself.

"You're right," I giggle. "The company is pleasant."

We walk side by side through the tangle of streets, and Leib's melodic voice distracts me from the stares of the passers-by. The route keeps getting longer, for we turn down one of the many alleys every time Leib spots German soldiers. I don't complain. I'm grateful to him for peeling off a bit of the harrowing loneliness.

We stop at the first stall in the market, and, with pleasure, I sniff the unfamiliar cheeses. It's been so many years since I've visited the market. It was always our maid's job to do the grocery shopping, and now I feel like a child discovering a hidden magical world.

I go from stall to stall, curiously scrutinizing the produce, and put the finest products I can find into my basket.

All the stallholders wear yellow armbands, and there are very few customers at the market – just a few young women pushing baby carriages, some older men, and lots of noisy children. Every few minutes, Leib deposits a penny into the outstretched hands of the beggars who keep passing us.

"Look down when the Germans pass by," Leib whispers behind me; I take a quick look to the left and see four soldiers in gray uniforms. They saunter among the stalls with their clubs drawn, reviewing the goods and roughly shoving anyone who crosses their path. Silence falls in the market. The stallholders don't say a word, even when the soldiers taste their produce. One of the soldiers stuffs a piece of hard cheese into his mouth, then spits it out onto the ground and rams his club into the stallholder's shoulder.

I inhale sharply and look away. My gaze falls on a broad back in a blue uniform. The man is tall, with thick, light brown hair. He turns around as though he can feel my eyes on his back.

My breath catches in my throat.

I'm gripped by excitement and my heart beats wildly. I smile at Anton and raise my hand to wave hello to him.

His eyes are fixed on the group of soldiers, and his expression remains frozen. He turns his back to me.

My heart constricts painfully, and a loud moan escapes my throat.

"He can't say hello to you," Leib whispers. "Don't look at him!"

I lower my head and shiver.

The sudden noise of screeching tires breaks the silence. Shaking like a leaf, I stare at the two trucks that have stopped at the market's entrance. Soldiers jump out of one of the vehicles with their clubs drawn. They rush forward, shoot into the market, and randomly drag men into the other truck. I tear up at the sound of the screams, cries, and pleas.

"What... What are they doing?" I whisper.

"Kidnapping men and taking them to labor camps." Leib seizes my arm and tugs me back. "We have to get out of here."

The stallholder on my left is trying to resist the two soldiers holding him. He desperately shields his head as they pummel him mercilessly.

"Ania," Leib hollers. "We have to get out of here *now*."

"You!" A shout in German is directed at us, and I stare in terror at the soldier running toward us.

A large figure walks up next to me. "Leib. Run. Now," Anton's deep voice commands quietly.

I watch the events in front of me unfolding like images on a movie screen. I hear the sound of Leib's feet hitting the cobblestones behind me, but the soldier is too close. My legs move forward on their own, blocking the soldier's way. My cheek trembles from the impact of his punch, and my body flies to the side. The basket falls from my hands, and the groceries roll every which way. I look up just in time to see a fleeting twitch of Anton's jaw. His beautiful eyes turn from brown to red. He grabs the club out of the soldier's hand and lifts it high into the air. A voice inside me screams that once Anton lands a blow, it will be the end. It will be the end of *him*. I hurl myself forward and block the blow of Anton's stick with my body. My back shakes from the force of the impact, but I don't feel any pain, only immense relief.

Anton's eyes open wide in horror, and the club falls out of his hand.

The soldier must think that Anton meant to assist him in thwarting the attack of a hysterical girl because he bends down to pick up the stick, thanks Anton with a slight bow of his head, and continues chasing Leib.

I crawl over the dirty cobblestones, groping for an escape route underneath the stalls. The screaming won't stop, and I nearly gag as I bump into an elderly man lying on the ground, blood spurting from his forehead. His eyes are wide open, unseeing, and his chest is still. I mumble a feeble apology and climb over him. I keep crawling until I reach an avenue of trees, where I stand, take off my high heels, and break into a sprint.

Bypassing the main streets makes the route longer. Night falls as I dash through the alleyways, the harsh wind whipping across my face.

When I finally reach the gate of my building, I crash through it and walk inside the dimly lit lobby.

"Ania." The whisper makes me jump in fright.

"Leib?"

"Are you all right? Did they hurt you?" He pushes my hair aside and looks at my bruised cheek, his eyes stricken with grief.

"Get away from her!" An aggressive whisper rings out, enraged.

The sound of his voice makes my heart contract in pain and my eyes fill with tears. I'm incapable of facing him. I turn to the staircase, grab onto the banister, and climb wearily.

"Are you insane?" Anton says to Leib. "How could you take her to the Jewish market and put her into such danger?"

"How was I supposed to know that the Germans would come to the market?" Leib responds in the same tone. "I finally convinced her to leave the house after she shut herself up inside for two whole weeks."

"I suggest you stop taking her on dangerous trips." I heard the sound of a fist hitting the wall.

"You're being unreasonable." Leib's tone softens. "You asked me to take care of her. I can't in good conscience encourage her to be a shut-in."

They keep arguing, and I keep climbing the stairs step by step until I reach my apartment door and slam it shut behind me.

I bend over behind the door, pain coursing through my body. I tear the fastener from my head, throw it aside, and pull off my torn coat. The burning sensation on my back causes me to cry out in pain. I'm covered in filth from the market's cobblestones, and I squirm around, trying to open the hooks on the back of my dress. My head pounds as though the club were hitting me over and over again. I rip the hooks open and finally manage to get the dress off.

The door opens, and Anton stands in front of me.

He stares at my chemise for a split second and then averts his gaze.

"Ania," he says, with torment in his voice, "the club wasn't directed at you. I would never hurt you."

"Anton," I whisper. It's obvious to me that he's telling the truth, but I still feel that my soul is injured.

He looks at me, his eyes revealing his pain.

"It hurt me more that you ignored me," I tell him as tears blur my vision.

"I didn't want you to be in danger." He steps forward hesitantly and slams the door behind him. "I had to muster up all my strength not to run and embrace you in the middle of the market."

"So embrace me now," I beg him.

He inhales sharply and, in one step, closes the distance between us and lifts me into the air. I wrap my legs around him, hug him around the neck, and rest my head on his shoulder.

"You're safe now," he tells me as he tenderly strokes my head.

"I know." I sigh into his neck.

He carries me down the hall and then sits down in the armchair. I sit on his lap with my legs spread wide, still wrapped around him.

"Are you in pain?"

I don't answer, just burrow my head deeper into his neck.

"Do you want me to take care of your injuries?"

I don't answer; I just nestle against his body.

"Please say something – anything." He caresses my head again.

"I'm afraid," I whisper miserably. "I'm afraid that no matter what I say, the conversation will be over and you'll leave."

I lift my face and look into his eyes.

He doesn't say anything. His hands slide gently over the thin satin fabric covering my back.

"What did you think would happen after you hit a German soldier?" I run a finger along his jawline.

"I didn't think." His eyes go toward the plunging neckline of my chemise. "At that moment I realized that if something happened to you, I would have no reason to be here." He exhales sharply, and I tremble. "I keep trying to remind myself that I'm just supposed to keep you safe. That we have nothing in common and that I simply promised to look out for you, but I can't seem to get you out of my head."

I bite my bottom lip and am suddenly acutely aware of how thin the cloth covering my body is.

"I think about you all the time," I find the courage to confess. "I know I'm not your first choice, but I'm willing to settle for what we have now."

He doesn't correct me, and I don't care anymore. I'm desperate to be held in the comfort of his arms, to absorb the feeling of safety and security. I'm thinking only of myself.

"I would prefer that you stop spending time with Leib." His throaty breathing causes the cloth covering my breasts to flutter. "Going to the market was dangerous and unnecessary."

"He wouldn't put me in danger on purpose." I defend him. "His visits are a comfort to me, and I know he's looking out for me."

"I'm the one who should be looking out for you," he murmurs angrily and looks at me intensely.

His declaration makes my heart pound rapidly.

"The groceries you brought me ran out." My bosom rubs against his chest, and I lick my lips. "All he did was come with me to the market so I wouldn't starve. I like him."

He narrows his eyes as if I've just said the last thing he wanted to hear, and I shudder at the thought that I've upset him and now he'll leave me.

"Don't be angry." I wrinkle my nose. "I don't want to talk about another man right now."

My last sentence seems to console him because he goes back to stroking my back. My thighs close against his. A moan of pleasure escapes my lips as the private spot between my legs rubs up against the fabric of his trousers. I forget the pain of my injuries and a pleasant warmth flares inside me, making my limbs quiver.

"I must look absolutely dreadful." I touch my swollen cheek.

"You're breathtaking." His palms skate up my legs, his eyes penetrate mine, and his fingers glide over my bare thighs. I feel the rough fabric around his manhood stretch, and a flame is ignited between my legs.

An awkward groan emanates from my mouth, and a dark blush rises on my cheeks. I feel an incomprehensible longing for his body so close to mine, and my hips cling to him involuntarily.

He groans hoarsely in my ear, and the intense desire I feel for him stirs my blood.

"I'm in pain," I pant into his mouth.

He puts his hands down and tightens his lips.

"Anton, it hurts here." I take his hands and draw a path with his fingers down the thin satin straps to my bosom. His fingers flutter over my protruding nipples. I open my eyes and stare deep into his burning brown eyes. "Why does it hurt so much?" I moan softly and writhe on top of him.

His raspy groan is music to my ears. His thumbs trace the satin around my nipples, and I arch my back and moan as tingles of pleasure shake my breasts.

"You're so beautiful..." He lowers his arms and cups my bottom. A loud moan erupts from his throat as he thrusts his hardness toward me. "You're breathtaking." He bites his lip with the same painful pleasure that I'm trying to subdue.

"Stay with me," I plead in a whisper and press my breasts to his chest. "Stay with me and make the pain go away."

"I… I don't think that's a good idea," he mumbles.

"Please, Anton." I stroke his arm.

"Ania, are you sure that this is what you want?" He grabs my buttocks and growls as I moan.

"Very sure." My nails dig deep into his shoulders.

He stands up with me wrapped around him and walks out into the hall.

"To the right." I pant and gesture with my head towards my bedroom.

But he steps to the left and opens the door to Michalina's room.

This act of sheer betrayal hits me like a club to the chest. Within a split second, my body goes cold, and I wriggle out of his arms and stand facing him.

"I hate you!" my voice shakes, and I attack him, slapping him on the cheek.

He furrows his brows, scans the bedroom, and he then blinks in confusion as if awakening from a daydream. His eyes search for my sister's beauty mark.

"I hate you!" Tears pour from my eyes, and I slap him again. "I hate you so much!" My voice breaks, and I sidestep him and run to my bedroom. I slam the door and turn the key, then collapse onto the floor, crying bitterly.

"Ania," he says my name in a tortured whisper and tries to open the door. "I'm sorry, I was distracted. I didn't mean to take you into M…"

"Go away," I shout, crying.

"Please let me in." He jiggles the door knob.

"No!" I sniffle and hug my knees to my chest. "I want you to leave now and never come back."

"Ania…"

"Go away!" I shout and throw the lamp from my night table at the door.

"I didn't mean to hurt your feelings," he sighs, and adds, "I can't stop thinking about you."

"About *her*," I wail. "You can't stop thinking about *her*."

No answer.

"You nearly caused me to make a terrible mistake," I whimper. "You took advantage of my weakness. I'll never forgive you for that."

"You're right." He sounds grief-stricken. "I'm sorry. I will honor your wishes and I won't come back."

The sound of his steps fades as he makes his way down the hall, and the apartment's door slams shut.

CHAPTER 20

There are two piles of clothes on the dining room table: the ones I've finished sewing and the ones I haven't sewn yet.

Leib is sitting across from me, smoking a cigarette and watching me quietly as I slip a ring into the hem of one of the sleeves of a brown dress. Ida is flipping through a magazine on the bench in the foyer, trying to give us some semblance of privacy.

More than a year has passed since I said goodbye to my father and sister at the train station, and the longing for them still burns inside me. Many months have passed since I kicked Anton out and he hasn't been back here since. Still, when he left, he ripped out a piece of my heart and took it with him, and my yearning for him gives me no respite. He's the first thing I think about every morning and the last thing I think about before I fall asleep every night. I thought my longing would fade as time went by, but it only intensifies.

I thread the needle again and scan the pile of clothes that awaits me. Word of my unique services has spread throughout the Jewish neighborhoods, and Ida and Leib bring me more clothes every day. I don't know my clients, and they don't know me, but I'm eternally grateful to them for giving me a reason to get up every morning.

I throw Leib a quick smile and make sure that the ring can't be seen in the sleeve's fold. The siblings' visits help ease my loneliness a bit, and from time to time I agree to go with Leib for a short walk around the block.

Our visit to the Jewish market left me with an emotional injury that torments me every day, while my broken heart torments my nights. A reminder of Anton's presence in my life materializes weekly, embodied by a basket full of groceries at the entrance to my apartment. Yet his concern doesn't lend me comfort. Instead, it fuels the searing pain in my heart every single time – a pain that has become an inseparable part of me.

"It's been almost four months since France was occupied by the Nazis." Leib smacks the radio receiver that hasn't been working properly since the Germans busted it when they broke in. "I believed with all my heart that their great leadership would devise some unpredictable strategies to win France back and crush the Führer," he says as he pretends to spit on the floor.

"There's no one left to fight for us." I pout.

"There's still hope for the British." He tries to tune the radio, but it only produces shrill static. "And who knows? Maybe your father and sister will be able to convince the Americans to quit sitting on the fence."

The pit of my stomach quakes with an intense, painful sensation, and I close my eyes for a minute. I have to change the topic of our conversation. "Are you coming again tomorrow?"

"Tomorrow is Yom Kippur." He takes a sip of water. "We won't leave the house except to go to synagogue."

"What are you celebrating?" I focus on another stitch.

"We're not exactly celebrating," he chuckles. "We're fasting."

"Ah…" I look up at him for a second and then continue sewing. "Why are you fasting?"

"To atone for our sins." He takes another sip of water.

"You and Ida? What sins have you committed, exactly?" I ask, puzzled.

"I don't know about Ida," he chuckles again, "But I've definitely committed a few."

"Then why does Ida need to fast?" I flinch as the needle pricks my finger.

"All Jewish people fast," he replies calmly. "Yom Kippur is a day of introspection. We beg God to forgive us for our sins and ask for forgiveness from everyone we believe that we have hurt."

"It sounds bizarre..." I say as I suck the blood that is dripping from my fingertip. "If I hurt someone, they probably deserved it. And actually, now that I think about it, you shouldn't have to fast this year at all. The German bastards should have to fast, not you."

"I happen to agree with you." He laughs. "I'll bring up your intriguing suggestion with the Judenrat."

I giggle when I realize that he's teasing me.

"Ania, you're welcome to stay with us during the holiday," Ida joins the conversation for the first time.

"And torture myself for sins I didn't commit?" I roll my eyes. "I didn't hurt anyone, even though everyone keeps trying to hurt me." I slide my finger over the perfect seam and put the dress on top of the tall stack of finished clothes.

"Then I'll come over and take you out for a walk when the fast is over." Leib hands me a black coat, and I pull a heavy gold bracelet from its pocket.

"Dziecko and I would love to get some fresh air." I quickly undo the stitches of the fur that adorns the coat's collar.

"Do you need anything?" He asks his usual question.

"I lack for nothing," I respond with my usual answer.

"Did a basket arrive from Anton this week, too?"

"Yes, and I don't want to talk about him." I almost rip the fabric, pushing the bracelet into the down lining.

Leib lights another cigarette and doesn't say anything.

Ida stands up and hovers by the table. "Ania, I don't know why you're mad at him, but there isn't a day that goes by that he doesn't ask about you. Tell her," she entreats angrily of Leib.

"I don't want to talk about him," I raise my voice.

Ida sighs and goes back to flipping through her magazine on the bench.

"I think if you leave him a note in the basket saying that you forgive him, he'll start visiting you again." Leib blows his smoke to the side. "Every time I see him, the first thing he does is ask about you."

"If he's so important to you, why haven't you tried to fix him up with your beloved sister?" I snap. The legs of the bench creak, and Ida's attention turns to us.

"I thought his heart belonged to someone else." He avoids my gaze. "And in any case, my sister cannot marry a Pole."

"Because a Pole wouldn't want a Jewish woman?"

"Because a Jewish woman wouldn't marry a gentile," Leib retorts obstinately.

"You basically just told me that you don't see me as Jewish." I smirk in satisfaction.

"That's not what I meant," he replies, bewildered. "I didn't think Anton was courting you. I thought..."

"He wasn't courting me!" I berate myself for the false impression I've created. "He was a friend, nothing more."

Leib and Ida exchange looks.

I go back to sewing and grumble, "I always thought that the Poles were the ones who despised the Jews. I'm amazed to find out that the hatred is mutual."

"For us, it isn't hatred," Leib insists on explaining himself. "We avoid intermarriage to guarantee the continued survival of the Jewish people."

"That's not a very convincing argument." I shrug my shoulders. "Maybe that's why the Germans hate you so much."

"Us," Ida states and stands up. "They hate you, too."

I clench my teeth and poke the needle into the fabric.

"We Jews would never harm someone else because of their religion," Ida bursts out in a forceful speech. "We don't try to convince the gentiles to convert, we don't beat innocent bystanders, and we don't burn down shops that belong to members of other religions. We live our lives quietly, but our silence scares them. It's like they think that while we're going about our business, we're actually secretly planning to take over the world and destroy them."

I stare at my needle in embarrassment but will never admit my ignorance.

"If you would only allow yourself to open up and learn new things, you could discover magical things in our religion." She puts her hand on my shoulder.

"I'm finished." I put the coat on the table, acting as if I didn't hear her speech. "You can take the clothes and leave. I don't want to keep you. I'm sure you need to prepare for your holiday."

Leib arranges some of the clothes in one basket, and Ida puts the rest in her basket.

"I have to understand what I can do so our next visit doesn't end in banishment," says Leib, laughing. "It's becoming a pattern."

"During your fast, you're welcome to reflect on all the times you've upset me," I tell him and stick out my chin.

"Then it's going to be an extremely tough fast." He flashes me his most beautiful smile. "Therefore I'll take this opportunity to apologize to you." He bows exaggeratedly.

"Dearest Ania, I also apologize if I hurt you." Ida bends down and kisses my cheek.

"Now it's your turn." Leib points at me.

I wrinkle my brow, and after quick consideration, reply, "I thought about it, and I have nothing to apologize to you for. I will try to commit more sins before next Yom Kippur." I try to keep my expression serious but to no avail as a smile lights up my face.

They both laugh and head toward the stairs.

I leave the apartment, lean over the railing, and watch them walk down. They seem so strongly connected to each other, like partners in fate. I feel a pang of envy, and I go back inside the apartment and lock the door behind me.

I pick up the cat and cradle him in my lap.

This feeling of intense loneliness has become an inseparable part of me.

I sit by the river and throw a rock into the water. The sun beats down on my head, and I'm enveloped in a feeling of absolute tranquility. I glance at Michalina, lying on a blanket next to me and reading a book. Her hair is in a long braid down the back of her neck, and the beauty mark on her cheek is visible.

"I miss you." I snatch the book from her hands.

"How can you miss me if I'm with you?" she giggles.

"I don't feel like you're with me," I answer, my voice quivering. "I feel like you abandoned me."

"Anushka, don't be silly." She grabs her book. "We're always together, never apart." She touches her triangle pendant and smiles. "Father explained that the star requires both of us in order to light our way."

"I have the strange feeling," I sigh, "that I don't really know you."

Michalina sits up and closes the book. "Well, you always prefer to listen to yourself." She wrinkles her nose apologetically. "Forgive me, dear sister. I didn't mean to hurt your feelings."

"You didn't." I bring my hand to her face, but I can't feel the softness of her skin on my fingers. "You're right, I'm afraid. I was so self-absorbed, thinking only of my own happiness, that I never actually took the time to get to know you. To truly get to know you."

"You shared a womb with me," Michalina giggles. "No one in the world knows me better than you."

"I wish I felt that that was true." I gnaw on my bottom lip. "Maybe if I actually knew you, I would have trusted you, heeded your warning, and joined you in America." I try to reach out and touch her beauty spot, but my finger remains cold and unfeeling. "Michalina, I'm so lonely."

"You're not alone." She puts her hand on mine. "Mother is with you. Mother is taking care of you."

"But Mother isn't with me." I swallow the lump in my throat.

"Then you must be surrounded by all your girlfriends and your dozens of suitors."

"My girlfriends are gone, and my suitors with them." I sigh.

"Don't be sad." Michalina gives me a naughty smile. "I left Anton with you to care for you. He's the best man in the whole wide world."

I avoid meeting her gaze.

"Ania, take care of him," she says, in a serious tone. "I'll come back. I'll come back to you and him."

I close my eyes tightly.

"There's someone at the door," she whispers.

I sit up and take a deep breath. The dream was so realistic that it takes me a minute to realize I'm sitting in an armchair in the parlor. A full day has passed since Leib and Ida left. My longing for Anton makes my entire body ache.

Loud knocking is coming from the door, but I hug my knees and keep panting. I wish they would just leave me alone. I need a few minutes to myself to understand the meaning of my dream.

The knocking continues. I stand up and hesitantly go to the door. "Ania, open up!" I hear Leib's voice and breathe a sigh of relief.

Limping, the cat walks ahead of me and meows with enthusiasm. Stupid me! His holiday must surely be over by now and he has come to take me for a walk as he promised.

"Ania!" he yells my name again.

"Why are you shouting?" I open the door. "Are you that eager to see me?" I joke.

My laughter dies down at the sight of the siblings. Ida is holding a hefty suitcase, and it's clear that she's been crying. Leib has a brown burlap sack on his back and he's looking at me with a grim expression.

"What happened to you?" I whisper, disoriented. "Were you kicked out of your house?" A dim fear creeps into my heart that they're planning to ask if they can stay at my house.

"This is all clothing and jewelry our people sent for you to sew," says Ida, her voice trembling.

"That much?"

"Haven't you heard the news?" Leib nudges Ida into the apartment and shuts the door.

"What news? I haven't heard anything since the Germans broke my radio, and I'm better off for it."

"Ania," Ida utters my name shakily, "the district commander issued an order saying that the Jews cannot stay in their homes and that we have to all move to the residential area assigned to us."

"Why would he order such a thing? They've already put warning signs at the entrance to your neighborhoods. Aren't they afraid you'll spread typhus if you move to another area?"

Ida drops her suitcase and bursts into tears, and Leib glares at me.

"What? What did I say?" I ask, embarrassed.

"You've truly outdone yourself." Leib pulls a handkerchief out of his shirt pocket and hands it to Ida. "I thought the time you spent with us helped open your eyes. I thought you finally understood that the despicable lies they spread about us are all part of the German propaganda designed to make everyone hate us."

"But I have changed." I bite my lip. "I provide services for Jewish people, and I like you even though you are Jews."

"I have to calm down. It's unlike me to be so panicky." Ida blows her nose and sits on a chair in the dining room. "Leib, we've discussed this. We can't expect Ania to change her entire worldview just because we've become part of her life. The roots of her ignorance are too deep and too strong."

"Ida, we keep failing with her. I'm beginning to lose hope." Leib lights a cigarette and paces back and forth restlessly. "I didn't think for a minute that our Polish neighbors would rally to help us, but I also didn't think they'd celebrate the Germans' abusing us."

I look from Leib to Ida but don't dare open my mouth to talk. The debate between them is about me, but it doesn't seem like I'm welcome to participate.

"It isn't like you to be so naïve." Ida rubs her eyes. "The pogroms began long before the Germans were struck with delusions of grandeur. The Polish hate us because we manage to prosper economically despite the hardships that continuously rain down on us."

"What economic prosperity are you babbling about?" Leib snorts derisively. "Hundreds of thousands of Jews in Warsaw had trouble making a living even before the war broke out, and now even the wealthiest of our community are forced to sell their belongings to survive. How long do you think we'll be able to survive on the jewelry that Mother and Father left us?"

"We'll manage." She corrects her posture. "As long as we're together, we'll get along fine."

Leib doesn't answer her and his face is contorted in distress. His silence worries me.

"We have to stick together," Ida says, clutching his arm.

"We've talked about this," he tells her, avoiding her gaze. "We've talked about this more than once."

"No." She shakes her head from side to side. "You talked. I refuse to stay here without you."

I furrow my brows, puzzled.

"Then come to the woods with me." He falls to his knees in front of her, and I cover my mouth with my hands and stifle a yelp of alarm. "Dearest sister, please come to the woods with me. We'll join the resistance together."

"Leib..." she whispers his name in despair and strokes his cheek, "You know I could never survive in such conditions. What do I know about war? I'm a teacher, an educator of morality and justice. Do you really think I'm capable of carrying a weapon and shooting another human being?"

"Ida, I can't stay here much longer," his voice is shaky. "I cannot just sit by while the Germans continue to persecute us. I need your blessing to leave you and go fight them." He lays his head on her knees and hugs her legs.

Ida bursts into tears, and I wipe away the tears flowing uncontrollably down my own cheeks.

"I don't think I can manage without you." She strokes his head. "But you know that you have my blessing, whatever your decision."

"No!" A shout erupts from my mouth, and their eyes pivot to me. "You can't leave Ida," I say firmly. "You can't leave her alone."

"I'm not leaving her alone." Leib stands up and adjusts the hat on his head. "We have many close friends who will take care of her, and you'll be with her as well." His green eyes flicker with concern. "Ania, I'm sure you'll look after her the same way we've looked after you."

"But... But she has to move to another area, and I'm staying here."

Ida sighs, and Leib exhales exaggeratedly.

"Ania, the way I see it, you have two options." He tosses the cigarette butt into the glass of water on the table. "The first is that you carefully pack your things and move with Ida to the ghetto like you were ordered. The second is that you wait here until the Germans arrive to take you there." He lights another cigarette, and his expression hardens, "Just keep in mind that they won't come in a royal carriage decorated with flowers. They'll beat you and drag you by the hair through the streets of the city for everyone to see. They'll make an example of you."

His description makes me shudder, and I look to Ida, hoping she'll scold him.

"He's right, Ania, my dear." Ida sighs again. "You're shut up here at home all day and haven't been exposed to their barbaric cruelty. They break into Jewish homes and beat women, men, and children for no reason at all. What do you think they'll do to you when you give them a reason to be cruel to you? They're inhuman." She shakes her head from side to side. "They're terrible beasts, and we're their prey."

I won't let them frighten me with horror stories.

"I'm not leaving my house." I cross my arms over my chest. "I'm sure someone in their offices has already realized that there's been a mistake. I don't visit your neighborhoods, I don't go to your places of worship, and I'm not harming anyone here. I'll explain to them that..."

"That you're not Jewish." Leib smirks.

"Exactly." I jut out my chin.

"I have to find out who your teacher was." He drops down into a chair as if our conversation has exhausted him. "When I have children, I only want her to teach them. She did such a good job with you."

"Maybe you should have fasted for a few more hours," I yell at him, "because if I'm not mistaken, insulting another person is also considered a sin."

"Ania." He jumps up and comes toward me with a conciliatory smile. "I don't think you're stupid. Just incorrigibly optimistic." He grabs one of my curls and wraps it around his finger. "I don't think anyone taught you that outside your perfect little world, there is unimaginable evil. And I believe with all my heart that my and Ida's role in your life is to support you while you learn this lesson." He drops the ringlet with troubled eyes. "You're hiding, sheltered here in your little bubble, and you have no clue about what's happening outside." He gestures toward the window. "Not only are Jews being kidnapped and taken to labor camps, the Polish are suffering, too, but the situation of the Jewish people has never been worse. The Nazis hunt us in the streets, taking away our property, our businesses, and our self-respect. And as if their brutality isn't enough, many Poles have joined the festivities. Pogroms take place on a daily basis. Even our visits here have become risky. Ania, I've genuinely begun to hope that maybe their decision to shut us up in a ghetto will at least protect us from the cruel abuse of our neighbors."

I look at his beautiful face and don't see even a trace of evil in his eyes. He wants the best for me; I know it with all my heart. And a little voice inside warns me that this nightmare has only just begun.

"Maybe there's another option?" I step back. "Maybe I can hide whenever they come."

"Where are you going to hide?" Ida interjects. "In your closet?"

"At one of my Polish neighbor's apartments." I nod to myself. "I'm sure one of the neighbors will agree to hide me whenever necessary, out of respect for my father. They've known him since he was a little boy."

"That's actually not a bad idea." Leib drums a finger on his lips. "Our Polish neighbors have shown such inspiring kindness." His tone is sarcastic. "We'll wait here while you ask them." He pulls up a chair and sits leaning over the backrest with his legs spread out to the sides.

"Right now?" I ask, perplexed.

"Why not?"

I know he thinks I'm bound to fail in my endeavor, so I accept the challenge to prove him wrong.

I leave my apartment, walk one floor up, and knock on the door. I hear a rustling noise from inside the apartment, but no one comes to the door. I knock again.

The old woman peeks through the half-open door looking terrified.

"Good evening to you." I give her my most charming smile. "We know each other. I'm Ania, the neighbor from down…"

"I know who you are," she replies coldly.

"Then you know I've lived here for many years." I continue smiling. "And now, with the unpleasant situation that has arisen, I may be forced to leave my home."

She doesn't bat an eyelid.

"There was a notarization error, and they mistakenly suspect that I'm a Jew." I wave my hand dismissively. "Until the mistake is fixed, I would appreciate it if you would consider hosting me if the Germans come looking for me."

"Hosting you?" She echoes my words. "Do you have any idea what the Germans did to us when they last came to the building?"

"I heard." I nod vigorously. "It's just awful."

"And did you know that while you receive baskets full of food every week, we are starving to death?"

"I didn't know your situation was so bad. I didn't think..."

"You didn't think of coming, even once, to check how we've been doing?" She shakes her head in disappointment. "Didn't it ever occur to you to visit your elderly neighbors to see if we're still breathing?"

I lower my eyes in embarrassment. "Listen, I endured a horrible visit from the Germans too, and..."

"Spoiled girl," she chastises me. "You're asking us to risk our lives for you, a girl who wouldn't shed a tear for us."

"That's not true." I shake my head, but deep inside, I know she's right. "I'm sure I would be sad if something were to happen to you."

"Just so you know, if it was your sister asking, I wouldn't hesitate," she concludes and slams the door in my face.

I stand in front of the closed door for a few more seconds, gasping for breath. Stupid old lady.

I spin around and walk to the other door. This neighbor knows me. She's the one who informed me when the war broke out.

I knock softly so as not to startle her, and when the door creaks open, the woman stares straight through me like she's sleepwalking.

"I thought it was the Germans." She shudders. "What were you thinking knocking on the door like that? Haven't you learned not to go knocking on stranger's doors?"

"But we're not strangers." I smile. "We're neighbors."

"Not for much longer," she responds with a smile that doesn't reach her eyes. "It's about time they cleansed this building of Jews."

I open my eyes wide in dismay.

"Did you think you could hide it?" She smirks. "Your stench reached all the way upstairs." She spits on the floor at my feet.

I back away, my heart pounding, alarmed by her burning hatred.

"Did you want to ask me something, Żydówka?" she asks, leaning against the doorframe, her voice dripping with venom.

"No. Nothing special." I turn and run down the stairs.

I reach my door and lean on the stair railing. Her words threw me off, and I just want to go inside my house and cuddle my cat. But the thought of Leib and Ida sitting there laughing at my expense provokes me to give it one last try.

I walk down the stairs and confidently head to the door of the lonely old neighbor. I knock once and then twice until I hear the noise of his feet dragging over.

The door opens a crack, and the old man standing in front of me doesn't look scared, just tired.

"How may I help you?"

"Mr... Umm..." I knit my brow, trying to remember his name. "You know who I am, right?!"

"Of course, Miss Ania Orzeszkowa," he replies with a yawn.

I decide to forgo my long persuasive speech and get straight to the point. "I need your help, I'm afraid the Germans are going to try to kick me out of my apartment, and I would like to know if you'd agree to hide me when they come to the building."

"In my innocence, I thought you needed a little milk or sugar." He grabs his back and moans. "I find it hard to believe you're requesting such a serious thing from a stranger."

"But..."

"Do you know what my name is?" He raises an eyebrow.

"Yes, but at the moment, I'm confused and can't remember."

"Then maybe when you remember, we can talk about it." He takes a step back and slams the door in my face.

I bang on my head and swear under my breath. Why can't I remember his name?

My eyes dart left and right, but I know there are no other tenants in the building. The glimmer of hope that sparked in me has gone out, and I clutch the railing and climb upstairs to my apartment.

Ida and Leib stand up the second I walk in and look at me in anticipation.

As I stand in front of them, tears stream down my cheeks. "Don't gloat. No one agreed to host me, but I can't leave. Mother will be so angry with me."

"Oh, Ania, we would never gloat." Ida rushes over to hug me. "And I'm sure your mother wouldn't want any harm to come to you. She would want you to do everything to survive."

"I wish she were here with me," I wail. "I'm tired of facing everything alone."

"You're not alone," Ida squeezes my arm. "I'm with you, and I won't leave you."

"You're probably happy I failed," I wipe my tears on the sleeve of my dress. "I was sure one of them would agree to hide me."

"We're happy when you're happy and safe," Leib says with no trace of amusement. "And we're sad when you're sad." He spreads his arms wide and pulls us both into a hug.

I close my eyes and inhale deeply. Their embrace is very comforting, but I painfully long for the embrace of another.

CHAPTER 21

I carry two heavy suitcases, and Dziecko limps rhythmically in front of me. My petticoats are rustling, and my heels are clacking on the cobblestones. I put down one of the suitcases for a moment, tighten the belt of my coat, and straighten the lace of my fastener.

"The Muranów neighborhood is the thriving center of Jewish commerce," Ida says, dragging a cart full of her belongings. "*Was* the thriving center of commerce," she corrects herself and greets a family passing by us with a smile. "I'm sure we'll get along fine there. Right, Ania?"

I don't respond. I don't have the emotional capability to comfort her at the moment. I'm walking through crowds of people wearing yellow armbands in a humiliating procession, the likes of which has never been seen before. Families walk together; elderly people trudge on alone; children carry sacks larger than their bodies on their backs. Some of the people look like beggars, while others look decidedly well off. I stuck to my guns and refused to vacate my apartment until yesterday evening when Ida arrived and handed me a letter in Anton's handwriting. For a fleeting moment, I hoped it would be a confession of his feelings towards me and word that he'd found a way to let me stay in my home, but the letter contained only one sentence: *Pack your things and move to the ghetto with Ida tomorrow morning!*

He wrote me a goddamn command. My heart broke the moment he walked out of my apartment, and it continues to crumble with each day that passes without him. Ida senses my pain and tries to cheer me up, but nothing has the power to make me feel better. I considered refusing his orders. I considered hiding in my parents' bedroom until the Germans came and forced me to leave, but Ida begged me not to leave her alone, and I no longer have anyone to wait in the apartment for.

I stare at the yellow armband on my sleeve and at the figures walking next to me. I hear my mother admonishing me in my head. Her voice is cold and disappointed. *You failed, Ania. You failed to save my boutique. You failed to protect our beautiful home. I warned you, and now you're one of them.*

I moan under my breath, and we overtake a group of men in black hats and coats pushing a giant cart.

"Talmidim hachamim – Bible scholars." Ida sighs.

"Everyone looks stupid to me at the moment," I mutter, "marching like sheep to the slaughter instead of fighting the Germans."

"And what exactly do you expect them to fight with? Bibles?"

"And how is their Bible helping them now?" I push Ida aside to dodge the spittle of two Poles spitting at us from the sidewalk.

"It gives them hope." Ida stops to help a golden-haired girl pick up items that fell out of her sack.

"I wish I had hope, too." I direct a proud look at the Poles watching us in silence from the sides of the road. It's positively preposterous that I'm forced to be part of this dreadful parade instead of standing with them.

"We'll give each other hope," Ida replies confidently.

I freeze in my tracks when I recognize a familiar face among the Polish bystanders. Paulina smiles at me, and I see Nina standing next to her, looking grief-stricken.

"Why are you stopping?" Ida nudges me to keep walking.

"My... my friends," I gulp.

Paulina removes an imaginary crown from her head and mimics throwing it on the pavement. She bends her knee and then kicks the pavement with her foot.

"Your crown has fallen," she announces with a wicked smile and slides her forefinger against her throat in a beheading motion.

I snarl in anger and move forward to hit her.

"No!" Ida commands me firmly and grabs my arm.

"I'll get her," I mutter angrily through clenched teeth.

"The Germans won't hesitate to shoot you." Ida sighs. "Ignore her, and let's keep walking."

"Stinking pig," I mutter and swear to myself that I'll get even with her.

"Don't poison your soul." Ida clings to me and urges me to keep walking. "Your best revenge will be surviving these terrible times and finding happiness when it's all over."

"My best revenge will be catching her in a deserted alley and strangling her."

Ida giggles at my colorful description.

I almost stumble when I notice another familiar face.

Stinky Masza is leaning against the wall of a building. She straightens up when she notices me. I remember how my sister protested so vehemently when I insulted her in front of Łukasz and Stanisław, back when I still thought they were my friends.

I clench my teeth, expecting to see her laughing at my bitter fate, but instead she puts her hand on her heart and bursts into tears.

I find the fact that she feels sorry for me extremely unnerving; I avert my gaze and continue walking.

"Even Stinky Masza is crying for me," I grumble and kick a rock on the road. "I would rather she laugh at me."

"We're almost there," Ida tries to cheer me up.

I put down my luggage, rub the back of my neck, and gasp. Two Polish policemen stand on the street corner, watching the procession with blank expressions. The taller of the two makes my heart skip a beat.

Anton's gaze wanders over the crowd, and his eyes focus when he notices me. I can't breathe; my need to run into his arms and feel the comfort of his embrace is so strong. His eyes are fixed on me and me alone, and the world stops. The longing I feel for him numbs my senses, and I take two quick steps toward him. Abruptly, he opens his eyes wider in a noiseless warning and looks away.

My whole body shakes, and my eyes fill with tears.

"You cannot expose your special relationship," Ida whispers. "It's too dangerous." She picks up my suitcases and shoves them into my hands. "Keep walking and looking straight ahead."

I carry my suitcases and continue walking, but I'm slumped over. With great difficulty, I manage to pass by Anton without looking at him, but when I'm confident that I've walked far enough away, I give in and turn around. His eyes are fixed on me, and on me alone.

* * *

Ida and I stand in the middle of our new apartment and study the modest space. There is only one room and a kitchen. In the room there are two faded cloth sofas next to a low table and a single bed under the window. The kitchen has a small ice box, a moldy oven, and a few cracked and peeling cabinets.

Ida turns towards a black door, opens it, then grimaces and holds her nose. "Oh, my goodness, Ania, it's truly a hovel."

Dziecko stretches his hind legs, yowls, and refuses to come inside the apartment.

"Where's the bathroom?" I ask, looking around.

Ida points at the black door in horror.

"And where's my room?"

"This room is for both of us." She goes to the window and pulls back the stained curtains.

"There must have been some mistake," I mumble. "Let's go find whoever is in charge and demand a bigger apartment."

The door to the apartment swings open, and I turn around and gawk at the smiling face in front of me.

"Good evening to my lovely ladies."

"Peter!" Ida runs forward and throws her arms around him.

I stare at him as if a shining piece of my former life has suddenly landed in front of me.

"Do you have room for another tenant?" He twirls the ends of his mustache and peers at the small space.

I sit on top of my two suitcases and can't get a word out. He's wearing a perfectly pressed three-piece suit and a fashionable hat. His appearance completely contradicts the filthy apartment. My eyes are glued to the yellow band on his arm, and I wonder if his visit is a joke at our expense.

"Frau Orzeszkowa," he mimics a German accent. "This is how you welcome a dear friend?"

"I... I don't understand what you're doing here."

"First and foremost, I'm making sure that you don't wrinkle your gorgeous skirt." He helps me stand up. "The Germans can force us to stay here, but we shan't allow them to damage your haute couture," he clucks in pompously.

My lips stretch into a little smile.

"That's the smile I wanted to see. Mission complete." He waves his hand in the air with a feminine flourish and starts parading around the apartment, shaking his hips to and fro. "Terrible." He points to the bed. "Just terrible." He points at the peeling walls. "They're forcing princesses to live in a kennel. I'm afraid there's no alternative. We'll have to lodge an official complaint with the Führer. How can we send a telegram from here?" He's standing in the center of the room, waving his hands exaggeratedly.

Ida bursts out laughing, and I join in.

Peter is like a beacon of light in the never-ending darkness around us.

"I didn't know you were Jewish." I eye his armband. "Or did the Nazis force you to come live here because you are..." I fall silent and blush, incapable of saying what everyone knows about Peter aloud.

"Special?" He raises an eyebrow.

"Um... No... I meant because you prefer..."

"You can say it," he chuckles and then whispers, "I indeed prefer men to women." He rolls his eyes. "Women cause too much drama." He lights a cigarette and blows the smoke up toward the ceiling.

Ida nods, giggling.

"So they moved you here because of your disease?" I take a seat on the sofa and leap back up when a cloud of dust engulfs the room.

"Ania!" Ida scolds me.

"It's not a disease!" Peter cries out. "It's a sexual preference. I never chose to be attracted to men, but I knew I was attracted to them from a very young age. If they forced people like me to wear an armband, the wretched Germans would probably make it a pink armband."

"But surely you don't want to be so different." My curiosity has gotten the better of me. "Isn't there some kind of treatment for that?"

"Ania!" Ida chides imploringly.

"My father asked the same question." Peter blinks and flicks his ashes into a murky glass on the table. "Mother didn't waste the opportunity to tell me that Father died of a broken heart." He smiles, but I see the sadness behind his eyes. "Imagine how a respected rabbi from Krakow felt when he found out that his son was playing doctor with the Polish neighbor's boy."

I put my hand on my mouth, and Peter says something in the Jewish language that I don't understand.

"Lying with man is an unpardonable sin," Ida translates and smiles at Peter as if sharing in his sorrow.

"So they forced you to move here because you're Jewish," I sigh. "I would never have guessed."

"I moved to Warsaw to start a new life." He shrugs. "I hoped that in this modern city there would be more tolerance for people like me, but even here they smash the windows of my café once a month." He opens the black door and peeks into the bathroom. His entire body shudders in revulsion. "If my father were alive, he would say all this is happening because of my sin and the sins of people like me."

"Of course it's not," Ida quickly reassures him. "You are kind, pleasant, and gentle. You always help those in need, and you are a true friend. Anyone who can't accept your uniqueness is a sinner himself."

"She's right," I lament, and lean against the wall. "I wish all men were like you."

"Heaven forbid." Peter feigns an angry expression. "If all the men were like me, who would court beautiful maidens like the two of you?"

I bite my lip and try to banish Anton's stony expression from my mind.

"But I have a dream." He walks to the door, sashaying his hips. "I have a dream that the day will come when instead of the horrific procession we participated in today, there will be a different procession." He strides around the room, waving his arms every which way. "A procession for men like me, dancing and celebrating their sexuality while spectators cheer them on from the sidewalks. And at the end of the parade, instead of locking us up in a ghetto, we continue marching towards our freedom."

"Peter," Ida chortles, "maybe you should think of a more realistic dream. A dream like that won't come true even in 1,000 years."

"I can actually see it in my mind's eye." I stand next to Peter and imitate his arm motions. "If I'm forced to be Jewish, then the end of the world must already be here." I keep shaking my hips and waving my arms. "And if the end of the world has arrived, such a parade can surely take place as well."

"I get the bed!" Peter giggles and jumps onto it. Its metal legs creak jarringly, and Peter lands on the floor as it breaks. "Actually, I think I prefer a stable mattress on the floor." He laughs, patting the dust off his clothes.

"Peter, I would love for you to live here with us," Ida says awkwardly, "But you're a man, and we're two single women. I'm afraid such a thing won't be well received in the community."

The expression on my face changes instantaneously.

"Rubbish!" Peter stands and tidies his jacket, "They've housed several families in each apartment. I saw smaller apartments with four adults and eight children."

Incredulous, I open my eyes wide.

"Somebody must really be looking out for you if you got this chateau all to yourselves." He peeks into the kitchen. "The small ghetto is only for the privileged. Go to the large ghetto if you want to see what harsh conditions really look like."

"But..." Ida still seems unsure.

"Darling Ida," he falls to his knees in front of her and presses his palms together, imploring. "The Judenrat assigned me to a one-room apartment with eight Bible students. They gawk at me like I'm a leper. Please don't make me stay there."

"I..."

"I promise that if your good name is damaged, I'll repent for my sins and marry you." He wrinkles his nose in despair. "Think about the beautiful, intelligent children we'll have."

With bated breath I wait for Ida's answer.

"Stop talking nonsense," she says through her laughter. "You know I would never abandon a dear friend in his hour of need."

I run over and hug her.

"I'm so happy!" Peter stands up and embraces us both. "Hopefully, there will be enough room for all my things." He dashes to the front door and whistles.

Four boys walk into the apartment, one after the other, and each one puts two suitcases against the wall.

"Many thanks to you." Peter pulls some bills out of his pants pocket and hands them to the boys.

Suddenly, the room looks much smaller.

"Do you want to earn double?" He turns to the boys.

They nod enthusiastically.

"Go find some cleaning supplies and scrub our kingdom clean." He hands each of them a wad of bills. "Also, buy mattresses, sheets, and a wardrobe for Ania's beautiful dresses."

I gasp in surprise.

"While you tidy up our chateau, I'll take these two lovely ladies out to a restaurant."

A restaurant? Are there any restaurants in this wretched place? I stare at him without uttering a word. The universe that has been so cruel to me until now has given me the gift that is Peter. I feel love in the place where I've been imprisoned out of hate.

CHAPTER 22

The apartment is spotless. Three mattresses lie in a pile against the wall, and there are clean sheets neatly folded on the couch. Ida pats the couch and smiles. Peter examines the bathroom with satisfaction, and I finger the doors of my new wardrobe.

I open one of my suitcases, take out the hangers, and carefully hang up my dresses. My thoughts wander to our excursion outdoors earlier. The "Small Ghetto," as Peter and Ida call it, is a neighborhood of crowded streets where all the signs are written in the alphabet of the Jews. We saw throngs of people lugging their belongings to the new quarters assigned to them. The general feeling of despair that reigns outside cannot be ignored. There are German soldiers everywhere, abusing everyone who passes by them. They look at the Jews with revulsion as if they were stray rats. Facing this great mass of beggars are the wealthy Jews; we saw some of them at the restaurant where we sat to dine. It seems that the Germans don't differentiate between the rich and the poor, and from what I've seen, they apparently derive great pleasure from harassing the Jews whose financial situation is good. Ida, Peter, and I managed to avoid them this time – but what will happen next time?

The waiter at the restaurant addressed us in their foreign Jewish language, and when I asked for golonka in breadcrumbs, he reacted with an appalling stare. I had no choice but to tell Ida to order for me what she'd chosen for herself, and the flavor of the salty pickled fish they served us makes me nauseous even now when I think about it. I feel like I've been torn from my life and flung into a parallel universe – a universe where the language, food, and culture are foreign and strange.

I want to go home.

The flood of tears that I can't control blurs my vision and makes it difficult for me to hang up my dresses. I pull out a handkerchief to wipe my eyes and suddenly feel like all the air has been sucked out of the room. Gasping in panic, I run to the window and open it wide.

The sound of shouting in German rises from the street, and my eyes widen in horror when I notice a man lying in the street and four soldiers kicking every part of his body.

"I need to get out of here," I whisper hysterically and turn around. "I can't breathe." I clutch my neck and wail, "I need to get out of here and go home." I burst into tears. "I want to get Mother and go with her to Father and Michalina in America." I run to the door, and my legs keep moving in the air as Peter grabs me by the waist. "Leave me alone!" I shout. "I don't belong here. I want to go home!"

"I want to go home, too." He hugs me from behind. I shake my arms and legs and wriggle my body, trying to break free of his grip, but he doesn't let go. "Ida also wants to go home. But this is our home now."

"But I don't want to be here." I stop struggling and cover my face with my hands. "I'm being punished for my stupidity. Why didn't I leave with Father? Why didn't I escape when I had the chance?"

"You're not the only one who committed such folly." Peter leads me to the couch, and he and Ida sit on either side of me. "People warned me, too." He sighs. "Friends urged me to move to England with them. I could've opened up a café on Oxford Street and learned English. But I didn't believe what they said." He pulls my hand to his lips and kisses it. "I ignored their ominous prophecies.

My café had become a place of pilgrimage for anyone who wanted a pleasant corner to go out to, and I laughed when anyone mentioned the looming threats to the Jewish people." He pulls a pack of cigarettes from his pocket and offers me one. I decline with a shake of my head, but Ida accepts it in my stead. "I told anyone willing to listen that I'd left that religion and had no intention of going back." He leans down to light Ida's cigarette. "I know our history, and I know that a different group tries to obliterate us in every generation."

I listen to his words, and the tears continue streaming down my cheeks.

"I knew the Germans were cruel to the Jews, and I knew that they had passed terrible laws against men like me. But it all seemed so far removed from my life. I thought that if they occupied Poland, the worst thing that could happen was that they would deport the Jews, and I, after all, am no longer Jewish." He lights his cigarette and blows the smoke out the corner of his mouth. "Who could force me to be part of a religion I don't believe in?"

Choking up, I nod vigorously.

"When I renounced Judaism, I chose not to join any other religion. I don't want to belong to a religion that doesn't accept my uniqueness. Christianity is disgusted by us, and Islam..." He doesn't bother finishing his sentence and chuckles bitterly. "In any case, I was mistaken. They didn't lock me in here because of my sexual preferences. They locked me in here because I'm registered as a Jew, and nothing will change that, even if I stand in the platz and declare that I'm a proud atheist."

I nod, fully identifying with every word.

Ida shifts in discomfort and then stands up and goes to the kitchen. She comes back holding a saucer that she ashes into.

"Peter." She moves the saucer towards him. "If they asked you to stand in the square and declare that your sexual preferences are a disease, would you be willing to do so?"

"No," he replies without hesitation. "I've lost so much to maintain my identity. I wouldn't declare it a disease even if they held a gun to my head."

"I feel the same way about my Judaism." She puts out her cigarette and sits on the table in front of us. "I understand that you both detest our religion, each for your own reason, but for me, it's my lifeblood. It's an inseparable part of who I am. The Germans can try to parade me as some sort of vermin, as something rotten, as if Judaism is some kind of disease, but I'm not sick. I'm proud of my identity. I'm proud that my people brought the values of law, morality, and justice to the world." She straightens up and puts her hands on her knees. "As far as I'm concerned, our role as Jews is to continue spreading light in the world, particularly in dark times like these."

Peter bends forward and takes her hand. "Ida, I apologize if I offended you." He bows his head and continues. "When you sit in front of me and feel like you need to justify yourself, I understand that I have sinned against you." He stands at the sound of screams coming up from the street and closes the window. "I shouldn't judge those who choose to adhere to their faith, just as I hope not to be judged for my lack of faith."

I don't share in his discomfort. I'm too absorbed in my own agony.

Abruptly Peter raises his hands as if disgusted with himself. "This conversation is too solemn for our housewarming party." He winks and opens one of his suitcases. "I brought the one thing that can change the atmosphere." He pulls out a bottle of brandy and waves it in the air.

I lick my lips and nod earnestly. He's right. It's exactly what I need.

"I thought they forbade you from running the café." Ida looks at the bottle with yearning.

"I didn't close it," he whispers as if confiding a secret. "I turned it into a grocery store, and the Nazis have permitted me to run it even while living in the ghetto. Luckily I managed to stash the spirits in an incredible hiding place."

Ida claps cheerily, then rushes to the kitchen and returns with three glasses.

Peter opens the bottle and generously pours brandy into the glasses. He hands them to us and raises his own glass high.

"Tonight, we celebrate our new accommodations in this majestic chateau." He clinks his glass to mine, but Ida moves hers away.

"I want to add," she says with a smile, "that we're also celebrating the fact that we have the privilege of being in this palace together. I pray that we will celebrate again when we're free to toast our unique differences with pride."

"I joyfully welcome your prayer." Peter clinks his glass with hers.

I sit up straight and take a deep breath. "We'll save what's left in this bottle for that celebration." I stand up and stash the bottle at the bottom of the garbage bin. "Promise me you won't give in to temptation and drink from it until we can honor the fulfillment of Ida's prayer."

"We promise," Ida and Peter reply in unison, clinking their glasses to mine.

Sipping the drink with pleasure, I close my eyes and pray that Father, Mother, and Michalina will be with us at our future celebration. I take another sip and add a small request that pains me in particular: that Anton will get to see Michalina again.

CHAPTER 23

The seams of the brown coat's lining are undone, and I carefully tuck the two rings into the narrow opening. I'm sitting on the couch with my legs crossed and the cat curled up in my lap. I hear a noisy commotion coming from the street, but I continue concentrating on my sewing.

From daybreak until curfew, I spend my time alone in the apartment, un-sewing and re-sewing the clothes that Ida brings me from the ghetto's wealthy residents who fear German break-ins. When the Germans break into apartments during the day, the screams are drowned out by the sounds of the bustling street life. But when it happens at night, the terrible cries penetrate the walls and claw at my heart.

I thread a needle and hold my breath at the sound of footsteps outside the apartment. The footsteps move away, and I steal a breath. I've forgotten how it feels to breathe normally. The smell of fear wafts off everyone around me. I've forgotten that other odors exist in the world.

I refuse to be afraid.

My way of coping with the situation is seclusion. I leave the apartment just once a day, at noon. I put a chair out on the sidewalk, against the wall near the entrance to the building, and let

Dziecko drink milk from a bowl that I put on the ground next to me. These are the only times that I allow myself to look at the passers-by, the only moments during which I slacken my many layers of protection a bit and observe the poverty that is growing around me. The ghetto has been blocked off by a three-meter-high wall topped with barbed wire and broken glass – as if we are the most dangerous criminals in the world. Throngs of men, women, and children run back and forth, looking for a way to make a living, or reaching out their hands to beg for money. My new street exists in perpetual darkness even when the sun is shining. In the row of buildings across the street, there's a building that was destroyed in the air raids and still hasn't been rebuilt, yet entire families live there anyway. Women, men, and youngsters sleep between shattered stones, breathing in clouds of dust. During the day, they beg for help and sometimes even receive it. The Jewish community has managed to create some kind of new order. There are communal kitchens, infirmaries, and other basic services. Thankfully, I don't need to use any of them. My tiny sphere is enough for me and helps me repress what is happening, although my ability to repress is ruptured every time a shot rings out and every time a defenseless individual encounters the Nazi patrol. No one can anticipate their cruelty, and it seems to evolve with each passing day.

I stroke the lining of the fur coat and sigh. I still can't understand the class distinctions in the ghetto. The wealthy residents spend their time dining out in restaurants, enjoying cultural performances, and maintaining their sanity in this loathsome place. A lucky few even get to work outside the ghetto walls. Everyone else wakes up every morning with no goal other than to survive another day.

Peter is among the fortunate ones to have obtained a special permit to work outside the ghetto. In the mornings, he leaves for the café, which has become a successful grocery store, returning just before curfew with a basket full of provisions.

I don't know where I stand in the hierarchy. Thanks to the groceries Peter brings home and the baskets Anton makes sure to send us, I don't go hungry. But the only reason I keep breathing is to survive another day. My life is meaningless.

The door opens, and I smile at Ida. None of us knocks on doors; knocking has become taboo.

Ida hangs her bag on the rack and sits next to me; she looks downtrodden. Dziecko senses her distress and hops into her lap.

"I don't want to hear bad news," I beg her.

"Then I'll shut up." She pets the cat and sighs.

I try to continue my work, but her sighs grow louder and more frequent.

"Fine." I stick the needle into the fabric and turn to face her. "You can tell me."

She gasps with relief, and her eyes fill with tears. "It's been over a month since we were moved in here, and the situation is only getting worse." She takes off her hat and throws it on the table. "There are so many children and far too few teachers. No one wants to work as a teacher for such pitiful compensation." She bites her lip. "I know I have no right to judge anyone because I don't lack food, thanks to Peter and Anton. But…"

My heart constricts in pain when she mentions his name. I want to interrupt her and tell her how my longing for him keeps me sleepless every night, but I don't say a word.

"And I saw a dreadful sight today," she wipes away a tear, "Two soldiers chopped off the sidelocks of a respected rabbi, and seconds later…"

"I don't want to know." I cover my ears with my hands. "Forgive me, but please spare me these stories." I shake my head. "I'm still trying to forget the way they brutally beat those two women for no reason."

"Ania." Her expression becomes earnest. "How can you forget? I try to fall asleep at night, but I'm bombarded over and over by the cruel images I see all day. I think I even hear the cries and pleas in my sleep."

"I don't make eye contact, and I don't look at the neighbors' faces." I pull the needle out of the fabric and resume my sewing. "When you don't see their faces, all the people become blurry. They're like faded pigments that pass in front of me."

"I can't do that." She shrugs. "I look at the people to remember what 'good' looks like and avert my gaze in front of the German soldiers to forget what 'evil' looks like."

The door opens, and Peter steps in with a shake of his hips. He arranges two baskets on the table in front of us and twirls his handlebar mustache with his fingers.

"Did I interrupt a nasty girl talk?" He peers at us slyly. "Because I would love to join in."

Ida laughs and dries her tears, and I roll my eyes and grin.

"I have exciting news." Peter lights a cigarette and turns off all the lights except the small lamp on the stool under the window.

"Are the Germans leaving Poland?" I ask sarcastically.

"Not yet," he says, pulling a bottle of wine from one of the baskets. "But I've obtained a permit for you to come to work with me in the store." He holds the bottle up. "Tomorrow morning, you will leave the ghetto walls with me and accompany me – dancing all the way – to my magical store."

I gape at him silently for a few seconds and then shake my head no. "I don't think I want to."

"Are you mad?" Ida cuts in. "You never leave the apartment. This isolation is really bad. Look how pale you are. Practically transparent."

"You have to go out." Peter flutters his lashes. "After all, you can't abandon a dear friend in need."

"But..."

"It's not up for debate." He waves a cautionary finger at me. "It will encourage you to see that there are good Poles who frequent my store even though I've been marked as a Jew."

"I hate the Poles." I clench my fists. "And I hate the Germans. And I hate the French who lost to them, and I hate…"

"I'm delighted to learn that you can feel something," he clucks. "Your indifference worries me sometimes."

"Peter…" Ida scolds him gently.

"What?" He shrugs. "Doesn't it bother you that she sits here all day as if the Nazis aren't right under her window? Doesn't it bother you that when she goes outside with her cat, she sits like a statue on her chair and stares blankly at the horrors taking place right before her eyes?"

"And what do you expect me to do?" I blurt out. "My hatred for this world is too powerful. If I start allowing sorrow and despair to seep in, I won't be able to get out of bed in the morning."

"I just wanted to make sure that you still had a pulse." He bats his eyelashes at me and disappears into the kitchen.

He returns with three glasses and pours the wine. He squeezes between us on the couch and puts his feet up on the table.

Ida pulls the coat towards her, examines the stitching, then stares at the pile of folded clothes I've finished sewing. "I'm afraid you won't be able to continue doing this."

"Why not?" I ask, astonished. "If they can't pay me, I'll do it for free. I enjoy the work, and I like keeping busy."

"It's too risky." She sighs. "What would happen if the Germans broke in here in the middle of the day?" She stands up and starts hanging the clothes up in the closet. Dziecko moves to cuddle on Peter's lap. "Imagine what would happen to us if the Germans found all this jewelry in our apartment?" She shudders.

"I'm not afraid of them," I grumble.

"Then it's about time you start." Peter pats my thigh. "I like breathing." His nose flares as he takes a deep breath, "I wouldn't want to stop breathing because the Germans put a bullet in each of our heads."

I scowl.

"I promised Leib we would be careful." Ida walks toward the kitchen and leans on the doorframe. "And also..." She pauses, staring at Peter as if she expects him to continue her sentence.

"And Anton also asked that you stop," Peter completes her statement.

"How does he know that this is what I do?" I snap. "He hasn't seen me since we were locked in here, and I haven't seen him."

"He asked me." Peter twirls his mustache. "He asks me about you every time he delivers a package for you."

"For us," I correct him, irritated.

"Ania, Ania, Ania..." Peter cackles. "The three of us know that he puts exactly what you like in those baskets." He leans down and pulls pork knuckles wrapped in paper out of the basket. "Ida and I prefer not to eat this animal." He chuckles, and Ida waves her hand in disgust.

I don't want to talk about him anymore. I have the privilege of living with two friends who are dear to my heart, and they are enough for me. The fear that they, too, will disappear and leave me entirely alone nags at me constantly.

I hang the finished coat in the closet and step over to the window. The street is dark and quiet, and dim lights fleck the building across the road. I watch the families sitting around their tables to eat dinner together. Suddenly, two trucks turn onto our street. They stop, their brakes screeching, and soldiers jump out and dash into the building next door. My breath catches in my throat.

I only realize that Peter and Ida are standing next to me when Peter switches off the lamp on the stool next to us. A second later, all the lights in all the houses are off, and a shadow descends on the street.

As if in a nightmare, I stare at the men being dragged into the street to the sound of the desperate pleas of the women and children running outside after them. The men are thrown into the back of the truck, and the pleading cries get louder.

"They're taking them to the labor camps," Peter whispers, pulling me back. Ida draws the curtains closed, panting rapidly.

The sound of a gunshot jostles me.

The screaming stops, and I don't dare turn around.

Ida bursts into mute tears, and Peter clutches her, whispering soothing words in her ear.

"It could be you next time," she says in horror, and I cover my mouth with my hand, stifling a shout.

"Narishkeit. Nonsense!" He waves his hand dismissively and throws us a reassuring smile, but his eyes betray his unease. "Why would they want someone like me? My attire is quite unsuitable for forced labor." He puts his hands on his hips and pirouettes.

Ida and I can't bring ourselves to smile. She pulls down her mattress, pushes it next to the wall, and lies down fully clothed. I move my mattress next to hers and lie down next to her. Peter sighs and lies down on his mattress on my other side. We remain in our clothes, cover ourselves with blankets, and Dziecko snuggles between us. It seems that they, like me, lost their appetite for dinner.

I wait for sleep to come and for my dreams to take me far away from here, to my family, to a world without Germans, without screams, and without gunshots.

* * *

Peter and I stand side by side in the crowd near the gates of the ghetto. One by one, the people present their documents to the soldiers and walk outside to the Polish streets of Warsaw.

I tighten the belt of my coat and grip the handle of my basket. Suddenly, they start kicking the man standing in front of me, and I spin around, determined to run back to my apartment.

"Don't look right at them. Just show them your papers," Peter whispers and clutches my arm tightly.

I snarl under my breath and turn back around.

"Kennkarte. Documents," barks the soldier, and I hand them to him, staring determinedly at my shoes. He pushes me forward, and I gasp for breath. I want to glance back to make sure that Peter is following me, but the thought of having to watch him endure some brutal humiliation stops me from doing so. I finally let out a sigh of relief when, after a few seconds, Peter puts his arm in mine and urges me to pick up my pace.

"Look around." He chuckles. "The world you once knew still exists outside the ghetto walls." He points to the tram and the cars driving up and down the road.

"It's nothing like the world I knew." I finger the armband displayed on my sleeve and watch a coachman transporting goods instead of people. "In my world, I would gesture to that coachman right now, and he would take us directly to your café. People would be staring at my elegant dress and hat and not at the hideous armband on my sleeve. And I would be on my way to my mother's boutique instead of being haunted by the thought of her two despicable seamstresses stealing it from her while I stood there powerless and unable to do anything to stop them."

"I'm glad you're looking on the bright side." Peter chuckles and hurries to pull me down to the street at the sight of soldiers marching towards us on the sidewalk.

"We're not allowed to walk on the sidewalk now either?" I grumble indignantly.

"Basically, if they could stop us from breathing, they would." He bumps his hip to mine. "But beautiful Miss Ania, they haven't managed to steal the fresh air from us yet, so let's try to enjoy it while we can."

I inhale deeply and nod. His words don't improve my sullen mood, but I decide to stop dampening the day.

We walk for more than an hour, bypassing the gardens and parks time and again because Jews are prohibited from entering. I notice the disgusted looks of the Poles but every so often, see a look of sympathy. The damage caused by the air raids is still evident on every corner, many shops remain closed, and mainly soldiers sit in the cafés. The city is dark and dirty. I don't love Warsaw anymore. I wish I could be anywhere but here in this city where evil reigns.

We cross Jerozolimskie Avenue, and I hurry to look away so as not to have to see Mother's boutique. The air refuses to enter my lungs, and I pant laboriously.

"You're allowed to dream, too, you know." Peter pats my arm. "Dreams help us maintain our sanity."

"I dream that my mother's seamstresses will be kidnapped and put into forced labor."

"That's not as far-fetched a dream as you think." With his basket, Peter gestures to the boarded-up shops in front of us. "The Germans took the owners of those shops to the labor camps, and believe me, they're not Jewish. They held celebrations when we were sent to the ghetto."

"Sometimes I think the Poles hate the Jews more than the Germans do."

"To be fair, you're not wrong." He grins bitterly. "But they're not all like that. There are Poles whom I'm proud to count among my friends."

I bravely glance at the street in front of me again and don't see a single person wearing a yellow armband. The Nazis have imprisoned all the Jews in the ghetto, and the world stands silently by.

We stop in front of the café, and I am astounded by the change it has undergone.

Massive profanity is smeared across the large glass of the front door, and an official sign is affixed above it, announcing that the business is Jewish-owned.

"Don't worry, I'll clean the window," I tell him, teary-eyed.

"Don't bother." He disregards it and unlocks the door. "I've decided to stop being ashamed of the labels people give me."

I bite my lip and follow him inside. If I hadn't frequented the café so often in the past, I would have been sure I had the wrong address. The tables and chairs stand in a jumbled heap in the corner of the room – a sad monument to what was once a bustling hub of entertainment. The bar's counter is cracked and covered with black stains, and the shelves behind it are devoid of drinks. In their place are small bags tied with brown strings.

"Welcome to my kingdom." Peter gives me an exaggerated bow and then pulls my hand to his lips and kisses it. "May I offer you a sack of rice? Or perhaps a sack of fine flour?"

"I can't decide!" I drum my fingers on my lips. "Everything looks so tempting."

We burst out laughing, and I decide to make the best of the day.

Peter leads me to the door at the rear of the café and ushers me into a storeroom packed with huge sacks.

"We fill small bags with rice and flour and then sell them to the many customers who come in," he explains, hanging his coat on a hook by the door.

I hand him my coat and get to work. I like the quiet of the storeroom.

Peter glances at his watch, nods to himself and carries the filled bags into the store. I hear the bell on the front door ring. The first customer has entered.

Their conversation sounds cordial and pleasant, and I smile to myself and continue filling the bags. Over the next few hours, the bell continues to ring, but I stay put in my safe corner of the storeroom.

"Noble lady," Peter scolds me from the doorway. "I didn't bring you here for forced labor. In three hours, you've filled enough bags to last us a week. Come on." He gestures toward the front room. "Join me and greet our customers."

I frown, feeling uncomfortable, but when the bell rings again, I stand up, stretch my arms and legs, and join him. He stands at the front of the counter, and I remain behind him.

He warmly welcomes every man and woman who walks in, and they respond with beaming smiles. None of them wears an armband on their arm, and yet they treat him with great respect. Miraculously, he charges each of them a different amount for the same goods, and some of them don't pay at all.

A woman pushing a baby carriage hugs him when he hands her two bags and refuses to take the zlotys she passes him.

"Thank you very much," she says with tears in her eyes and then turns to me and says, "Thank you very much as well."

I nod but immediately avert my gaze. I prefer not to see their faces.

In the late afternoon, the line gets shorter and shorter until there are no more customers, and when the bell rings, a young, muscular man walks in. He's wearing faded overalls, and when he takes his hat off and combs his light hair back, I squint, trying to remember where I know him from.

Peter rushes over to him with an excited grin and momentarily strokes his arm.

I stare at him in curiosity and then remember that I saw him here when I came with Anton.

"Ania, this is Olek." Peter motions with his hand for me to come out from behind the bar.

I approach them hesitantly, trying not to make eye contact.

"How can they imprison a woman as beautiful as you behind the terrible walls of the ghetto," Olek says in a low masculine voice. He takes my hand and kisses it.

I stretch my lips into a smile, but I don't look at him.

"Dear Ania, would you be willing to safeguard my kingdom while I show Olek something in the storeroom?" Peter implores.

"Umm..." I'm not sure I feel comfortable at the front of the store by myself.

"We won't be long. I promise." He pulls Olek by the arm and closes the storeroom door.

I go back behind the counter and organize the bags that are left on the shelves. The minutes tick by, and my eyes dart toward the storeroom.

The shop door opens with a ring, and I spread my lips into a fake smile, determined to welcome Peter's customers warmly.

The smile freezes on my face when I notice uniforms.

Two German soldiers stride in. Their heels click harshly on the floor tiles, and their eyes are cold and wicked.

"Heil Hitler!" they call out with a Nazi salute.

My arms turn to stone at my sides, and I bite my bottom lip and nod. I don't know how I'm supposed to respond.

"Our sacks," the German barks in my face.

I turn to the shelves and put bags of rice and flour on the counter.

The face of the soldier on the left is contorted with rage, and he flings the bags to the floor, their contents spilling every which way.

"You filthy Jewess," he roars. "Where are our sacks?"

I throw a desperate look in the direction of the storeroom and turn pale as chalk when I realize my look is drawing their attention toward the couple inside.

The soldiers click their heels and march to the back room.

My heart pounds wildly, and I dash past them and open the door hesitantly. Peter and Olek are sitting behind two large sacks and filling bags, their eyes downcast.

The Germans push me inside and look with disgust at the couple, who are flushed and disheveled.

"Do they look like two perverted rats to you, too?" The soldier addresses his friend in German and taps the butt of the gun clipped to his belt.

I stifle a gasp and force myself to regain my composure. "My love," I address Peter in German, "The honorable soldiers have come to collect their sacks."

Peter wrinkles his forehead, confused, and the Germans peer at him in suspicion.

"The sacks," I bark in Polish. "Which sacks belong to the Germans?"

Peter nods energetically and points to two huge sacks in the corner of the storeroom. His suspicious behavior is annoying me. I step over to the sacks and, with incredible difficulty, pick up the first one. A growl yearns to escape my throat, but instead, I smile at the soldier as I pass him the sack.

"Get back to work!" I shout at Peter and Olek in German, and the soldiers burst out laughing.

My arms almost tear off my body as I pass the other sack to the other soldier. I shake my hands and complain, "Men are useless."

"Filthy Jews!" The soldier picks up the sack, spitting on the floor as they leave the storeroom. I lean against the wall, panting. I break into a cold sweat that coats my entire body.

"Thank you, Ania." Peter pouts apologetically, then stands up and buttons his pants. "What did those villains say about us?"

"That we look like two perverts." Olek stands up and closes the buckles of his overalls. "Your clever friend saved us." He cups Peter's cheeks and kisses him lightly on the lips.

I look on in silence, watching this intimate and tender moment between them, and I can't understand how I ever thought such affection between two men was a disease.

"We have to be more careful." Olek caresses Peter's arm and then moves away from him and towards me. "I'm sorry we put you in such an uncomfortable situation." He gives me a grateful hug and then smiles at Peter. "I hope you understand how hard it is for me to keep my distance from him." He winks at me and leaves the storeroom.

"I'm sorry, Ania." Peter wrinkles his nose like an abandoned puppy again. "Please tell me you forgive me."

"Of course, I forgive you." I sit down, leaning against the wall with my legs stretched out in front of me. "Until those despicable Nazis arrived, you helped me regain a taste of what a normal, sane life feels like, and for that I thank you from the bottom of my heart."

"That's definitely a cause for celebration." He rubs his hands together with delight and bends down to the floor. He moves the filthy carpet, and the wooden board under it creaks as Peter lifts it up and slips his arm inside. He pulls out a bottle of Żubrówka and chuckles. "I promise you we'll never run out of vodka."

I reach out my hands and lick my lips in anticipation.

"We don't have much time." He twists off the cap and chugs directly from the bottle. "We need to get back to our other kingdom before curfew."

"Don't mention the ghetto." I grab the bottle. "Let me have a few minutes more to imagine we're just spending time here like two friends." I take two big gulps and hand the bottle back to him.

"I can do that easily." His eyes gleam. "Tell me what you think of Olek. Isn't he handsome?"

I nod and motion for Peter to hand me back the bottle. I take three more long sips, and a warm blush rises on my cheeks.

"Ania, have you ever been in love?"

I don't answer and quickly take two more sips.

"Have you ever known a man who made your heart pound wildly every time you saw him?"

I cough and take another gulp.

"You're not being very cooperative," Peter whines and tries to grab the bottle from me. Suddenly, we hear the doorbell ringing, and he stands up straight. The sound of footsteps echoes through the store, and Peter steps back and signals to me to lie down behind a large sack of flour. I hug the bottle to my body and lie on my back.

The storeroom door opens, and I cover my mouth with my hand.

"Peter."

The deep voice causes my heart to pound.

"Mr. Mrożek." I can hear Peter's relief. "How nice to see you."

"Unfortunately, I don't have time to chat with you," Anton replies impatiently. "I came to tell you to pack everything you can and take it with you to the ghetto. Tomorrow the gates close, and you won't be able to leave again."

"What do you mean?" Peter asks, panicked.

There is no reply.

"What will I do with all the goods?" I hear Peter's footsteps pacing back and forth. "I won't be able to get a cart on such short notice."

"I'm sorry. The goods left here will be confiscated."

"That's terrible." Peter sounds bewildered.

"Ania," the deep voice speaks my name softly. "Please tell me how she's doing. Does she lack for anything? Does she need me to bring her..."

"You can ask her yourself," Peter interrupts him.

I keep hugging the bottle and sit up.

Anton's torso tenses up, and he turns around slowly. His usually serene brown eyes look feverish.

Panting in excitement, I rise to my feet without putting the bottle down.

Anton's gaze never leaves me. He examines me from head to toe, and then our eyes meet. He takes one step toward me and stops.

"Umm... I think I'll leave you two here alone," Peter mumbles. "I'll go clean the store before the Germans come," he whines, closing the storeroom door behind him.

"Ania..." Anton whispers my name and takes one step toward me. My heart bruises my rib cage as it beats against it mercilessly.

"I miss you so much." He presses his palm to my cheek.

I close my eyes and tilt my head toward him.

"I apologize for the way my last visit ended. I apologize for not being able to control my emotions, and I apologize for taking advantage of…"

"I forgive you." I rub my cheek against his palm. "I forgave you a long time ago."

"I wish I could visit you in the ghetto." He sighs heavily.

"You're here now." His touch feels so good.

"Do you need anything?" He moves closer again, and his body brushes against mine. "Please tell me if you need anything, and I'll try to get it for you."

"I need your arms around me." The bottle slips from my fingers, and I open my eyes and stare deep into his.

Before I have the chance to blink, he clasps me by the waist and hoists me into the air. My arms wrap around his neck, and my legs around his body. My buttocks rest on the flour counter, and Anton stands between my legs.

I feel drunk, but not from the vodka I drank. His protective touch dulls my senses, and I want to lock the storeroom door and beg him to stay here with me forever.

"I've missed you," he whispers into my mouth.

"I think I've missed you more," I tell him as my eyes fill with tears.

"I'll make sure I'm transferred to guard your neighborhood of the ghetto." He wipes away my tears with his thumb. "You have to understand. Knowing you're so close and I can't visit you drives me mad." He clenches his jaw, and his cheeks quiver.

"I'm not sure that's a good idea." I slide my palms over his chest and sigh. "When I don't see you, it's easy for me to convince myself that you cannot visit me. I don't think I can handle being ignored by you every day."

"I tried to persuade myself that you would be better off without me." His cheek quivers again. "Every day I convinced myself that if I didn't see you, I wouldn't be able to hurt you, but…" He pauses for a moment and caresses my cheek. "I don't want to hurt you. I want to protect you and to know that you're still thinking of me."

I welcome the words that I've hungered to hear into my heart and dare not wonder if his feelings are real — or just an echo of the memory of my other half.

"I think about you all the time."

"Then we'll invent a special signal," his thumb flicks over my lower lip, and I lick my upper lip. "When you see me drumming on the butt of my gun, you'll know that I long to come to you, even if I can't."

My eyes move down to the butt of his gun, "All right." I look up again at his strong face. "When I lick my lips, you'll know I'm thinking of you."

"You should think of another signal," he says hoarsely, staring at my lips.

"I'll twirl a curl around my finger?" I tilt my head to the side and wrap a ringlet around my finger.

"I think that'll drive me crazy as well." He smiles his dazzling smile at me.

I blink hard, proving to myself that I'm not dreaming. After such a long time, he's actually here with me. I lean against the wall behind me, and he strokes my hair, pushes it behind my ears, and runs his fingers along my jawline. His thumb approaches the spot where her beauty mark should to be, and I tremble and grab his hand, refusing to allow him to discover that the marking isn't there. At this moment, I need to believe that he's not looking for her in me. That I am enough.

"I wish I could snap my fingers and change the scenery." His hand clings to my waist, and his entire body presses against mine. "I would surround you with a field of flowers right now. Another country. Another reality."

His hands send warm currents through every part of my body. "Anton, right now, I want to be right here." My bosom rises and falls heavily, and I dig my fingernails into his arms.

He inhales sharply, as if I've said exactly what he needed to hear, and his face moves nearer to mine. I close my eyes. I feel his breath so close to my lips.

The storeroom door swings open, and I open my eyes in alarm. Anton straightens up and carefully helps me down from the counter. Stupefied, I stagger to my feet, staring at Peter's apologetic smile.

"Curfew is coming up," he tells us as he taps his wristwatch. "The lovely young lady and I, her handsome friend, must return to the ghetto."

"Of course." Anton continues looking at me and only me. He lifts my hand and presses it to his lips. His kiss is more intimate and sensual than any kiss he could have given me on the lips.

The realization that my time with him is over distresses me. "Promise me that..." I stammer, "Promise me that you'll come to visit me at our apartment in the ghetto soon."

"I never make a promise I'm not sure I'll be able to keep." He kisses my hand once more and turns away. "Take care of her," he tells Peter gruffly as he leaves the storeroom.

A searing pain rips through the pit of my stomach, and I bend down and grope for the bottle. "You're the one who abandoned me, Michalina," I mutter to myself. "Don't be selfish. Let me take comfort in him." I quickly take a sip, ignoring the strange look Peter gives me.

* * *

Peter and I leave the café and walk together towards the gates of the ghetto. I'm carrying two heavy baskets, and Peter is toting a giant sack of rice on his back.

I giggle, and he looks at me inquiringly.

"I liked the cleaning job you did in honor of the Germans' forthcoming visit to the café," I explain, my tone amused.

"Do you think they'll appreciate the path of rice and flour I paved for them?" He raises an eyebrow.

"I'd love to see them get down on all fours and lick it off the floor."

We burst out laughing.

I look at the beautiful sunset and latch onto my feeling of happiness. The brief meeting with Anton was all I needed to feel sane and shake off my constant despair. I know this pleasant sensation is temporary, so I try and hold onto it with all my might.

"Peter," I address him. Questions crowd my head. "Do you think taking such a risk with Olek was worth it? After all, physical pleasure is only momentary."

"It's so much more than that." He smiles dreamily. "Some people think it's just a physical relationship between two people, but the truth is that sexual relations reflect the true essence of your connection with your partner."

"I don't know what you mean." I blush.

"You don't know *yet*," he corrects me. "The day will come when you consummate your love in the purest, most natural, age-old way, and you'll realize how much you need his touch and how much you long to share such thrilling passions with your partner."

I long to put down the baskets and rub my face. Peter's words make my skin feel hot, and I can't stop picturing Anton touching me the way I long to touch him.

"You're imagining it, aren't you?" Peter giggles and affectionately bumps his hips to mine.

"No, no," I lie. "I need to experience such strong feelings towards someone first in order to be able to imagine it."

"It's odd..." Peter mumbles. "I always thought his heart belonged to your sister."

A sharp pain shoots through my chest.

"I was wrong," Peter says confidently. "I swear to you that I never saw him look at her the way he looked at you today."

I should feel satisfied by his remark, but the pain returns, and all I feel is guilt.

"Anton is just a good friend." I say and turn down a side street after Peter. "My sister asked him to look after me while she and Father are away. He's only doing what she asked."

Peter stops walking and looks at me like I've sustained a head injury.

"I promised her I would look after him, as well," I say, my voice trembling. "I'm looking after him for her."

Peter's eyes suddenly look sad, and he nods in understanding. "Betraying a family member is out of the question, no matter what."

I avoid his gaze.

"But the heart is a crafty organ." Peter gives me a knowing smile. "It's the most selfish organ of all. It doesn't care about any organ but itself."

He starts walking again, and I pick up my pace to keep up. The streets are getting emptier, the people who pass by us are hurrying home, and my despair returns as I see the walls of the ghetto unfurling before our eyes.

We avoid the park and turn down another side street.

A pair of soldiers walk towards us on the sidewalk, and I step down into the street without Peter having to ask me to. They're engrossed in their conversation and don't seem to notice us at all. I snicker bitterly to myself when I think about how they always walk in couples. It's as if their great Führer realized that each of them had been blessed with an exceptionally small brain and that maybe they'd only be able to face the wicked challenges he set for them in pairs.

"Walk closer to me," Peter whispers sternly. I don't understand why he's so nervous. The soldiers have walked away, and it doesn't seem like we're in any danger. I look up ahead and see a man wearing a yellow armband, trying to hide his two daughters behind his back. Three Polish boys are pestering him.

Peter crosses the road to avoid the scene, and I cling to him but continue staring at the horrifying assemblage.

One boy throws the Jew's hat into the street, the second slaps him across the face, and the third rummages through his basket.

"Look down," Peter hisses angrily.

I can't take my eyes off the two distraught girls, desperately trying to help their father.

"Meat?" The boy pulls something out of the basket and presses it against the man's face. "All we have to eat is peas and rice while you dirty Jews steal our meat?"

"I'm a butcher," the man says, trying to remain composed. "If you come to my butcher shop tomorrow, I'll gladly give you a few cuts of meat."

"We want these cuts." One of the other boys slaps him in the face several times.

"Okay, they're yours," the man replies, gesturing with his hands in an attempt to comfort the crying girls.

"We don't need your permission." The third boy kicks him in the belly, and the man crumples to the ground. "And we don't need your permission to have our way with your beautiful girls either."

"No!" The man shouts, and I cover my mouth with my hands when I realize I screamed along with him.

"Ania, look away!" Peter pleads.

It's too late. The boys are already running towards us. The man gathers his daughters, and they run down an alley and are quickly swallowed up.

The boys stand in front of us, the meat in their hands. They study us carefully.

"Forgive her," Peter stammers. "She didn't mean to interfere."

A thumping noise shocks my ears, and I look on in terror as Peter crashes into the street.

The blood drains from my face, and my body freezes, petrified.

"So the pervert from the café found a new girlfriend?" asks one of the boys maliciously, kicking Peter in the belly. "What happened? Did you get tired of being fucked by men?"

His friends laugh and kick Peter, who is cowering on the ground.

"Stop! You're hurting him," I shout and drop the baskets. His fragile appearance makes my heart ache, and I lay shielding him, without thinking twice. A boot strikes me in the ribs.

"We don't mind beating up Jew girls." One of the boys laughs. "But I'd rather we finish with the degenerate first." He kicks Peter's legs. I hear him moaning with pain underneath me and hug him tightly, wrapping myself around him like a protective barrier.

Suddenly, as if in a dream, I hear thumps and screams of pain, but they aren't coming from me, rather from the three boys. I look up cautiously, and, to my amazement, I see four men in black suits beating up the boys. Yellow bands are tied to their arms, and with each additional blow, I begin to see the Star of David in a different light. Suddenly it doesn't seem like a symbol of weakness and defeat to me anymore, but rather a symbol of strength that was just waiting for its moment to shine.

The boys run away down the alley, and the men chase them. One of them turns around and runs back to us.

He gives me his hand and addresses me in a language I don't understand.

"I... I don't understand." I stand up and rub my ribs.

"I wanted to know if you are all right," he says in Polish and leans down to check on Peter.

I choke up as Peter comes to his feet. Blood is dripping from his forehead and lips, and bruises and scrapes cover his face.

"Adank, thank you," Peter thanks him in both languages and attempts to smile. He touches his face in discomfort, then clutches his hips and bends over.

"You better hurry to the ghetto." The man looks at Peter in concern. "Do you think you can help him walk?" He turns to look at me, and I lower my eyes, trying my best not to commit his face to memory. But it's too late. I could draw him in my sleep. His features are chiseled and sharp, simultaneously manly and pleasant. A short beard decorates his jawline, and his sidelocks are tucked behind his ears.

"We'll manage," I position Peter's arm over my shoulder and lead him forward carefully. After three steps, I stop and look back helplessly at the baskets and sacks strewn all over the street.

The man swings the sack over his shoulder and picks up the two baskets.

"Go ahead. I'll make sure to bring you your things." He motions with his head for us to keep going.

"But how will you find us?" I ask, bewildered.

"Easily." He winks at me and turns down the alley.

CHAPTER 24

Dziecko is cradled in my arms, and I swing my legs off the chair and watch the passers-by indifferently. The streets of the ghetto are unbearably crowded. We are like sardines in a can. Bodies colliding with more bodies, peddlers trying to sell their meager wares, beggars, weak starving men and women, and children who no longer make noise. Everyone is equally anxious for the inevitable moment when the patrol of soldiers will pass by.

The skirt of my dress rustles in the breeze, and I put my gloves on. My beret is pinned on my head, and this morning, like every morning, I'm perfumed and made up as if I'm about to leave for another day of work at a boutique. No one looks at me. Not even the Nazis who passed by here a few minutes ago. Maybe they think I've lost my mind. A girl who's wobbling between total denial and complete despair.

A day has passed since Peter was brutally beaten. He's lying on a mattress in the apartment, and Ida is nursing him. She won't leave him, even for a second.

I, on the other hand, am having a hard time being around him. I'm plagued by a guilty conscience. He asked me to look down and walk away, but I was unable to comply; now he lies broken, bruised, and in agonizing pain. All because of me.

I sense an unfamiliar figure looming over me, and I look up anxiously. The man who helped us yesterday puts the two baskets down at my feet and then stands in front of me. He takes off his black hat and holds it to his chest.

"I would love to make your acquaintance properly." He smiles, and I look down, avoiding eye contact. "Bruno Stern," he says his name.

"Ania..."

"Orzeszkowa," he completes my sentence.

I straighten up in surprise.

"And you live with Miss Ida Hirsch."

"How do you know?" I shift in discomfort.

"When you live in the Jewish community, all you need is one prayer service at the synagogue to get information about anyone," he replies in an amused tone.

I smile, remembering my pleasant conversations with Leib. Something about this fellow makes me feel at ease, like how I felt with Ida's older brother.

"I don't pray."

"Not at all?" he asks in nonjudgmental astonishment.

"Sometimes in my heart," I confess, surprising myself, and pet the cat's fur.

"That's what matters." He takes a step back.

"My prayers are never really answered." I sigh, still not looking at him.

"It can take some time."

I fight the need to look at his face and instead enjoy his pleasant and soothing voice.

"Mr. Stern, thank you for helping us yesterday," I say awkwardly, remembering that I haven't yet thanked him properly.

"You can call me Bruno, and we were honored to help you." He makes no comment on the fact that I'm not looking at him.

"You weren't afraid that intervening would lead to them taking revenge on you? Or that German soldiers would pass by and do something terrible to you?"

"Weren't you afraid when you intervened on behalf of the Rosenfeld family?"

I raise my eyes for a moment, meet his handsome smile, and immediately avert my gaze again.

"I didn't know their last name," I say thoughtfully. "The truth is that at that moment, I wasn't afraid. I just felt that if I didn't intervene, I would explode."

"It's a great virtue to help people you don't know, especially when it could put your own life in danger."

His compliment embarrasses me. I don't deserve it. "Are you complimenting yourself because you chose to help us?" I tease him to overcome my embarrassment.

His throaty laugh is music to my ears.

Two women passing by us slow their pace.

"Oh my, by tomorrow, everyone will be talking about how Bruno Stern is courting Miss Ania Orzeszkowa." He chuckles. "Believe me, it's hard to keep anything private in our community."

His insinuation makes me nervous, and I bite my lip.

"I didn't mean to upset you." He takes another step back. "Of course, I wouldn't do such a thing without your consent."

I frown. I don't know why I'm nervous. After all, I was surrounded by suitors my whole life. I flirted, giggled, and demanded attention. Suddenly my old behavior seems so ridiculous and inappropriate.

"I would be happy to carry the baskets up to the apartment for you." He interrupts my thoughts.

"No need. I can do it myself."

"I considered bringing the sack as well but decided to use it as an excuse to visit you one more time."

"I'm sure Peter would like to see you and thank you again," I answer evasively.

"If you need anything else, I'd be happy to try and obtain it for you."

"No one offers to help without expecting something in return."

"I think you are mistaken, and so I'll ask you again. Do you need anything else? I won't ask for anything in return."

I want to say no, but his offer has come just when we need it the most. "I'm afraid that Ida hasn't been able to get any pain medication for Peter. If you could . . ."

"I can't promise, but I will definitely try."

I nod in thanks.

"Until we meet again." He leans forward in a little bow and turns to go.

I look up and watch him walking away in his black suit, upright and proud, through the crowds of stooped-over people.

A broad-shouldered figure in a blue uniform stands with his back to me. He drums his fingers on the butt of his gun and then grips it tightly.

I gasp. The excitement of Anton being here, so close to me, makes my limbs tremble. I long to be in his arms. I'll tell him about the harrowing experience we had, and he'll comfort me and enfold me in his strength. I embrace Dziecko and force myself to keep sitting and staring at the building across from me.

"Was that man bothering you?" Anton's voice sounds cold and aggravated.

"On the contrary. I'm glad he came. This way, I could thank him properly," I whisper. If anyone was to look at me now, they would think I was talking to myself.

"And what do you need to thank a strange man for?" He takes a step to the side, still with his back to me.

I hold Dziecko to my cheek and whisper last night's events into his fur.

"Why didn't you listen to Peter?" he whispers angrily. "Why would you put yourself at risk like that?" Groaning under his breath, he lights a cigarette.

I had hoped that he would say a kind word to me, that he would comfort me, that he would tell me that he would never let anyone hurt me ever again. But instead, he's scolding me like I'm some stupid little girl. My eyes fill with tears, and I sniffle, holding back tears.

"I apologize." He drums frantically on the butt of his gun. The passers-by move away from him and walk one after the other to the opposite side of the street. They're afraid of him, of Anton, of the man who has become my pillar. "The thought that I couldn't be there to protect you makes me angry. The thought of your thanking another man for something I should have done for you drives me insane."

Wiping away my tears, I hug my cat. "This abominable reality is driving me crazy, and I miss my family so much that it hurts."

"There's no news from your Mother," his voice softens, "And when there's no news, it's good news."

I sigh with relief.

"What about Father and Michalina?"

"I don't know." He takes another step to the side, and I stare at his back, the bulwark between me and the street. "I believe that they're already in America and are unable to make contact."

"I want to be happy for them." A sharp pain in the pit of my stomach makes me moan. "But I can't do it. I'm still mad at them. Everyone abandons me."

"I'm here with you," he whispers and clutches the butt of his gun tightly.

Dziecko pounces from my lap and claws at Anton's pants. Anton doesn't look down.

The quiet intensity that surrounds him like a magnetic field whispers to me to move closer to him and take comfort in his arms. The cramps in my stomach intensify, and unrelenting feelings of guilt overcome me. The realization that Bruno's veiled remark about courtship made me nervous reminds me of how stupid I was in my former life. The fact that my heart is bursting with emotion for my sister's beau suddenly shocks me. What the hell am I doing? How have I allowed myself to betray her?

"Anton, do you miss her?" The question escapes my mouth, and I bite my lip anxiously.

He doesn't look at me, but his silence speaks volumes.

I feel a new crack beginning in my heart.

"You're here with me to take care of me for her." I bend down and pull Dziecko back into my arms. "And I, too, am supposed to take care of you for her." I stand up and put the cat on the sidewalk.

"Ania..." His whisper sounds pained.

"We can't forget it."

"Of course," he replies with a sigh. "Then I suggest you change your wardrobe. You can't sit here in your fancy dresses and your eye-catching hats. You need to be less conspicuous. You attract too much attention."

"What does it matter what I wear?" I chuckle bitterly. "After all, for the Nazis it's only a disguise to mask the rot hiding underneath."

"Don't be a smart aleck," he mutters angrily through clenched teeth.

"Maybe instead of pestering me, you should ask me what I need." I pick up the two baskets.

He blows the cigarette smoke out the side of his mouth and nods his head to two German soldiers passing by him. I stare evil in the face. Their ice-cold eyes and the sound of their heels clicking on the cobblestones make my chest quake. Everyone on the street hurries to elude their gaze, as if that way they will become invisible to these birds of prey. Suddenly, I'm struck with rage.

"Peter needs pain medication," I whisper, "And I need you to leave me alone." I turn on my heel and go inside the building.

* * *

A knock on the door makes Ida and me sit up on our mattresses and stare apprehensively at the door. Peter opens his eyes and moans softly.

The knocking stops, and we both exhale in relief.

"It's not the Germans," Ida whispers confidently and stands up. She wraps herself in her robe and throws my robe at me.

We tiptoe to the door, and Ida rests her hands on it and presses her ear to the wood.

Dziecko yowls and scratches the door with his claws. I hurry to pick him up and pet him, while whispering soothing words.

"Bruno Stern," comes a hushed murmur from the other side of the door.

Ida opens the door, pulls him inside, and hastily latches it after him.

"What are you doing here in the middle of the night?" she scolds him, rubbing her eyes. "If the Germans find out you're here..."

"No one saw me come in. They're patrolling the parallel street." He takes off his hat and holds it to his chest. "Miss Orzeszkowa asked me to try and obtain some pain medication for your friend." He nods his head at me and pulls a vial of capsules from the pocket of his pants.

Ida's gaze wanders back and forth from him to me.

I lower the cat to the floor and tighten the belt of my robe. Dziecko sniffs Bruno's feet, and Bruno gets down on his knees to pet him.

"Do you still need the medicine?" He presents the vial to Ida.

She nods vigorously and takes it from him. I can't read her expression. She goes over to the mattresses, puts the vial on the floor, and offers Peter some water.

Peter groans and closes his eyes.

"Forgive me for the cold welcome." She stands up straight, combs her hair with her fingers, and smiles in embarrassment. "Ania didn't tell me we were expecting such an important guest."

He waves his hand in dismissal.

"I would love to offer you a cup of tea." Her eyes dart hesitantly toward the kitchen. "But when the water comes to a boil, the kettle will whistle and..."

"I cannot stay," he replies apologetically, "I have to head back to my apartment before the Germans start patrolling this street again."

I don't utter a single syllable and painstakingly make sure not to look at his face.

"You're welcome to come back to visit us another time," she says as she walks him to the door.

"I already forced an invitation out of Ania." He smiles at me, and I still don't look right at him. I got distracted and accidentally looked into his kind eyes. Now he's become a real live person to me, and my heart trembles in pain. Now I'll have to fear for his fate as well.

Ida closes the door and pulls me onto the couch next to her.

"Ania, he seems to like you." She puts her arm in mine. "He risked his life breaking the curfew."

"Men don't interest me." I shrug.

"Because he's Jewish?" She glowers.

"No," I reply honestly. "I didn't think of him as a Jew. When he and his friends came to our aid and chased away those horrible boys, I looked at their armbands and felt something different. The armbands didn't make me feel embarrassed. They made me feel proud."

She presses her lips together, and her eyes fill with tears.

"Do you think Peter is mad at me?" My voice shakes. "Are *you* mad at me?"

"Why would we be?" She opens her eyes wide in disbelief.

"Because… Because if I hadn't gotten involved, the boys wouldn't have noticed us, and Peter wouldn't be lying here in agony."

Peter shifts on the mattress and sits up, hugging his arms to his body.

"Ania, I'm not mad at you." He closes his eyes for a minute. "I'm mad at myself."

I shake my head, confused.

"I've been called numerous names throughout my life," he whispers, pained. "Jew, pervert, sick – but never 'gutless coward.'"

"No one thinks you're a coward," I reply, stunned.

"But I think of myself as one." He arranges his pillow and leans back on it. "I was so afraid for you and me that I chose to turn my back on a father trying to protect his daughters."

"But... But what could you have done to stop such evil?"

"Scream like you screamed," he moans.

"I made a mistake!" I bite my lip. "They beat you up because of my scream."

He smiles with difficulty and says, "I don't usually quote my father, but I will deviate from my custom just this once. There's a saying he used to repeat – he recites something in a language I don't understand.

"Whoever saves one life, saves the world entire," Ida translates.

"My mother would say that your father is talking nonsense," I grumble. "First and foremost, we have to protect our loved ones, and we certainly shouldn't endanger ourselves for strangers."

Peter laughs and clutches his chest. "I would like to meet the lady who would dare argue with the renowned rabbi."

I'm tormented with longing for my strong, proud mother. I get up from the couch and lie down on the mattress next to him.

"Peter, I put you in danger to help people I don't even know."

"Don't you understand? *That's* what distinguishes us from them!" He lies on his side and squeezes my hand. "Oddly enough, moving to the ghetto has reminded me of what I loved about my parents' religion. For us, every soul, every person, is important. Maybe that's why they're so repulsed by us."

Ida lies down on my other side and snuggles up against me.

"Am I the only one who's still shocked that Bruno Stern broke the curfew to fulfill Ania's request?" she asks pensively. "I hope you're not stringing him along and have been honest regarding your intentions towards him."

"I have no intentions towards him." I roll over onto my back and sigh. "He offered help, and I accepted."

"I'm happy to hear it." Ida covers us both with a blanket. "The attention my brother showed you didn't concern me because he understands both worlds. He knows that girls sometimes flirt for no reason. He does the same thing himself, leaving a trail of broken hearts in his wake. But Bruno is a different kind of man. He comes from a distinguished family of rabbis and being matched with him means a lot."

"Are you trying to imply that I'm not good enough for him?" I move away from her.

"Of course not." She nestles close to me again. "But you need to know that if he courts you and wins your heart, his family will still never approve of you. It'll only cause suffering for you both."

I close my eyes and ponder her words.

"Ida, if you had said such a thing to me in my previous life, I would have done everything to prove to you that there's no challenge I cannot meet, especially regarding members of the opposite sex." I yawn. "But the truth is, it honestly doesn't concern me now. I'm not interested in suitors. There isn't a single man in the world that interests me right now. I just want them all to leave me alone."

Peter coughs as if trying to correct my mistake, and I open my eyes in annoyance. If he weren't injured, I'd punch him.

Ida sits up, supporting herself with her elbow. "Maybe I should have told you that while you were in the bathroom, the neighbor's son brought us a basket." She stares at me, analyzing my reaction. But I don't bat an eyelid. "Among your cheeses, bread, and gentile provisions, there was also pain medication."

I turn my back to her. I had no doubt that Anton would bring what I requested. I know with all my heart that I am important to him, but I find no comfort in this knowledge. My feelings for him torment me and overwhelm me with unbearable guilt. The moment my sister comes back, he won't be obligated to keep his promise. He'll choose my better half, and I'll give her my place with a broken heart from which I will never recover.

www.ingramcontent.com/pod-product-compliance
Lightning Source LLC
LaVergne TN
LVHW020426070526
838199LV00004B/301